GRAVE SURPRISE

GRAVE SURPRISE

CHARLAINE HARRIS

WHEELER
CHIVERS

This Large Print edition is published by Wheeler Publishing, Waterville, Maine USA and by BBC Audiobooks Ltd, Bath, England.

Wheeler Publishing is an imprint of Thomson Gale, a part of The Thomson Corporation.

Wheeler is a trademark and used herein under license.

The text of this Large Print edition is unabridged.

Other aspects of the book may vary from the original edition.

Set in 16 pt. Plantin.

LIBRARY OF CONGRESS CATALOGING-IN-PUBLICATION DATA

Harris, Charlaine.
 Grave surprise / by Charlaine Harris.
  p. cm.
 ISBN-13: 978-1-59722-440-6 (lg. print : alk. paper)
 ISBN-10: 1-59722-440-5 (lg. print : alk. paper)
 1. Clairvoyants — Fiction. 2. Brothers and sisters — Fiction. 3. Children — Crimes against — Fiction. 4. Tennessee — Fiction. I. Title.
 PS3558.A6427G733 2007
 813'.54—dc22   2006033326

BRITISH LIBRARY CATALOGUING-IN-PUBLICATION DATA AVAILABLE

Published in 2007 in the U.S. by arrangement with
The Berkley Publishing Group, a member of Penguin Group (USA) Inc.
Published in 2007 in the U.K. by arrangement with
The Orion Publishing Group Ltd.

U.K. Hardcover: 978 1 405 64016 9 (Chivers Large Print)
U.K. Softcover: 978 1 405 64017 6 (Camden Large Print)

Printed in the United States of America on permanent paper
10 9 8 7 6 5 4 3 2 1

This book is dedicated to a tiny minority of the American population: people who have survived a lightning strike. Members of a small and exclusive club, some of these survivors spend the rest of their lives trying to convince doctors of the validity of the myriad of ongoing problems plaguing them. The other survivors simply try to go on with their lives, though they're invariably altered by the experience. I wish you all freedom from pain and anxiety, and I thank you for letting me share your experiences.

ACKNOWLEDGMENTS

There are several people who helped me with information for this book, and though I may not have used it correctly, I want to acknowledge their good intentions and their freely given time. First and foremost is my friend Treva Jackson, who has helped me with details in this book and a few others. Her daughter Miller has chimed in, too, from time to time. My fellow writer Robin Burcell was also a great help, not only in giving me some tips on police procedure but in introducing me to FBI Agent George Fong, who is nothing like the agent in this book. My college pal Ed Uthman also provided some funny reminiscences about his college years in Memphis. Julie Wray Herman and Rochelle Krich straightened out some of my mistaken ideas about the Jewish faith in the kindest way possible. I appreciate you all very much.

ONE

I didn't like Clyde Nunley the first time I met him face-to-face in the old cemetery. There was nothing wrong with the exterior of the man: he was dressed like a regular person would dress for the mild winter weather of southern Tennessee, especially considering the task at hand. His old blue jeans, work boots, shapeless hat, flannel shirt, and down vest were reasonable attire. But Dr. Nunley had a smug, smooth, air about him that said that he'd brought me here to be an object of derision, said he'd never believed I was anything but a fraud.

He shook my hand, standing right in front of me. He was having a great time, scanning the faces of my brother and me, as we waited side by side for his directions.

Offered under the aegis of the anthropology department of Bingham College, the course Dr. Clyde Nunley taught was titled "An Open Mind: Experiences Outside the

Box." I noted the irony.

"Last week we had a medium," he said.

"For lunch?" I asked, and got a scowl for my reward.

I glanced sideways at Tolliver. His eyes narrowed slightly, letting me know he was amused but warning me to play nice.

If it hadn't been for the presence of that asshole of a professor, I would have been brimming with anticipation. I drew in a deep breath as I glanced past Dr. Nunley at the tombstones, worn and weathered. This was my kind of place.

By American standards, the cemetery was an old one. The trees had had nearly two centuries to mature. Some of these hardwoods could have been saplings when the denizens of St. Margaret's churchyard had been laid to rest. Now they were tall, with thick branches; in the summer, their shade would be a blessing. Right now, in November, the branches were bare, and the grass was bleached and strewn with dead leaves. The sky was that chill, leaden gray that makes the heart sad.

I would have been as subdued as the rest of the people gathered there if I hadn't had a treat in store. The headstones still upright were uneven, both in lodgment and in color. Below them, the dead waited for me.

It hadn't rained in a week or two, so I was wearing Pumas rather than boots. I would have better contact if I took the Pumas off, but the students and the professor would doubtless interpret that as further evidence of my eccentricity. Also, it was a bit too cold for going around barefoot.

Nunley's students were there to watch my "demonstration." That was the point. Of the twenty or so in the group, two were older; one, a woman, was in her forties. I was willing to bet she'd arrived in the minivan now sitting frumpily among the other vehicles pulled up to the wire strung between white posts to separate the gravel parking lot from the grass of the churchyard. Her face was open and curious as she evaluated me.

The other "nontraditional" class member was a man I placed in his early thirties, who was dressed in cords and a heathery sweater. The thirties man was the shining Colorado pickup. Clyde Nunley would be the ancient Toyota. The four other cars, battered and small, would be those of the traditional students who formed the bulk of the little crowd here to watch. Though St. Margaret's was actually on the campus grounds, the old church was tucked far back into the reaches of Bingham College, beyond the little stadium, the tennis courts, the soccer field — so it wasn't surprising that the students who could, had driven, especially in the chilly weather. The kids were in the typical college eighteen-to-twenty-one age bracket, and with an odd jolt I realized that made them only a bit younger than me. They were wearing the usual uniform of blue jeans, sneakers, and padded jackets — more or less what Tolliver and I were wearing.

Tolliver's jacket was from Lands' End, bright red with a blue lining. Red looked good with his black hair, and the jacket was warm enough for most situations in the South. I was wearing my bright blue padded jacket, because it made me feel safe and soft, and because Tolliver had given it to me.

We were spots of color in the overall grayness. The trees that surrounded the old church, its yard, and its cemetery gave us a feeling of privacy, as if we'd been marooned at the back of the Bingham campus.

"Miss Connelly, we're all anxious to see your demonstration," Dr. Nunley said, practically laughing in my face. He made an elaborate sweeping gesture with his arm that encompassed the gaggle of headstones. The students didn't look anxious. They looked cold, bored, or mildly curious. I wondered who the medium had been. There weren't many with genuine gifts.

I glanced at Tolliver again. *Fuck him,* his eyes said, and I smiled.

They all had clipboards, all the students. And all the clipboards had diagrams of the old graveyard, with the gravesites neatly drawn in and labeled. Though this information wasn't on their clipboards, I knew there was a detailed record of the burials in this particular graveyard, a record containing the cause of death of most of the bodies buried in it. The parish priest had kept this record for the forty years he'd served St. Margaret's church, keeping up the custom of his predecessor. But Dr. Nunley had informed me that no one had been buried here for fifty years.

The St. Margaret records had been discovered three months ago in a box in the most remote storeroom of the Bingham College library. So there was no way I could have found out the information the registers contained beforehand. Dr. Nunley, who had originated the occult studies class, had heard of me somehow. He wouldn't say exactly how my name had come to his attention, but that didn't surprise me. There are websites that connect to websites that connect to other websites; and in a very subterranean circle, I'm famous.

Clyde Nunley thought he was paying me to be exposed in front of the "An Open Mind" class. He thought I considered myself some form of psychic, or maybe a Wiccan.

Of course, that made no sense. Nothing I did was occult. I didn't pray to any god before I got in touch with the dead. I do believe in God, but I don't consider my little talent a gift from Him.

I got it from a bolt of lightning. So if you think God causes natural disasters, then I suppose God is responsible.

When I was fifteen, I was struck through an open window of the trailer where we lived. At that time, my mother was married to Tolliver's father, Matt Lang, and they had had two children, Gracie and Mariella. Crowded into the trailer (besides that lovely nuclear family) were the rest of us — me, my sister Cameron, Tolliver, and his brother Mark. I don't remember how long Mark was actually in residence. He's several years older than Tolliver. Anyway, Mark wasn't at the trailer that afternoon.

It was Tolliver who performed CPR until the ambulance got there.

My stepfather gave Cameron hell for calling the ambulance. It was expensive, and of course, we didn't have any insurance. The doctor who wanted to keep me overnight for observation got an earful. I never saw him again, or any other doctor. But from the Internet list I'm on, a list for lightning strike survivors, I've gathered it wouldn't have done me a lot of good, anyway.

I recovered — more or less. I have a strange spiderweb pattern of red on my torso and right leg. That leg has episodes of weakness. Sometimes my right hand shakes. I have headaches. I have many fears. And I can find dead people. If their location is known, I can diagnose the cause of death.

That was the part that interested the professor. He had a record of the cause of death of almost every person in this cemetery, a record to which I'd had no access. This was his idea of a perfect test, a test that would expose me for the fraud I was. With an almost jaunty air, he led our little party through the dilapidated iron fence that had guarded the cemetery for so many decades.

"Where would you like me to begin?" I asked, with perfect courtesy. I had been raised well, until my parents started using drugs.

Clyde Nunley smirked at his students. "Why, this one would be fine," he said, gesturing to the grave to his right. Of course, there was no mound, probably hadn't been in a hundred and seventy years. The headstone was indecipherable, at least to my unaided eyes. If I bent down with a flashlight, maybe I could read it. But they didn't care about that part of it; they wanted to know what I would say about the cause of death.

The faint tremor, the vibration I'd been feeling since I'd neared the cemetery, increased in frequency as I stepped onto the grave. I'd been feeling the hum in the air even before I'd passed through the rusted gate, and now it increased in intensity, vibrating just below the surface of my skin. It was like getting closer and closer to a hive of bees.

I shut my eyes, because it was easier to concentrate that way. The bones were directly underneath me, waiting for me. I sent that extra sense down into the ground under my feet, and the knowledge entered me with the familiarity of a lover.

"Cart fell on him," I said. "This is a man, I think in his thirties. Ephraim? Something like that? His leg was crushed, and he went into shock. He bled out."

There was a long silence. I opened my eyes. The professor had stopped smirking.

The students were busily making notations on their clipboards. One girl's eyes were wide as she looked at me.

"All right," said Dr. Clyde Nunley, his voice suddenly a lot less scornful. "Let's try another one."

Gotcha, I thought.

The next grave was Ephraim's wife. The bones didn't tell me that; I deduced her identity from the similar headstone positioned side by side with Ephraim's. "Isabelle," I said with certainty. "Isabelle. Oh, she died in childbirth." My hand grazed my lower stomach. Isabelle must have been pregnant when her husband met with his accident. Hard luck. "Wait a minute," I said. I wanted to interpret that faint echo I was picking up underneath Isabelle's. To hell with what they thought. I pulled off my shoes, but kept my socks on in a compromise with the cold weather. "The baby's in there with her," I told them. "Poor little thing," I added very softly. There was no pain in the baby's death.

I opened my eyes.

The group had shifted its configuration. They stood closer to each other, but farther from me.

"Next?" I asked.

Clyde Nunley, his mouth compressed into

a straight line, gestured toward a grave so old its headstone had split and fallen. The marble had been white when it had been situated.

As Tolliver and I went over to the next body, his hand on my back, one of the students said, "He should stand somewhere else. What if he's somehow feeding her information?"

It was the older male student, the guy in his thirties. He had brown hair, a thread or two of gray mixed in. He had a narrow face and the broad shoulders of a swimmer. He didn't sound as if he actually suspected me. He sounded objective.

"Good point, Rick. Mr. Lang, if you'd stand out of Miss Connelly's sight?"

I felt a tiny flutter of anxiety. But I made myself nod at Tolliver in a calm way. He went back to lean against our car, parked outside what remained of the cemetery fence. While I watched him, another car pulled up, and a young black man with a camera got out. It was a dilapidated car, dented and scraped, but clean.

"Hey, y'all," the newcomer called, and several of the younger students waved at him. "Sorry I'm late."

The professor said, "Miss Connelly, this is Clark. I forgot to tell you that the student newspaper wanted to get a few shots."

I didn't think he'd forgotten. He just didn't care if I objected or not.

I considered for a moment. I really didn't care. I was ready to have a good fight with Clyde Nunley, but not a frivolous one. I shrugged. "I don't mind," I said. I stepped onto the grave, close to the headstone, and focused my whole attention on ground below me. This one was hard to decipher. It was very old, and the bones were scattered; the coffin had disintegrated. I hardly felt my right hand begin to twitch, or my head begin to turn from side to side. My facial muscles danced beneath my skin.

"Kidneys," I said, at last. "Something with his kidneys." The ache in my back swelled to a level of pain that was almost unbearable, and then it was gone. I opened my eyes and took a deep breath. I fought the impulse to turn to look at my brother.

One of the youngest of the students was white as a sheet. I'd spooked her good. I smiled at her, trying to look friendly and reassuring. I don't think I achieved it. She took another step away from me. I sighed and turned my attention back to my job.

Next, I found a woman who'd died of pneumonia; a child who'd died of an infected appendix; a baby who'd had a heart malformation; a baby who'd had a blood problem — I suspected he was the second child of a couple with conflicting Rh factors — and a pre-teen boy who'd had one of the fevers, scarlet, maybe. Every now and then I heard the photographer snap a picture, but it really didn't bother me. I don't care much about my physical appearance when I'm working.

After thirty or forty minutes, Nunley seemed almost won over. He pointed to a grave in the corner of the cemetery farthest from the gate. The plot he indicated lay right by the fence, which had collapsed almost completely in that area. The headstone was partially obscured by the overhanging branches of a live oak, and the light was especially bad. This is a draining process, so I was beginning to get tired. At first I attributed my extraordinary reading to that. I opened my eyes, frowned.

"It's a girl," I said.

"Ha!" Nunley chose to regard himself as vindicated. He kind of overdid his glee, he was so happy to be proved right. "Wrong!" he said. Mr. Open Mind.

"I'm not wrong," I said, though I really wasn't thinking about him, or the students, or even Tolliver. I was thinking about the puzzle under the ground. I was thinking

20

about solving it.

I took off my socks. My feet felt fragile in the chilly air. I stepped back onto the dead grass in line with the headstone to get a fresh outlook. For the first time, I noticed that though an attempt had been made to level this grave — it bore the flattened spots that blows with a shovel on soft dirt would have produced — the earth had been recently turned.

Well, well, well. I stood still for a moment, the implications working their way through my brain. I had the ominous creeping feeling you get when you just know something's right outside your realm of knowledge — a bad piece of future poised to jump out from behind a door and scream in your face.

Though the kids were muttering to each other and the two older students were having a low-voiced conversation, I squatted down to decipher the headstone. It read, JOSIAH POUNDSTONE, 1839–1858, REST IN PEACE BELOVED BROTHER. No mention of a wife, or a twin, or . . .

Okay, maybe the ground had shifted a bit and the body buried next to Josiah's had sort of wandered over.

I stepped back onto the grave, and I squatted. Distantly, I heard the click of the camera, but it was not relevant. I laid my

hand on the turned earth. I was as connected as I could be without lying full
length on the ground.

I glanced over at Tolliver. "Something's
wrong here," I said, loudly enough for him
to hear. He started over.

"A problem, Miss Connelly?" Dr. Nunley
asked, scorn lending his voice fiery edges.
This was a man who loved to be right.

"Yes." I stepped off the grave, shook
myself, and tried again. Standing right
above Josiah Poundstone, I reached down
again.

Same result.

"There are two bodies here, not one," I
said.

Nunley made the predictable attempts to
find an explanation. "A coffin gave way in
the next grave," he said impatiently. "Or
something like that."

"No, the body that's lower is in an intact
coffin." I took a deep breath. "And the upper body isn't. It's much newer. This ground
has been turned over recently."

Finally interested, the students quieted
down. Dr. Nunley consulted his papers.
"Who do you . . . see . . . in there?"

"The lower body, the older one . . ." I
closed my eyes, trying to peer through one
body to another. I'd never done this before.

"Is a young man named Josiah, like the headstone says. By the way, he died of blood poisoning from a cut." I could tell from Nunley's face that I was right. However the priest had described Josiah's death, modern knowledge could recognize the symptoms. What the priest may not have known, however, is that the cut had come from a stab wound, inflicted in a fight. I could see the knife sliding into the young man's flesh, feel him staunch the blood. But the infection had carried him off.

"The upper body, the newer one, is a young girl."

There was sudden and absolute silence. I could hear the traffic rushing by on busy roads just yards away from the old graveyard.

"How recent is the second body?" Tolliver asked.

"Two years at the most," I said. I tilted my head from side to side, to get the most accurate "reading" I could. On the age of the bones, I mostly go by the intensity of the vibration and the feel of it. I never said I was a scientist. But I'm right.

"Oh, my God," whispered one of the female students, finally understanding the implication.

"She's a murder victim," I said. "Her

name was . . . Tabitha." As I heard what my voice was saying, an awful sense of doom flowed over me. The boogeyman jumped out from behind the door and screamed in my face.

My brother moved across the intervening ground like a quarterback who could see the end zone. He stopped just short of the grave, but he was close enough to take my hand. Our eyes met. His echoed the dismay in mine.

"Tell me it's not," Tolliver said. His dark brown eyes were steady on mine.

"It is," I said. "We finally found Tabitha Morgenstern."

After a moment, in which the younger people in the group turned to look at each other with inquiring faces, Clyde Nunley said, "You mean . . . the girl who was abducted from Nashville?"

"Yes," I said. "That's who I mean."

TWO

I'd been standing on two murder victims, one ancient (at least to me), and one modern. There were differences in the reading I got from the older one, in addition to the shock of finding Tabitha. I stowed Josiah Poundstone away to ponder later. No one here in St. Margaret's cemetery was concerned with him today.

"You got some explaining to do," the detective said. He was putting it mildly. We were at Homicide, and the carpeted partitions and the ringing phones and the flag tacked to the wall made the floor seem more like a modest company with a burgeoning business than a cop facility.

Sometimes I faint when I find a body that has passed in a violent way. It would have been good if I'd fainted this time. But I hadn't. I'd been all too conscious of the disbelief and outrage on the faces of the police, uniformed and plainclothes. The initial skepticism and anger on the part of the two uniforms who'd rolled up on the scene had been understandable and predictable. They didn't imagine anyone would dig up a centuries-old grave on the say-so of a lunatic woman who made her living as a con artist.

But the more Clyde Nunley explained, the more they began to look uneasy. After a lot of comparison of the grave's surface with the others around it, the larger black cop finally radioed in, calling a detective to the scene.

We'd gone over the whole sequence of events again. This took a lot of time. Tolliver and I were leaning against our car, getting progressively colder and wearier, while the slow and repetitive questioning went on and on. Everyone was angry with us. Everyone thought we were frauds. Clyde Nunley grew more defensive and loud with each amazed reaction he got from the cops. Yes, he conducted a course during which students "experienced" people who claimed they could communicate with the dead: ghost hunters, mediums, psychics, tarot readers, and other paranormal practitioners. Yes, people actually sent their kids to college to learn stuff like that, and yes, they paid a rather high tuition for it. Yes, the papers about the old cemetery had been kept quite secure, and Harper Connelly had had no chance to examine them. Yes, the box containing the papers had been sealed when the library staff had discovered it. No, neither Tolliver nor I had ever been a student at the college. (We had to smile when we heard that one.)

To no one's surprise, we were "asked" to come to the police station. And there we sat, answering all the same questions over and over again, until we were left to vegetate in an interview room. The garbage can was full of snack wrappers and stained Styrofoam coffee cups, and the walls needed a new coat of paint. In the past, someone had thrown the chair I was sitting on. I could tell, because one of the metal legs was slightly bowed. At least the room was warm enough. I'd gotten chilled down to my bones in the cemetery.

"You think it would look bad if I read?" Tolliver asked. Tolliver is twenty-eight now, and he likes to grow his black hair out, wear it long for a while, and then cut it drastically. At the moment, it was long enough to pull back into a short ponytail. He has a mustache and acne-scarred cheeks. He's a runner, like me. We spend a lot of hours in

cars, and running is a good way to counter-
act that.

"Yes, I think it would look callous," I said.
He glowered at me. "Well, you asked me," I
said. We sat in dreary silence for a minute
or two.

"I wonder if we'll have to see the Morgensterns again?" I said.

"You know we will," he said. "I bet they've
already called them, and they're driving over
from Nashville right now."

His cell phone rang.

He checked who was calling, looked as
blank as a man can look, and answered it.
"Hey," he said. "Yeah, it's true. Yes, we're
here in Memphis. I was going to call you
tonight. I'm sure we'll see each other. Yes.
Yes. All right, goodbye."

He didn't look happy as he snapped the
phone shut. Of course I wanted to know
who his caller had been, but I didn't say
anything. If anything could have made me
gloomier, it was the idea that sooner or later
we'd have to see Joel and Diane Morgenstern again.

When I'd realized whom the bones belonged to, my dismay was more overwhelming than my feeling of triumph. I'd failed
the Morgensterns eighteen months ago,
though I'd tried as hard as I could to find

their daughter. Now I'd finally come through for them, but the success was bitter.

"How'd she die?" Tolliver asked very quietly. You never knew who was listening, in a police station. I guess we're the suspicious sort.

"Suffocated," I said. Another silence. "With a blue pillow." We'd seen so many pictures of Tabitha alive: on the news broadcasts, pinned to the walls of her room, in her parents' hands, blown up to illustrate the fliers they'd given us. She'd been a very average girl of eleven, to everyone but her parents. Tabitha had had bushy reddish-brown hair she hadn't yet learned to deal with. She'd had big brown eyes, and braces, and she hadn't begun to mature physically. She'd liked gymnastics, and art lessons, and she'd hated making her bed and taking out the trash. I remembered all this from talking to her parents; or more accurately, listening to their monologues. Joel and Diane had seemed to believe that if they made Tabitha real to me, I would work harder at finding her.

"You think she's been down there since she was missing?" Tolliver asked, finally.

It had been the spring of the preceding year when we'd been summoned to Nashville by the Morgenstern family. By then, Tabitha had been gone a month. The police had just cut back on their search, since they'd looked everywhere they could. The FBI had scaled back its presence, also. The extra equipment that had been installed to trace phone calls had been removed, because there hadn't been any ransom demands. By then, no one was expecting such a demand.

"No," I said. "The ground was too freshly disturbed. But I think she's been dead the whole time. I really hope so." The only thing more awful than a murdered child was a murdered child who'd been subjected to prolonged torture or sexual abuse.

"There was no way you could have found her," Tolliver said. "Back then."

"No," I agreed. "There wasn't."

But it hadn't been for lack of trying. The Morgensterns had called me when they'd exhausted all the traditional methods of finding their lost child.

Yes, I had failed; but I had given it my all. I'd been over the house, the yard, the neighborhood, into the yards of anyone with a police record who lived in the surrounding area. Some I'd done at night because the homeowner wouldn't consent. Not only was I risking arrest, but injury. A dog had almost gotten me the second night.

I'd toured nearby junkyards, ponds, parks, landfills, and cemeteries, in the process finding one other murder victim in the trunk of a junked car (a freebie for the Nashville police — they'd been so pleased to have another murder victim on the books), and one natural death, a homeless man in a park. But I hadn't found any eleven-year-old girls. For nine days I'd searched, until the time came when I'd had to tell Diane and Joel Morgenstern that I could not find their child.

Tabitha had been snatched from her yard in an upscale Nashville suburb while she was watering the flowers in the beds around the front door of the house on a warm morning during spring break. When Diane had come out to go to the grocery, she'd discovered Tabitha was nowhere to be found. The hose was still running.

Daughter of a senior accountant with a firm that handled lots of Nashville singers and record people, Tabitha had had a blessed childhood. Though she had a step-brother because Joel had been married and widowed previously, Tabitha had obviously enjoyed a well-regulated home life centered on maintaining her health and happiness, and incidentally that of Victor, her half sib.

My childhood, and Tolliver's, had not been like that — at least, after a certain point. That was the point where our lawyer parents began using drugs and drinking with their clients. After a while, the clients had ceased to be clients, and had become peers. That downward slide had brought me to the moment in time when I'd been standing in the bathroom in that trailer in Texarkana and the lightning had come through the window.

Trips down memory lane aren't happy jaunts for me.

I was almost glad when the detective — Corbett Lacey was his name — came back with cups of coffee for both of us. He was trying the soft approach. Sooner or later (probably later) someone else would try the hard approach.

"Tell me how you came to be here this morning," suggested Corbett Lacey. He was a burly man with receding blond hair, a large belly, and quick blue eyes like restless marbles.

"We were invited by Dr. Nunley to come to the old cemetery. I was supposed to show the students what I do."

"What exactly do you do?" He looked so sincere, as if he would believe any answer I gave him.

"I find the dead."

"You track people?"

"No, I find corpses. People call me in, and I find the bodies of those who've passed on." That was my favorite euphemism. I have quite a repertoire. "If the location of the corpse is already known, I can tell you the cause of death. That was what I was doing at the cemetery today."

"What's your success rate?"

Okay, that was unexpected. I'd assumed he'd sneer, at this point. "If the relatives or the police can give me a bead on the location, I can find the body," I said matter-of-factly. "When I find the body, I know the cause of death. In the case of Tabitha Morgenstern, when the family called me in, I could never find her. She'd been taken from her yard and put in a car pretty quick, I guess, and her corpse just wasn't there for me to sense."

"How does this work?"

Another unexpected question. "I feel them, like a buzz in my head," I said. "The closer I get, the more intense the buzz, the vibration, is. When I'm on top of them, I can reach down and tell how they died. I'm not a psychic. I'm not a precognate, or a telepath. I don't see who killed them. I only see the death when I'm near the bones."

He hadn't expected such a matter-of-fact reply. He looked at me, leaning forward on the other side of the table. His own cup of coffee was forgotten in front of him. "Why would anyone believe that?" Lacey asked wonderingly.

"Because I produce results," I said.

"Don't you think it's quite a coincidence? That you were called in by the Morgensterns when they were looking for their little girl, and now, months later, in a different city, you say you've found her? How do you think those poor folks are going to feel when the area's dug and there's nothing there? You should be ashamed of yourself." The detective regarded me with profound disgust.

"That's not going to happen." I shrugged. "I'm not ashamed of anything. She's there." I glanced at my watch. "They should have reached her by now."

Detective Lacey's cell phone rang. He answered, "Yeah?" As he listened, his face changed. He looked harder and older. His eyes fell on me with a look I've seen often — a stare compounded of distaste, fear, and a dawning belief.

"They've reached some bones in a garbage bag," he said heavily. "Too small to be an adult's."

I tried very hard to look neutral.

"A foot below the garbage bag bones, there are wood remnants. Probably a coffin. So there may be another set of bones." He breathed heavily. "There's no trace of a coffin around the upper bones."

I nodded. Tolliver squeezed my hand.

"We'll get a very preliminary identification in a couple hours, if it's the Morgenstern girl. The dental records have been faxed from Nashville. Of course, a solid ID will have to wait on a full exam of the body. Well, what's left of the body." Detective Lacey set his own personal coffee mug on the battered table with unnecessary force. "Nashville police are sending the X-rays by car, and the car should be here in a couple of hours. The local FBI office is sending someone to witness the full autopsy. The Fibbies are offering their lab for the trace stuff. You are not to say anything about this to anyone until we've talked to the family."

I nodded again.

"Good," Tolliver said, just to goose the silence.

Corbett Lacey gave us a steady glare. "We've had to call her parents, and if this isn't her, I don't even like to think about what they'll feel. If you hadn't broadcast her name to the whole group standing there, we could have kept this quiet until we had something solid to tell them. Now, we've had to talk to them because it looks like the damn television will have it on the air soon."

"I'm sorry about that. I just wasn't thinking." I should have kept my mouth shut. He had a good point.

"Why do you even do this, anyway?" He gave me a puzzled face, as if he really couldn't figure me out. I didn't think he was completely sincere, but I was.

"It's always better to know. That's why I do it."

"You seem to make quite a bit of money, too," Corbett Lacey observed.

"I have to make a living, same as anybody else." I wasn't going to act ashamed of that. But, truly, I sometimes wished I worked at Wal-Mart, or Starbucks, and let the dead lie unfound.

"So, I guess Joel and Diane started out right away," Tolliver said. He was right; a change of subject was in order. "It'll take them how long to get here?"

Detective Lacey looked puzzled.

"The Morgensterns. How long a drive is it, Nashville to Memphis?" I said.

He gave us an unreadable look. "Like you didn't know."

Okay, I wasn't getting this at all. "Know

. . . ?" I looked at Tolliver. He shrugged, as bewildered as I was. A possibility occurred to me. "Tell me they're not dead!" I said. I'd liked them, and I didn't often have feelings for clients.

It was Lacey's turn to look uncertain. "You really don't know?"

"We don't understand what you're talking about," Tolliver said. "Just tell us."

"The Morgensterns left Nashville about a year after the little girl was abducted," Lacey said. He ran a hand over his thinning blond hair. "They live here in Memphis now. He manages the Memphis branch of the same accounting firm, and his wife's pregnant again. Maybe you didn't know that he and his first wife were both from Memphis, and since Diane Morgenstern's family lives overseas, back here was where they needed to be if they wanted the support of family during the pregnancy and birth."

I suspected my mouth was hanging open, but for the moment I didn't care. I had so many thoughts I couldn't process them all at once. The Morgensterns being here turned everything upside down. If I'd thought we were placed in a bad situation, ours was nothing compared to theirs. It looked so bad for them, Tabitha's body being found here. And their presence here in

Memphis made the fact that I'd been the one to finally find her even fishier, since they'd employed me before.

I simply couldn't think of any explanation that cleared the couple of some involvement in their daughter's death.

My stunned reaction struck true to the detective, and Tolliver's was even more obvious. Lacey nodded sharply, as if he were reluctantly convinced of something.

After that, there weren't any more questions. We were released to go back to our motel, an absolutely typical airport motel in a medium-range chain that we'd picked because it was right off the interstate and not too far from the college. On our way back, we'd gone through a Wendy's drive-through to pick up sandwiches, and before we went up to our room we each pulled a soft drink from the ice chest in the back seat. Our room was wonderfully quiet and warm. I gulped my soda down right away, because I needed the sugar after our experience in the cemetery. (We've found, by trial and error, that sugar really helps get me up and running after a job.) Sure enough, after the sugar hit me, I was able to eat my sandwich at a calm pace. I felt much better. After we'd cleared away the debris, Tolliver stood and looked down from our second-story window.

"There are reporters already gathering," Tolliver said, after a minute. "It's only a matter of time before they come up to the room and knock on the door."

I should have thought of that already. "This will generate a lot of publicity," I said, and the ambivalence was clear in Tolliver's face, as I'm sure it was in mine.

"You think we need to call Art?" Art Barfield was our attorney, and his firm was based in Atlanta.

"That might be a good idea," I said. "Would you talk to him?"

"Sure." Tolliver pulled out his cell phone and dialed, while I went to the sink to wash my face. After I turned off the water, I could hear him talking. I was combing my hair in the mirror — my hair was almost as dark as Tolliver's — when he hung up.

"His secretary says he's with a client, but he'll call soonest possible. Of course, he'll charge an arm and a leg if we ask him to come. That is, if he can get away."

"He'll come, or he'll recommend someone local. We've only asked him once before, and we're his most . . . lurid clients," I said practically. "If he doesn't come, we'll be swamped."

Art called us back about an hour later.

From Tolliver's end of the conversation, you could tell Art was not too excited about the prospect of leaving home — Art was not young, and he liked his home comforts — but when Tolliver told Art about the reporters gathered at the police station, the lawyer allowed himself to be persuaded to get on a plane right away.

"Corinne'll call you with my plane information," Art said to Tolliver, but I could hear him clearly. Art has one of those carrying voices, which is really useful if you're a trial lawyer.

Art likes publicity almost as much as he loves his remote control and his wife's cooking. He's had a taste of it since he became our lawyer, and his practice has increased exponentially. His secretary, the middle-aged Corinne, called us within minutes to give us Art's flight number and his ETA.

"I don't think we'd better meet Art at the airport," I told Corinne. I watched another news van enter the parking lot. "I think we're going to have to go to a hotel, one with more security than this."

"You'd better make the change now, and I'll book Mr. Barfield a room at the same place," Corinne said practically. "I'll call him on his cell when he lands. In fact, I'll make a phone call or two, find the right place, and book the reservation for all of you. One room or two, for you and Mr. Lang?"

The hotel was sure to be very expensive. Normally I'd be inclined to share one room with Tolliver, as we were doing now. But if the newspapers were checking, better to err on the side of the Goddess of Rightness.

"Two," I said. "Adjacent. Or if we can get a suite, that would be good."

"I'll do some quick research, and then I'll confirm with you," the efficient Corinne said.

She called back to tell us we were booked into the Cleveland. It was, as I'd feared, way too expensive for my taste, but I'd pay the money to ensure the privacy. I didn't like being on television. Publicity was good for business, but only the right kind of publicity.

We left our motel, as disguised as we could be without looking ludicrous. Before strolling out one of the side doors and making a beeline to our car, we had bundled to the teeth. Because we looked so humble, Tolliver lugging the ice chest and me carrying our overnight bags, we managed to escape the attention of the news crew until we were pulling out of the parking lot. The newswoman, whose lips were so shiny they looked polyurethaned, made a flying leap to land right beside the driver's window. Tolliver couldn't see to turn left into the traffic flowing the way we needed to go, so we were more or less trapped. He rolled down the window and put on an agreeable smile.

"Shellie Quail from Channel Thirteen," the shiny woman said. She was the color of hot chocolate, and her black hair gleamed like it had been polished. It was in a smooth helmet style. Shellie Quail's makeup was equally warlike, lots of bright colors and definite lines. I wondered how long it took her to get ready to leave her house in the morning. She was wearing a tight pantsuit in a brownish, tweedy material, flecked with orange. The little flecks made her skin glow. "Mr. Lang, are you Miss Connelly's manager? Have I got that right?" the shining woman said.

"Yes, you do," Tolliver said agreeably. I knew the camera was rolling. But I had faith in my brother. He has a lot of charm when the occasion arises, especially if it arises in the presence of a pretty woman.

"Can you comment on this morning's happenings in the old St. Margaret's cemetery at Bingham College?" she asked. The microphone she'd been clutching was thrust at Tolliver's chin in what I considered a very aggressive way.

"Yes," he said. "We're waiting to hear if the body we discovered can be identified." I admired the way he kept his voice so level and calm — but serious, and worthy of being taken seriously.

"Is it true the police are considering the possibility that the skeleton may be that of Tabitha Morgenstern?"

Well, that hadn't taken long to leak out.

"Our thoughts and our prayers are with the Morgenstern family. Of course, like everyone else here, we're very anxious to hear some news," Tolliver said neutrally.

"Mr. Lang, is it true your sister stated that the body just exhumed from the cemetery is *definitely* that of the missing girl?"

We weren't going to get by with anything. "We believe that to be true," he said, indirectly.

"How do you explain the coincidence?"

"What coincidence?" Tolliver asked, which I thought was maybe a little over the top.

Even Shellie Quail looked disconcerted. But she got back on her roll. "That your sister was hired to look for Tabitha Morgenstern months ago in Nashville, and then hired to look at the graves in the old St. Margaret's cemetery here in Memphis. And that a body reported to be that of Tabitha

Morgenstern is found in that cemetery."

"We have no idea how this came about, and we're looking forward to hearing the explanation," Tolliver said sternly, as if we'd been mightily put-upon. Baffled, Shellie Quail paused to think of another question, and we took the opportunity to make our left turn.

THREE

The Cleveland was beautiful. The Cleveland was discreet. I was not going to want to see our credit card bill when it came next month.

A valet took our car, and we rolled into the lobby in a flurry of baggage and desperation, anxious to get away from the reporters who'd actually followed us to the new hotel. The staff was as courteous as if we'd stayed at the Cleveland four times a year. We were upstairs and out of reach of anyone in the twinkling of an eye. I was so glad to have time to regroup in relative safety and privacy, I could have cried.

The suite had a central living room with a bedroom on each side. Going directly to the bedroom on the right, I took off my shoes, lay down on my very own king-size bed, and surrounded myself with pillows. That's something I love about really good hotels: the abundance of pillows. Once I was padded and quiet and warm, I closed my eyes and let my thoughts drift. Of course, they drifted right to the little girl I'd found in the cemetery.

I'd assumed Tabitha was dead from the moment I'd read about her disappearance, weeks before the Morgensterns had asked me to find her body. Based on the information in the newspaper accounts and even more on my own experience, that was a logical assumption. In fact, I'd been fairly sure the child had been dead since scant hours after her disappearance.

That didn't mean I was happy to be right. I'm not callous about death; at least I don't think I am. I think of myself as more . . . matter-of-fact. And I'd seen the Morgensterns' anguish first-hand. Because of my sympathy for them, I'd persisted longer in the search than I'd thought was reasonable, and certainly long enough to cut into our profit very severely. Tolliver didn't even charge them the full amount; he didn't say anything to me, but when I went over our profits and expenses at the end of the year, I'd noticed.

Since Tabitha had been dead all this time, I thought it would be better for Joel and Diane to know what had happened to their daughter.

I could only hope that the sentiment I'd sprouted so glibly to the detective was valid. I could only hope that knowing for sure what had happened to Tabitha gave the Morgensterns some relief. At least they would know she wasn't in the hands of some madman, actively suffering.

I found myself wishing I'd had longer with the body. I'd been so startled at the identity of the grave's unauthorized inhabitant that I hadn't spent enough energy evaluating the girl's last moments. I'd only seen the blue cushion, a flash of the long seconds as Tabitha slipped into unconsciousness and then passed away — as she passed from the imitation of death to death itself.

I don't believe that death and life are two sides of the same coin. I think that's bullshit. I'm not going to say Tabitha was at peace with God, because God hasn't let me know on that one. And there'd been a strange feeling to my connection with the body; a sensation I'd seldom experienced before. I tried to analyze the difference, but I didn't come up with anything. That would bother me until I understood it.

I have seen a lot of death — a *lot*. I know death the way most people know sleep, or eating. Death is a fundamental human necessity, a solitary passage into the unknown. But Tabitha had made her passage years too early, at the end of a painful and frightening ordeal. I was sorry for the manner of her death. And something about it had marked her during that transition, in a way I had yet to understand. I filed it away to consider later; maybe another trip to the cemetery would help. It was hardly likely I'd be in contact with the body again.

I turned onto my side and stretched back to prop a pillow against my shoulders. I turned my thoughts down a mental path so familiar that it had ruts worn in it. That path led to my sister Cameron. Her face was fuzzy in my memory now, or it took on the contours of her last school picture, which I carried in my wallet.

Somehow, discovering Tabitha's corpse in such an indirect and unexpected way gave me hope that someday I might find my sister Cameron's remains.

Cameron has been gone for six years. Like Tabitha, she was snatched out of the stream of her life, leaving her backpack behind on the shore as witness to her departure. When Cameron had become way overdue at home that day, I started looking for her. I'd roused my mother enough to feel she could watch Mariella and Gracie for at least a little while, and I'd trudged through the sweltering heat, following the route Cameron took when she walked home from the high school. It was getting to be twilight by then. Cameron had stayed at school later than I because she was helping to decorate for a dance; the senior prom, I think.

I'd found her backpack, fully loaded with the schoolbooks, notebooks, notes passed to her in class, broken pencils, and small change. And that was all that was left of Cameron. The police had kept it for a long time, gone through its compartments, asked me about the content of every note. Then we'd asked for its return. Today, we carried that backpack in the trunk of our car.

When Tolliver came in, I was still lying on my bed. I'd rotated again, to lie flat on my back as I gazed at the ceiling, thinking about my sister.

"The car from the hotel's going to pick up Art at the airport," he said. "I got it all arranged."

"Thanks," I said, moving over to give him room. He lay on the other half of the vast king bed, shoes properly off. I let him have a pillow. Then I gave him another one.

"Looking back on the cemetery thing this morning," he began, and gave me a moment to fix my attention back on the nearer past.

49

"Okay," I said, to let him know I was ready to listen.

"Did you notice that man mixed in with the kids?"

"Yes, the guy who looked to be about thirty-five or so?"

"Dark brown hair, five ten, medium build."

"Right. Yes, of course I noticed him. He stood out."

"You think there was something fishy about him?"

"There was another older student," I said, not really protesting Tolliver's direction, but testing it out.

"Yeah, but she was a regular person. There was something off about this guy; he was there for a purpose, not because he had to be. You think he was some kind of professional debunker? There to spot how we did it, and expose us?"

"Well, I think that was Clyde Nunley's goal in teaching the course, don't you? Not an inquiry to stimulate students' minds to seriously consider spiritualism and the people who practice it, but to prove that it's all claptrap."

"But not as . . . I don't know, this guy seemed to have an agenda. He was purposeful."

"I know what you mean," I said.

"You think we've been set up?"

"Yes, I sure do think so. Unless this is most amazing coincidence in the history of coincidences."

"But why?" Tolliver turned his head to look at me.

"And who?" I countered.

The worry in his face mirrored my own.

My business would die without word of mouth. But it has to be a quiet word. If I brought a trail of newspaper and television reporters with me, half the people who use my services wouldn't want to see me coming. There are a few who'd love nothing better, but only a few. Most clients are embarrassed at hiring me at all, because they don't want to seem gullible. Some are desperate enough to be just that. But very few of them want any outside scrutiny.

So restrained coverage from time to time is okay. Once, a really good reporter wrote a story on me for a law enforcement journal, and I still get business from that exposure. Lots of officers clipped that story; when all else fails, they may get in touch with me through my website. My prices scare off some of the people who apply for my services. I'm not a lawyer, and no one asks me to do pro bono work.

Well, that's not true. People do. But I refuse.

However, I've never left a body unreported. If I find one in the course of a job, I'll report it, and I never ask for extra money for that.

If I got into the news too much, I'd be absolutely grabbing at pro bono work, just to get the good press. I didn't want to have to do that.

"Who do you think would hire such a person? Someone I didn't satisfy?" I asked the ceiling.

"We've found everyone since Tabitha," Tolliver said.

Yes, I'd had a long string of successes: cases with enough information to go on and enough persistence on my part. Bodies found, causes of death confirmed. Money in the bank.

"Maybe someone connected with the college who wanted to check on what the class was being exposed to?" I guessed.

"Could be. Or someone connected with St. Margaret's, who felt the cemetery was being used in some irreligious way."

We both fell silent, puzzled and unhappy about too many things at once.

"I'm glad I found her, though," I said. "No matter what."

My brother, who had followed my thoughts as he often did, said, "Yeah."

"Nice people," I said.

"You never thought what the police suspected — ?"

"No," I said. "I never believed Joel did it. These days, everyone looks at the dad first. Did he molest her?" I did my television announcer voice. "Were there dark secrets in the house that seemed so normal?" I smiled with a twist of my mouth. People sure loved believing there were dark secrets — they love discovering happy normal families are anything but. Truly, sometimes there were plenty of secrets, more than enough to go around. But Joel and Diane Morgenstern had struck me as truly devoted parents, and I'd seen enough of the kind of parents who weren't to recognize the ones who were.

"I never believed it," I repeated. "But — here they are. In Memphis." We looked at each other. "How the hell could it have happened that her body turned up here, the city where her parents are living now? Unless there's a connection."

There was a tap at our suite door.

"The troops are here," Tolliver said.

"Well. The troop."

Art was missing a lot of his hair. What remained was curly and white. He was very heavy, but he dressed very well. So he looked like an eminently respectable, sweet-natured grandpa — which just goes to show how deceptive appearances can be.

Art maintains the fiction that he is my father substitute.

"Harper!" he cried, throwing open his arms. I stepped in, gave him a light hug, and backed away when I could. Tolliver got a clap on the shoulder and a handshake.

We asked about his wife, and he told us what (but not how) Johanna was doing: taking art classes, keeping the grandchildren, remaining active in their church and several charities.

Not that we'd ever met Johanna.

I watched Art grope, trying to think of someone he could ask us about in return. He could hardly ask about our parents: my mother had died the previous year, in jail, of AIDS. Tolliver's mother had died years ago, of breast cancer, before we'd even met Art. Tolliver's dad, my stepfather, was in the wind since he'd gotten out of jail, having served his time on drug charges. My own father was still in big-boy prison, and would be for maybe five more years. He'd taken some money from his clients to support the drug habit he and my mother had developed. We never saw our little half sisters,

Gracie and Mariella, because my Aunt Iona, my mom's sister, had poisoned the girls against us. Tolliver's brother, Mark, had his own life, and didn't much approve of ours, but we called him at least once a month.

And of course, there was never any news about Cameron.

"It's great to see you two looking so healthy," Art said in his heartiest voice. "Now, let's order some room service, and you can tell me all about this." Art loved it when we ate together. Not only did it make the meal billable, but it also reassured Art that Tolliver and I were normal people and not some kind of vampires. After all, we ate and drank like the rest of the world.

"It should be up in a minute," Tolliver said, and Art had to go on and on about how amazed he was that Tolliver had been so farseeing.

Actually, I was pretty impressed myself.

Art made notes throughout the meal as we told him everything we remembered about our previous search for Tabitha Morgenstern. My brother got out his laptop and checked our records to be sure of how much the Morgensterns had paid us for our fruitless search. We assured Art that we had no intention of charging them anything for finding her today — in fact, the idea made me sick. Art looked kind of relieved when I told him that.

"There's no way we can leave here without seeing the Morgensterns or talking to the police?" I asked, knowing I sounded cowardly.

"No way in the world," Art said. For once, he sounded as hard as he actually was. "In fact, the sooner you talk to them, the better. And you have to issue a press statement."

"Why?" Tolliver asked.

"Silence is suspicious. You have to say clearly that you had no idea that you would find Tabitha's body, that you're shocked and saddened, and that you are praying for the Morgensterns."

"We already told Channel Thirteen that."

"You need to tell everyone."

"You'll do that for us?"

"Yes. We need to write a statement. I'll read it on-camera for you. I'll take a few questions from the press, just enough to establish who you are. After that, I think questions will just muddy the water, especially since I won't be able to answer them."

I looked at Art, perhaps with a certain skepticism; he gave me big hurt eyes. "Harper, you know I wouldn't put you all in a spot hotter than the one you're in already. But we have to set the record straight while we can."

"You think we're going to be arrested?"

"Not necessarily. I didn't say that. I meant, highly unlikely." Art was backpedaling to firmer ground. "I'm saying this is our chance to get in our licks with the public, while we can."

Tolliver looked at Art for a minute. "All right," he said, when he reached his conclusion. "Art, you stay here while Harper and I go in the other room and write the press statement. Then you can look it over."

Leaving our lawyer no chance to offer another plan, we retreated to Tolliver's room, with his laptop to act as our secretary.

Tolliver settled at the desk, while I flung myself across the bed. "Dr. Nunley never said anything to you, did he, about Tabitha? When he asked us to come here?" I asked.

"Not a word. I would have told you," Tolliver said. "He just talked about the old cemetery, about how it would be a true test, since you really had no idea who was buried there and there was no way you could find out. He wanted to know if you'd be comfortable with that. Of course, he thought I'd make some excuse for you, trying to back out. Nunley was really surprised when I emailed him back, told him to expect us. He'd just had Xylda Bernardo, the psychic.

She lives in this area, remember?"

I'd met Xylda once or twice, in the line of duty. "How'd she do?" I asked, out of sheer professional curiosity. Xylda, a colorful woman in her fifties, likes to dress in the traditional stage-gypsy style — lots of jewelry and scarves, long messy hair — which immediately makes people distrust her. But Xylda has a true gift. Unfortunately, like most commercial psychics, she embellishes that nugget of talent with a lot of theatrics and made-up flourishes, which she thinks lend her visions credibility.

Psychics — honest psychics — do receive a lot of information when they touch something a crime victim owned. The bad part is, quite often they receive information so vague it's almost useless ("The body's buried in the middle of an empty field"), unless you have a good idea what you're looking for to begin with. Even if there are a few psychics who can see a clear picture of, say, the house where a child's being held hostage, unless the psychic can also see the address, and the police find an identifiable suspect lives in that house, the building's appearance is almost irrelevant. There are even some psychics who can achieve all that, but then they have to get the police to believe them . . . since I've never met a single psychic who was also up on SWAT tactics.

"Oh, according to Nunley, Xylda did her usual," Tolliver said. "Vague stuff that sounded really good, like 'Your grandmother says to look for something unexpected in the attic, something that will make you very happy,' or 'Be careful of the dark man who comes unexpectedly, for he is not trustworthy,' and that's flexible enough to cover a lot of circumstances. The members of the class were pretty weirded out, since Xylda insists on touching the people she's reading. The students didn't want Xylda holding their hands. But that's the way it's done; for Xylda, touch is everything. You think she's for real?"

"I think most of what Xylda tells clients is bullshit. But I also think she actually has a few moments when she knows stuff."

Every now and then, I wonder: if the lightning had hit me a little harder, if I'd gotten a few more volts — would I have become able to see *who* caused the deaths of the people I find? Sometimes I think such a condition would be wonderful, a truly valuable gift. Sometimes it seems like my worst nightmare.

What if the lightning had entered through

my foot, or my head, instead of jumping from the sink to the electric hair curler I held in my hands . . . what would have happened then? I probably wouldn't be around to know. My heart would have stopped for good, instead of for a few seconds. The CPR wouldn't have worked.

By now, Tolliver might be married to some nice girl who liked to be pregnant, the kind of girl who enjoyed going to home decoration parties.

Carrying this stream of supposition to an extreme length — if I'd died that day, maybe, somehow, Cameron would not have been on the road on that day at that hour, and she would not have been taken.

It's stupid and profitless, thinking like that, of course. So I don't indulge in it very often. Right at this moment, I needed to force myself to throw off this train of thought. Instead of daydreaming, I needed to concentrate on helping Tolliver compose the press release. What he'd said to Shellie Quail had been the gist of our public policy. We began embroidering on that. It was hard to imagine that anyone would believe us; after all, what were the odds that the same people who had failed to find the body in Nashville would find it in Memphis? But we had to try.

We'd just finished printing out our statement when I had to answer the phone. The manager said, "Ms. Connelly, there are some people down here who want to come up to talk to you and Mr. Lang. Are you receiving guests?"

"Who are they, please?"

"The Morgensterns. And another lady."

Diane and Joel. My heart sank, but this had to be done. "Yes, send them up, please."

Tolliver stepped into the living room to update Art while I printed out the statement. Art read it and made a few minor changes while we waited. In two or three minutes a hand rapped on our door.

I took a deep breath and opened it, and received yet another shock in a day that had already been full of them. Detective Lacey had told us Diane was expecting another baby, but I hadn't gotten a visual with that fact. Seeing her now, there was no mistaking it. Diane Morgenstern was really, really pregnant — seven months along, at the least.

She was still beautiful. Her bitter-chocolate hair was smooth and short, and her big dark eyes owed nothing to makeup. Diane had a small mouth and a small nose. She looked like a really pretty lemur of some kind. Just at the moment, though, her expression was simply blank with shock.

Her husband, Joel, was maybe five foot ten and stocky, powerful looking. He'd been a wrestler in college. I remembered the trophies in his study in their Nashville house. He had light red hair and bright blue eyes, a ruddy complexion, and a square face with a nose like a knife blade. How did all this add to up to a man women could not ignore? I don't have the faintest idea. Joel Morgenstern was the kind of man who focused on the person to whom he was speaking, which might have been the secret of the magnetism he exuded. To Joel's credit, he didn't seem to be aware of this; or maybe he took it so for granted that he didn't even think of the effect he had on women.

In Nashville, even under the circumstances I'd noticed how the female representatives of the media clustered around him. Maybe they'd been thinking the father is always a likely suspect, maybe they'd been trying to pick holes in his story, but they'd hovered around him like hummingbirds at a big red blossom. Not too surprisingly, the police had checked over and over to see if Joel was having an affair. They hadn't found a trace of such a thing; in fact, everyone who knew Joel commented on how devoted he was to Diane. For that matter, it was universal knowledge how caring he'd been during his first wife's terminal illness.

Maybe because lightning had fried my brain, maybe because my standards of judgment were completely different, Joel just didn't affect me like he did most women.

Felicia Hart, whose sister had been Joel's first wife, trailed in after Diane and Joel. I remembered Felicia from my first encounter with the family. She had been trying hard to be a good aunt to Victor, the son that first marriage had produced. She'd been aware that Victor was a suspect in Tabitha's disappearance, and she'd been at the house constantly, perhaps imagining that the loss of their daughter had meant that Diane and Joel would not be able to focus on Victor's needs and on his legal position.

"You found her," Joel said, taking my hand and pumping it ferociously. "God bless you, you found her. The medical examiner says there's a long way to go before an official identification, but the dental charts do match. We have to keep this to ourselves, but Dr. Frierson was kind enough to let us know in person. Thank God, we can have some peace."

This was such a different reaction from the one I'd expected that I was unable to respond. Luckily, Tolliver was more collected.

"Please, Diane, Joel, sit down," he said. Tolliver is very reverent toward pregnant women.

Diane had always seemed the frailer partner in the couple, even when she wasn't so obviously carrying a child.

"Let me hug you first," she said in her soft voice, and she wrapped her arms around me. I felt her distended belly pressing against my flat one, and I felt something wiggle while she was hugging me. After a second, I realized it was the baby, kicking against her stomach. Something deep inside me clenched in a mixture of horror and longing. I let Diane go and backed away, trying to smile at her.

Felicia Hart was no hugger, to my relief. She gave me a firm handshake, though she did put her arms around Tolliver. In fact, she muttered something in his ear. I blinked at that. "Glad to see you," she said a bit loudly, addressing an area somewhere between us. Felicia was a single woman. I placed her in her early thirties. She had jaw-length glossy brown hair that curved forward, and her expertly cut bangs stayed where they were supposed to be. As a professional woman on her own, she could

64

spend all her money on herself, and her clothes and makeup showed it. If I remembered correctly, Felicia was a financial adviser employed by a national company. Though I hadn't talked to her at any length, I knew Felicia would have to be both intelligent and bold to hold down so responsible a job with such success.

When we were all seated, Joel and Diane on the love seat, Felicia perched on one arm of it by Diane, and Tolliver and I in wing chairs on the other side of the coffee table, with Art settled uncomfortably on a chair set a bit aside, I realized I had to somehow proceed with a conversation.

"I'm so sorry," I said finally, since that was the truth. "I'm sorry I found her so late, and I'm sorry the circumstances make life even more difficult for you." It made life a hell of a lot more difficult for us, too, but this didn't seem like the moment to dwell on it.

"You're right, this doesn't look good for us," Joel said. He took Diane's hand. "We were already under suspicion. Not Felicia, of course, but Diane and I and Victor, and now that . . ." He had trouble going on. "Now that her body has been found here — of all the places on earth — I think the police are going to decide it was one of us all along. I almost don't blame them. It just looks bad. If I didn't know how much we loved Tabitha . . ." He sighed heavily. "Maybe they think we conspired together to kill our daughter. They're paid to be suspicious. They can't know it's the last thing in the world we'd do. But as long as they're focusing on us, they won't be looking for the son of a bitch who actually took her."

"Exactly," Diane said, and her hand rubbed her stomach in a circular motion. I yanked my gaze away.

"How long have the police suspected you?" Tolliver asked. When we'd been there, Tabitha had been missing for several weeks, and the police hadn't been around so much any more. But we'd been impressed at how cordial the relationship that had formed between Detective Haines, who'd been the Last Man Standing on the case, and the Morgensterns had seemed. I should have realized that the other cops might have developed other suspicions. Haines had actually gotten to know the Morgensterns a lot better than her associates.

"From the get-go," Joel said, his voice resigned. "After nosing around Vic for a while, they got the idea that Diane was guilty."

I could almost see why they'd suspect Joel,

even Victor. But Diane?

"How could that be?" I said incautiously, and she flushed. "I'm sorry," I said instantly. "I'm not trying to dredge up bad memories. I was sure, always, that you and Joel were telling the truth."

"Tabitha and I had a fight that morning," Diane said. Big fat tears ran down her cheeks. "I was mad because we'd just given her a cell phone for her birthday, and she'd already exceeded her minutes. I took her cell away from her, and then I told her to go outside to water the plants around the front door, just to get her out of the house because I was so angry. She was furious, too. Spring break, and no way to communicate with her three hundred best friends. She was just into that 'Mo-THER!' stage, the eye-rolling thing." Diane wiped her face with Joel's handkerchief. "I didn't think we'd get to that until she was fifteen, and here she was, eleven years old, giving me the whole routine." She smiled in a watery sort of way. "I hated to tell the police about this really trivial conversation, but one of my neighbors overheard us arguing when she came over to ask if we were through with our paper. So then I had to relate the whole thing to the police, and they turned hostile so quickly, as if I'd been withholding important evidence from them!"

Of course, to the police, this was important evidence. The fact that Diane couldn't see that only proved what I'd suspected about her when I'd met her: Diane Morgenstern was no rocket scientist. I was willing to bet that she never read crime fiction, either. If she had, she'd have known that any such revelation would make the police suspicious.

All the incident really proved was that Diane was out of touch with popular culture, in the reading-and-television-watching category.

"When did you move to Memphis?" Tolliver asked.

"About a year ago," Joel said. "We couldn't wait there, in that house, any longer." He sat up a little straighter, and as if he were reciting a credo, he said, "We had to accept the fact that our daughter was gone, and we had to leave that house ourselves. It wouldn't be fair to the new family we're starting, to have the baby there. I actually grew up in Memphis, so it felt like coming home, to me. My parents are here. And Felicia was here, along with her parents, my first in-laws. She and Victor are very close, and we figured the move would be a good thing for him. He's had a very tough time."

So everyone was happy here, except possibly Diane. It hadn't been coming home for her. It had been a move to a strange city that held many memories for her husband, memories of his first wife.

"We'd had a lot of therapy, the whole family," Diane said softly.

"We all went, Diane and I and Victor," Joel said. "Even Felicia drove over to Nashville from Memphis to go to some of the sessions."

I'd been to therapy, too.

The high school guidance counselor had been horrified when Cameron's disappearance had exposed the conditions under which we lived. "Why didn't you come to me?" she'd asked, more than once. And one time she'd shaken her head and said, "I should have noticed." I didn't blame her for not noticing; after all, we'd gone to great efforts to conceal our home life, so we could stay together. Maybe a part of me had hoped that our substandard parents would be taken away and we would be given good parents, instead; but that hadn't happened.

"When is the new baby due?" Art asked in the cheerful voice parents used when they weren't going to be having any more babies themselves.

"In five weeks," Diane said, an involuntary

69

smile curving her lips even under the circumstances. "A healthy boy, the doctor says."

"That's great," Tolliver and I said, more or less in unison. I eyed Felicia Hart, who'd risen to stand behind the love seat. Felicia was looking less than ecstatic, perhaps even impatient. Maybe she thought the new baby would mean even more attention was diverted from Victor. It was also possible the childless Felicia was even more creeped out by pregnant women than I was.

"Today, we have to deal with Tabitha," Diane said, to give us an easement back into the grim reality of the body in the cemetery. "How . . . you know how she died?"

"She was suffocated," I said, not knowing any other way to say it. Severely deprived of air? Terminally oxygenless? I wasn't trying to tell myself jokes, but there are only so many ways to talk about the COD of any individual, even a child, especially to the mother.

The couple did their best to take the news on the chin, but Diane couldn't suppress a moan of horror. Felicia looked away, her face a hard mask concealing deep emotion.

There were many worse ways to die, but that would hardly be a consolation. Suffocation was bad enough. "It would be over in

70

seconds," I said, as gently as I could. "She would be unconscious, after a tiny bit." This was an exaggeration, but I thought Diane's condition called for as much cushioning as possible. I was terrified that she would go into labor right in front of us.

Art had the strangest expression as he looked at me. It was like he'd never seen me before; like the reality of me, of what I did, had just hit him in the portly belly he carried in front of him like an announcement of his own importance.

"We should call Vic," Joel said, in his warm voice. "Excuse me for a moment." He brushed at his eyes and groped in his pocket for his cell phone. Vic, Joel's son by his first marriage, had been a sullen fifteen-year-old at the time of Tabitha's abduction. I'd glimpsed him trying hard to be tough and contained in the face of an overwhelming situation.

Diane, who had seemed very fond of the boy and in fact had largely raised him — she'd married Joel when Victor was very young — said, "If he needs to talk to me, I'm okay," as Joel rose to walk a few feet away, his back to the room, to punch in the number.

"How's Victor done here in Memphis?" I asked Felicia, just to be saying something.

Victor and I had shared a strange moment when I'd been trying to find his half sister. The boy had come into the living room of the Morgenstern home and begun to curse a blue streak, evidently thinking he was by himself. When I'd moved, he'd clutched me, crying on my shoulder, having to bend a little to do so. People weren't given to touching me, and I'd been startled. But I knew grief, and I knew release, and I'd held him until he was through. When he'd done crying and my blouse was a blotched mess, Victor had drawn back, appalled at his breakdown. Anything I said would have been wrong, so I'd just given him a nod. He'd nodded back, and fled.

Felicia was giving a surprised look. I supposed she was astonished that I remembered Victor at all. "He's done . . . middling," she said. "Diane and Joel have sent him to a private school. I help them out a little. He's such a fragile kid, hanging in the balance. At that age, they can go either way, you feel, at any moment. And with this new baby coming . . ." Her voice trailed off, as if she couldn't imagine how to finish the sentence without criticizing Joel and Diane for their ill-timed fertility.

Joel came back and sat down by his wife, and he was frowning. "Victor isn't holding together very well," he said to us in general. Diane's face simply looked exhausted, as if she had no energy to spare for maintaining someone else's spirits when her own were so fraught with misery. "He came home from school early, after we called. We didn't want anyone to see it on the news at noon and tell him when they got back to campus," he explained.

We all nodded wisely, but my mind was on something entirely different.

"We never knew you moved," I said, wanting to get that absolutely clear, "so we were astonished when the police said they were contacting you. You don't have anything to do with the faculty at Bingham, do you? You're not an alumna, Diane?"

"No, I went to Vanderbilt, and Joel did, too," she said, bewildered. "Felicia, didn't you go to Bingham? With David?"

Felicia said, "More years ago than I care to remember. Yes, David was in my class. I don't believe you met him in Nashville, Harper. Joel's brother."

"Felicia's parents are here in Memphis, too," Diane said. "They both went to Bingham. And so did Joel's. It was quite a scandal when he decided to go to Vanderbilt. Why are you asking?"

"Just trying to think of some connection

between you and the school. Someone put Tabitha's . . . Tabitha there, and someone made sure we were hired for this job."

The couple sat and looked at me wide-eyed. I had the uncharitable thought that this increased Diane's resemblance to a lemur. Though the pregnant woman looked as though she were about to bolt, Joel was alert and intense. The man had an over-abundance of energy, and it boiled around him, even under these circumstances. Behind them, Felicia was staring at me with an incredulous face.

"Surely it's just a coincidence," Felicia said, finally, looking at me as though I were delusional. "You don't think . . . you can't imagine that someone created such an elaborate plot? How could someone have put Tabitha there, and then find you, get you here, make sure you found Tabitha? That's just incredible."

We all spent a second or two staring at each other. Art was looking from me to Felicia, as if we were playing Ping-Pong.

"I agree," I said. "But I can't make sense out of any other scenario. Actually, there's not much sense in that one."

"We have to issue some kind of statement to the press," Art said, when he realized the conversation had reached a stalemate. "It has to be a statement that treads a fine line. We can't rule anything out, like Diane just did. We can't make any fantastic claims, like Harper did. We have to regret everything and admit nothing about our personal feelings about what might have happened."

Tolliver was the only one who nodded his head in agreement.

"You know, our own lawyer is downstairs," Diane murmured.

At the same moment Joel erupted. "No!" he said. "No! We have to condemn whoever did this to our daughter in the strongest possible terms!" Diane and Felicia both nodded their agreement.

"Oh, of course," Art said. "Naturally, that, too."

FOUR

We turned on the television in the living room of the suite to watch Art meet the news cameras. There were three stations in Memphis, and all three had sent representatives to the press conference, which was held on the sidewalk outside the Cleveland. By that time, the Morgenstern family lawyer, a chic fortyish woman named Blythe Benson, had arrived on the scene. Joel and Diane had told us that Benson had insisted on the Morgenstern family issuing their own separate-but-equal statement. The local lawyer and Art made an impressive duo. Art had that older-man gravitas thing going, and Blythe was cool and blond and WASP-y to the nth degree.

Blythe had consulted with the Morgensterns at their home about what she was going to say on their behalf, Diane told us. Felicia shot me a glance as Diane said this, and I wondered what was coming. Felicia

Hart, as I've said, seemed way smarter than Diane. It made me wonder what Felicia's sister, Joel's first wife, had been like.

Downstairs and outside, Blythe Benson prepared to make the first statement. The family was most important, we had all agreed.

"Diane and Joel Morgenstern are devastated at the news that the body that may be that of their child, Tabitha, has been found in St. Margaret's cemetery. Though closure is something they have sought for many months, Diane and Joel Morgenstern had hoped that closure would come with the return of their living daughter. Instead, they have recovered what may well be her body." The blonde lawyer paused for effect. The newscasters were fairly quivering with the desire to ask questions, but Blythe plowed on. "The Morgenstern family would like to urge anyone who may have knowledge of the disappearance of Tabitha to come forward at this time. Though the reward for the discovery of her body is most likely out of consideration now, there is still a reward standing for the submission of facts about Tabitha's abduction."

I wasn't sure what that meant. I hadn't known there was a reward, since we hadn't maintained contact with the Morgensterns (naturally) after our failure to locate their daughter in Nashville.

Thinking that was the end of the statement, I'd turned to look at Tolliver to get his reaction when I heard Blythe Benson's precise voice continue. I looked back at the screen.

"As to what police have termed an 'amazing coincidence'— that the psychic Diane and Joel Morgenstern hired to find Tabitha's body actually did find the body, though in a different location . . ."

She's losing control of that sentence, I thought.

"The fact remains that there are coincidences in life, and this is one of them. Diane and Joel Morgenstern did not hire Harper Connelly to come to Memphis. They have not seen her or her manager since Miss Connelly arrived in Memphis. They did not know that Miss Connelly was scheduled to give a demonstration at the old cemetery of St. Margaret's this morning. Neither of the Morgensterns attended Bingham College. Neither has ever been connected with the college department that arranged Harper Connelly's visit to St. Margaret's cemetery. In fact, no member of the Morgenstern family has contacted Harper Connelly or her brother and manager, Tolliver Lang, since her unsuccessful attempt to find Tabitha over eighteen months ago. Thank you."

Though Art hadn't moved physically, the cameras caught him staring at Blythe Benson as though she'd just sprouted horns, and I didn't blame him for the look.

Just for openers, Benson's voice had emphasized "psychic" and "giving a demonstration" as if they were words for something far nastier and more disreputable. Then she'd gone on to sever her clients from us in every possible way. She'd all but said we were implicated somehow in the death of the girl.

We'd been hung out to dry.

As one, Tolliver and I turned to look at the couple on the couch. The Morgensterns seemed oblivious to the implications of the speech Blythe Benson had just read. They were staring at the television, waiting for Art's speech, in a kind of numb silence. Behind them, Felicia gave us a significant look that meant, "Ha! I told you so!" I exchanged a look with Tolliver, a look of sheer incredulity. He half-opened his mouth, and I reached over to touch his arm. "Not now," I said, very quietly.

I wasn't sure why I chose to be quiet, rather than confront Joel and Diane. God knows, even Diane was smart enough to realize that they'd just dumped us publicly, while sitting in our very own (temporarily) living room. They'd said, in effect, "Whatever these people claim, we're not responsible for it. We don't know them, we haven't seen them, we'd never collaborate with them, and they failed the first time we asked them to find our child."

Art took his place before the microphones. It's just strange seeing someone you know on television, not that it's an experience I've had often. The fact that the person who was just in the room with you is now on-camera, for the moment an icon, is weird and unsettling. It's as if they've become translated by the screen into another being — someone less flawed and more knowledgeable, someone smoother and smarter.

Art had our statement, the one Tolliver and I had written, but he was doing yet another rewrite in his head at just this minute; a hasty and public one. I could see it in the long downward focus of his eyes before he began speaking.

"My client, Harper Connelly, is astounded and grieved by the events of the day. At this moment Ms. Connelly is with Tabitha's parents, who came here to thank Harper, from their hearts, for her part in the discov-

80

ery of a body we believe to be that of their missing daughter."

Ha! Ball in your court, Blythe!

"Ms. Connelly is deeply saddened by the tragic end to her search for Tabitha Morgenstern. Though she did not maintain any contact whatsoever with the family during the months since her original employment, and though she had no knowledge that the Morgenstern family had moved to Memphis, Ms. Connelly is glad that circumstances brought about the discovery of the long-lost child the Morgensterns have been seeking. Perhaps, thanks to my client, the Morgensterns' long time of uncertainty has come to an end."

"When will Harper Connelly meet with us?" said a reporter, in a voice that was not awfully loud, but extremely piercing.

Art gave the reporter a wonderful look; it combined reproof with resignation. "Ms. Connelly does not talk to reporters," he said, as if that were a well-known fact. "Ms. Connelly lives a very private life."

"Is it true . . ." began a familiar voice, and the camera swung around to frame the shining Shellie Quail.

"For God's sake," I said. "She's everywhere."

Tolliver smiled. He thought the reporter's

81

doggedness was a little funny, maybe even admirable.

". . . that Miss Connelly charges a fee for finding bodies?"

"Ms. Connelly is a professional woman with an unusual gift," Art said. "She does not like to be in the spotlight of media attention, something she has never sought."

That's true enough, I thought. *Evasive, but true.*

"Is it true that your client will be claiming the reward for finding Tabitha's body?" asked Shellie Quail, and Tolliver's smile vanished in the blink of my eye.

"That's not a subject we've discussed," Art concluded. "I have no more to say at this time. Thank you for coming." And he turned to pace back inside the Cleveland's front door. The Morgensterns' lawyer was nowhere to be seen. Blythe Benson had slipped away in the preceding moments, apparently.

I hoped she didn't plan on coming up to the suite.

The cameras cut back to the scheduled program, and in a moment Art returned to the room, in actual reality. Again, I felt that curious jolt.

"That went well," Joel said without a touch of irony. Tolliver and I had to struggle to keep our faces neutral. "And of course, you'll get the reward." Joel got up, checked his watch. "Diane, we have to get home. We have people to call. I wonder how long it will take for them to be sure they've got . . . Tabitha's remains. When we can have them."

Felicia picked up her purse and Diane's, ready to help the pregnant woman return to their car.

With a heave, Diane got to her feet. She was absently rubbing her hand across her gravid stomach, as if to keep its contents calm. I remembered my own mother's pregnancies with Mariella and Gracie. I also couldn't help recalling *Rosemary's Baby;* Tolliver and I had watched it the week before on an old-movie channel.

"Thanks, Felicia," Diane said.

"Let us know how Victor's doing," Tolliver asked out of the clear blue sky.

"What?" Felicia turned, and her eyes pinned Tolliver to the wall. "Why, of course." There was a bite to her voice that I simply didn't understand. I looked from her to Tolliver, but didn't get an explanation.

"This has been harder on Victor than just about anyone," Joel said. "Kids can be so cruel."

"Victor's what, now? Sixteen?" I asked brightly, trying to ease the atmosphere. I don't know why. I should have stood in absolute silence until the party left.

"He's just turned seventeen," Diane said. Suddenly her face lost its Madonna-like sweetness. She had struck me, even when I'd first met her after the abduction, as a woman fed up to the teeth with her stepson's moody teenage behavior, and now her jaw had a certain set that gave her simple words a real edge. "I love that boy, but everything they say about teenagers is true, as far as Vic's concerned: he's been secretive and sullen or talking back for the past three years. When Tabitha began to show signs she was entering the same phase, I just wasn't ready for it. I overreacted."

Victor had been a spotty — but athletic and attractive — boy eighteen months before. I remembered him always skulking on the edge of any group of adults in the Morgenstern home, his face tight with suppressed — rage? Fear? I hoped for the boy's sake that his complexion and his attitude had cleared up now. I was willing to believe Victor had feelings and thoughts that were complicated and dealt with something besides himself, but only because I tried to believe that of all people.

"How can you say that, Diane?" Felicia asked, but without much real indignation.

"He's been yours since he was a baby. You have to love him, like I do."

"I do love him," Diane said, sounding as surprised as an emotionally exhausted pregnant woman can. "I've always loved him, at first for his mother's sake, but then because I raised him as my son. You, of all people, should know that. Even if he were my own biological child, I'd be having a hard time with him right now. It's not him, it's his stage of life."

"He doesn't like school here very much," Joel said. He sounded just as tired as his wife, as if dealing with Victor wore him out. "But he's great on the tennis team."

"Poor Victor," my brother said, somewhat to my surprise.

"Yes, the whole thing's been very hard on him, too," Joel said. "Of course, he was sure he was going to be arrested and executed instantly, the drastic way teenagers decide things, when the police questioned him very . . . persistently."

"They thought he might resent his little sister, the attention she got as the child of the second marriage." Then Diane went absolutely still, and I had a moment of panic, thinking something was happening with the baby. But it was just one of the moments when anguish comes sweeping down like an eagle from the air, to tear at you with cruel talons.

"Oh, Tabitha," Diane said, in a low voice that contained profound grief. "Oh, my girl." Large tears began to roll from her beautiful dark eyes.

Her husband put his arm around her and together they left to return to their new home. Felicia trailed after them, her face heavy with unhappiness.

I looked at the closed door a few minutes after they'd passed through it. I wondered if the baby's room was ready yet. I wondered what they'd done with all Tabitha's things.

With their departure, the tension eased out of the room. Art, Tolliver, and I looked at each other with some relief.

"That's great news, about the reward. Last I heard, it was up to twenty-five thousand dollars. Before taxes, of course." Art was reviewing the afternoon mentally, I could tell from the way he was drumming his fingers on the occasional table. "I'm glad I went second, after all," Art said next. "I've heard of Blythe Benson. She said a few things I took issue with."

"Yeah, we noticed." Tolliver got a cross-word puzzle book out of his laptop bag and began rummaging around in the bottom of the pocket for his pencil.

Art looked irritated. "You think I could have handled it differently, Tolliver, you say so."

Tolliver looked up, apparently surprised. "No, Art, no problem. You, Harper?"

"I noticed you didn't say Tolliver was your client, too, Art," I said.

Art did his best to seem surprised; though I thought his only real surprise was that we'd noticed the omission. "Tolliver's name hadn't been brought into the mix at that point, I was just trying to keep it that way," he said. "You want me to call all the reporters and correct myself?"

"No, Art, that's fine," I said. "Just, for future reference, be more thorough and include that little detail."

"Message received," Art said brightly. "It's been a long day for an old man, kids. I'm going to my room, call the office, catch up on my work."

"Sure, Art," Tolliver said, his attention on the puzzle open before him. "If you're not flying back to Atlanta until tomorrow, you'll have to join us for dinner."

"Thanks, we'll see how much work I have to do tonight. I may just get room service. But give me a call when you're ready to head out."

"See you later," I said.

When he was safely gone, I said, "What do you think he's heard?"

"I was trying to figure it out. Maybe the police think I had Tabitha's body all this time and moved it into the cemetery to prove you were a genuine sensitive."

I gaped at him and then laughed. It was just too ridiculous.

Tolliver put down his pencil and focused on me. "Yeah, right. I don't know where I'm supposed to have stowed the poor girl's body for eighteen months, or whatever."

"The trunk," I said, deadpan, and after a second he smiled at me. It was a real smile, something he didn't give me that often, and I enjoyed seeing it. Tolliver hadn't been struck by lightning, and his mom hadn't tried to sell him to one of her drug buddies for sexual use, it's true, but Tolliver has his own scars, and he's not any more fond of talking about them than I am.

"Tabitha was somewhere for eighteen months," Tolliver pointed out. "That is, her body was either in that grave, or in some other hiding place."

"Was she there all the time?" I asked, but I was just thinking out loud. "I don't think so. The earth was disturbed. The rest of the ground in the cemetery was smooth, but this ground had an uneven feeling, and there wasn't any grass on the grave."

"Well, we know she was buried somewhere during the last eighteen months," Tolliver pointed out reasonably.

"No, she could have been alive for part of that time. Or she could have been dead in a freezer, or a meat locker, or a morgue. Or buried somewhere else, as you say." I thought about the possibilities I'd raised. "But I don't think so. I still believe she's been dead since she was abducted, or very nearly the whole time. But she wasn't lying in St. Margaret's all that time. I just don't understand why she was put there, and how it happened that I was the one to find her. It's so strange."

"In fact, it's almost . . . unbelievable," Tolliver said, his voice quiet and thoughtful.

FIVE

The morning didn't start on any more of a positive note. I turned on CNN while I drank my morning coffee, the complimentary newspaper folded open to the page that featured an old picture of Tabitha, a recent shot of the Morgensterns, and a picture of me taken when I was at a crime scene about two years ago.

The TV coverage was just as hyper as the newspaper article. The FBI had definitely had a presence at the initial crime of Tabitha's kidnapping. Now, they'd put their expertise at the service of the Memphis police, including the resources of their lab.

"We are confident in the ability of the Memphis police to conduct this investigation," said an agent who looked like he ate nails for breakfast. "We'll have an agent in place who participated in the investigation of Tabitha's abduction, and he'll make available any service he can offer to local officials. All we want is to get justice for this little girl and her family."

I wondered if we'd be allowed to leave for our apartment in St. Louis — though it would be better yet if we could slip away to some unexpected destination, so we'd be harder to track. We weren't in residence at our apartment often, true, but it was our address of record, and the news media would definitely find us there.

I didn't remember what the next job on our list was, or even if we had one. Tolliver managed that side of our lives. I was already restless and bored, having finished the one book I'd brought in from our car. Ordinarily, I'd go out for a run.

There was no point whatsoever in trying to run today. Though I still felt a bit shaky from yesterday's discovery, I was definitely in the mood to get in a couple of miles, or more. But if I ran today, I'd be followed, and that was no fun.

Tolliver knocked at the connecting door, and I called to him to come in. He was toweling the wetness out of his hair.

"I went running on the treadmill in the health club," he said, in answer to my unspoken question. "It was better than nothing."

I hate running on treadmills. It just makes

me feel stupid. I'm not really going anywhere. But this morning I was willing, since I needed activity in the worst kind of way. While he poured his own cup of coffee, I was on the elevator in my running shoes and my shorts and my T-shirt.

There were several treadmills. One was already occupied by a man who was probably in his forties, dark hair just beginning to turn silvery at the edges. He was pounding along, his face set and remote. He gave me an absent nod, which I barely returned.

I studied the control panel and the instructions, since I couldn't imagine anything that would make me feel stupider than flying off the back of a treadmill. When I was confident I understood what I was doing, I started off slow, getting used to the feel of the rubber under my feet. I thought of nothing, just the feeling of my shoes hitting the treadmill, and then I reached down and pressed the control to increase the speed. Soon I was going at a good clip — and though I was indoors and not going anywhere and the damn scenery never changed, I was content. I began sweating, and gradually I began to feel that welcome exhaustion that tells you you've gone just about your limit. I slowed the pace a bit, and then slowed again, and finally I walked for about five minutes.

I'd been vaguely aware Mr. Silvertip was still in the room, moving from weight station to weight station, one of the hotel towels around his neck. I headed for the stack on a table by the door as soon as I was through, and while I was patting my face dry, a voice said, "It's good to run in the mornings, isn't it? Helps you to start your day on a good note."

I lowered the towel to appraise the speaker.

"FBI?" I asked.

He couldn't control his jerk of surprise. "You're really psychic," he said pleasantly after a moment.

"No, I'm not," I said. "Or only in the most limited way. Were you down here when Tolliver ran, too?"

He had dark blue eyes, and he examined me with them very carefully. I was exasperated. He'd had plenty of time to look me over while I was running. This wasn't about him deciding I was a hunkette of burning love. This was about something else.

"I decided you were more approachable," he said. "And you're the more interesting, of the two of you."

"You're wrong there," I said.

He looked down at my right leg. The top

part of the leg is marked with a fine spider's web of red lines. My Lycra running shorts stopped at mid-thigh, and the web was clearly visible if you looked at the right leg with attention. That's the leg that gives out, every now and then. That's another reason I need to run, to keep that leg strong.

"What happened to you?" he asked. "I've never seen marks like that." He was quite clinical.

"I was hit by lightning," I said.

He made an impatient movement, as if he'd read that and just recalled it. Or maybe he simply didn't believe me. "How'd it come about?" he asked.

I explained the circumstances. "I was doing my hair. I had a date," I said, remotely remembering that detail. "Of course, I never went out with that boy. The blast blew my shoe off and stopped my heart."

"What saved you?"

"My brother, Tolliver. Gave me CPR."

"I've never met anyone before who was hit by lightning and lived to tell about it."

"There are plenty of us around," I said, and I went out the glass door, towel still clutched in my hand.

"Wait," he said behind me. "I'd like to talk to you, if I may."

I turned to face him. A woman stepped

past us, ready for her own workout. She was wearing old shorts and a T-shirt dingy with age. She glanced at us curiously. I found myself glad to have a witness.

"What about?"

"I was there, in Nashville, for a while. That's why I got this assignment."

I waited.

"I really want to know how you knew ahead of time that Tabitha was in the graveyard."

"I didn't."

"But you did."

"If you're not in charge of the investigation, I don't have to talk to you, do I? And I can't think of any reason I'd want to."

"I'm Agent Seth Koenig." He said that as if I should have heard the name.

"I don't care." And I got into the elevator before he could, pressed the door close button, and smiled as he took a surprised step toward me, realizing I was actually leaving.

After I showered, I knocked on the door to Tolliver's room and told him what had happened.

"That bastard. That was an ambush," Tolliver said.

"That's putting it a little strong. It was more like a strategic approach," I said.

Tolliver recognized my description of Seth

Koenig. The agent had been in the exercise room when he was, sure enough. "He thought you would recognize his name, huh?" Tolliver said thoughtfully. "Well, let's see." Tolliver's laptop was already plugged in. He Googled the name and got several hits. Seth Koenig had been present at a few hunts for serial killers. Seth Koenig had been a heavy hitter.

"But all those are in the past," I said, reading the dates. "Nothing in the last four years or so."

"That's true," Tolliver said. "I wonder what happened to his career?"

"And I wonder why he's here. I haven't heard any suggestion that Tabitha's abduction and death was part of any serial killer's pattern. And I think I'd remember if another girl had shown up buried in a cemetery, miles away from her abduction site, buried on top of somebody else, right?" I thought that over. "Actually, other than her burial, there's nothing distinctive about Tabitha's case. That in itself is pretty awful, when you think about it."

Tolliver wasn't in the mood to discuss the degeneration of American society as exemplified by the emergence of the serial killer as common occurrence. He just nodded.

"He's different," I said. "Seth Koenig."

"Define."

I shook my head. "He's pretty intense, pretty deep. Not your regular law enforcement type."

"You hot for him?"

I laughed. "Nah. He's too old for me."

"How old?"

"Probably in his early forties."

"But in good shape, you said."

There are times when I just don't appreciate Tolliver's teasing. "I'm not talking about his body. I'm talking about his head."

"Can you pin that down a little?"

"I think . . ." I hesitated for a long moment, uneasy about putting my idea into words. "I think he's more than professionally interested. Maybe obsessed."

"With you," Tolliver said, very levelly.

"No, with Tabitha. Not her personally." I struggled to express what I felt. "He's obsessed with the puzzle of it. You know, how some people spend a large part of their lives rehashing the Lizzie Borden case? How futile that is, because all the people involved are dead and gone? But there are still books appearing all the time about it. I think that's how Seth Koenig is about Tabitha Morgenstern. Look at his work record. He hasn't done anything newsworthy since he worked her case. And here he is, Johnny-on-the-spot, when she's found. Not because of Tabitha as a person, or because of Joel and Diane, but because of the mystery of it. Like some of the law enforcement people in Colorado are about that little girl who was killed in her own home."

"The little beauty queen. You think Seth is as fascinated with Tabitha as some people are with her?"

"Yes, I think that's possible. And I think it's dangerous," I said.

I sat beside him on the end of his bed and found myself looking at the picture he'd stuck in the mirror frame, a picture he carried with him on the road. It was a snapshot of Cameron, Mark, Tolliver, and me. We're all smiling, but not genuinely. Mark's looking down a little, his stout build and round face distinguishing him from the rest of us. Cameron's to my left, in profile, looking away. Her light hair is pulled up in a ponytail. Tolliver and I are in the center, and his arm is around my shoulders. At first glance, you might assume that Tolliver and I were the brother and sister; we're both dark-headed and pale and slim. But if you spend any time with us, you notice that my face is longer and narrower than Tolliver's, which is practically square. And his eyes are a rich dark brown. Mine, though also dark and often mistaken for brown (since people see what they expect to see), are actually gray. Tolliver's mouth is thin and fine-lipped; mine is full. Tolliver had acne as a teen that went untreated, and he has scars on his cheeks as a result. My skin is smooth and fine. Tolliver has a lot of attraction for the opposite sex, and I don't seem to have much of that.

"You just scare them," Tolliver said quietly.

"Was I talking out loud?"

"No, I could just follow what you were thinking," he said. "You're the only psychic in this family." He put his arm around me and gave me a hug.

"You know I don't like to be called psychic," I said, but I wasn't really angry.

"I know, but what else would you call it?'

We'd had this discussion before. "I am a corpse-finder," I said, with mock hauteur. "I'm the Human Geiger-Counter."

"You need a superhero outfit. You'd look good in gray and red," Tolliver said. "Tights and a cape, maybe some red gloves, high red boots?" I smiled at the picture. "After this media hoopla is over, we can go to the apartment for about a week," Tolliver said. "We can catch up on our laundry and our sleep."

The apartment in St. Louis wasn't great,

but it beat living in a hotel, no matter how fancy. We could open our mail (what little we got), wash our clothes, cook a little.

The constant travel was getting increasingly old. We'd been at it for five years now, at first making almost nothing; in fact, we'd gone into debt. But the past three years, as the word spread, business had started becoming regular, and we'd even turned down a job or two. We'd paid back what we owed, and we'd saved a lot.

Someday, we wanted to buy a house, maybe in Texas, so we wouldn't be too far from our little sisters — though the chances were slim that we'd get to visit with them much, thanks to my aunt Iona and her husband. But we would be on hand when we were needed, and maybe seeing us from time to time would waken better memories for Mariella and Gracie.

When we had a house, we would buy a lawn mower, and I would mow every week. I would have a big planter, one of those that looked like a truncated barrel, and I'd fill it with flowers. Butterflies would perch on them, and bees would lumber in and out. I wanted one of those big Rubbermaid mailboxes, too. You could get them at Wal-Mart.

"Harper?"

"What?"

"You had that dazed look again. What's up?"

"Thinking about a house," I admitted.

"Well, maybe next year," Tolliver said.

"Really?"

"Yeah, our bank account is healthy. If we don't have any catastrophes . . ."

I sobered immediately. Of course, health insurance is hard to get for people like us, since we don't have what you'd call regular jobs, and the lightning strike was always classified as a pre-existing condition. That meant I couldn't claim coverage for anything that the insurance people could classify as resulting from the lightning strike. We had to pay an outrageous amount for the most basic policy. It made me angry every time I thought about it. I did everything I could to keep healthy.

"Okay, we won't wreck the car or break a bone or get sued," I said. We did a lot of doctoring on each other for the everyday sprains and cuts, and we'd spent a week in a motel in Montana when Tolliver had had the flu. But the only persistent health issues facing us were my continuing problems from the lightning strike.

You'd think after you'd recovered from the initial effects, that would be it. Most doctors believe that, too. But that's not the truth. I talk to other strike survivors on the Internet. Memory loss, severe headaches, depression, burning sensations in the feet, ringing in the ears, loss of mobility, and a host of other effects can manifest in the years afterward. Whether these are a result of the neuroses of the victims — which is what most doctors say — or a result of the mysterious reaction of the body to an almost unimaginable jolt of electricity . . . well, opinions vary.

I have my own set of problems, and luckily for me they're pretty consistent.

As far as I know, there is no other strike survivor who has become able to find dead people.

I'd had plenty of time to shower and dress and wonder what we were going to do with our day, when that problem was solved for us. The police came by again, to ask more questions.

Detective Lacey had a chaperone this time, another detective named Brittany Young. Detective Young was in her thirties, and she was a narrow-faced woman with short tousled brown hair and glasses. She had a huge handbag and comfortable shoes, clothes that were no higher-end than Sears, and a gold band on her left hand. She looked around the hotel room curiously, and then she examined me with even more curiosity.

"Do you always travel in this kind of style?" she asked, while Detective Lacey was talking to Tolliver. I sensed they had a plan. Why, gee, what could it be?

"Not hardly," I said. "We're more Holiday Inn or Motel 6 people. But we had to have the security."

She nodded, as if she really understood that and didn't think we were pretentious. Detective Brittany Young was establishing a rapport with me. She grinned at me. I grinned back. I'd done this dance before with other partners.

"We really need all the information you can give us," she said earnestly, still with the smile. "It's very important to our investigation to figure out how the body got here and how you came to find it."

No shit. I tried not to look like I thought she was an idiot. I said, "Well, I'll be glad to tell you everything I know. But I believe I covered it all yesterday." I added more sincerely, "I'm really sorry for the Morgensterns."

"Would you consider, say, that you and your brother are religious?"

Now she had actually surprised me. "That's a very personal question, and one I can't answer for my brother," I said.

"But you would describe yourself as Christians?"

"We were raised Christian." Cameron and I had been, at least; I didn't know what kind of faith education had taken place in the Lang household. Certainly by the time Tolliver's dad had married my mother, religious training for their children had not been a high priority. In fact, toward the end of our life as a family, my mother hardly knew when it was Sunday. While we'd thought of taking Gracie and Mariella to Sunday school — though they were very young — the thought of what the sharp-eyed church ladies might be able to tell about our home life had stopped us.

We tried so hard to stay together. It had all been for nothing.

"Did your parents have some reason to be prejudiced against Jews?"

What? Where had that come from?

"Some Christians don't like Jews," Brittany Young said, as if that would be news to me. But she was making a huge effort to keep her voice neutral. She didn't want to scare me off from offering her my true opinion, just in case I was a closet anti-Semite.

"I'm aware of that," I said, as mildly as I

could. "But I really don't care what people are." Then everything clicked. "So the Morgensterns are Jewish?" I said, genuinely surprised. I just hadn't thought about it, but now I recalled seeing one of those special candleholders in their home in Nashville. I might have missed a lot more symbols and signs. I don't know much about Judaism. The few Jewish kids I'd known in high school hadn't been interested in parading their differences in a Bible-belt area.

Detective Young gave me a look that was full of so much skepticism it almost stood and walked by itself.

"Yes," she said, as if I was funning with her. "As you know, the Morgensterns are Jewish."

"I guess I was too busy wondering where their child was to think about their religion," I said. "Probably I had my values backward."

Okay, maybe I'd overdone the sarcasm, or I was coming off as self-righteous. Detective Young eyed me with scorn. Or, that was the pose she was adopting, to see if it got a rise out of me.

I glanced around for Tolliver, and found that Detective Lacey had maneuvered him over to the other side of the room.

"Hey, Tolliver," I said. "Detective Young says the Morgensterns are Jewish! Did you know that?"

"I figured they were," he said, drifting over to us. "One of the men I met at their house in Nashville — I'm not sure you met him, you were talking to Joel — I think his name was Feldman . . . anyway, Feldman introduced himself as the Morgensterns' rabbi. So I knew they must be Jewish."

"I don't remember him." I really didn't. I still didn't get the relevance of the Morgensterns' faith. Then the lightbulb in my brain clicked on. "Oh," I said, "does that make it worse? That she was buried in a Christian cemetery? The St. Margaret's cemetery was Catholic or Episcopal, right?" All I knew about Jewish burial customs was that Jews were supposed to be buried quicker than Christians traditionally were interred. I didn't know why.

Both the officers looked startled, as if their original baseline for questioning had been completely misinterpreted.

"I would think," Tolliver said, "that the fact that it really was Tabitha would kind of overwhelm the religious consideration, but maybe not." He shrugged. "That's more important to some people than others. Are the Morgensterns really religious? Because

I've got to say, they've never mentioned anything about Judaism to us. Have they, Harper? Said anything to you?"

"No. All they said to me was, 'Please find my child.' They never said, 'Please find my *Jewish* child.' "

Tolliver sat by me on the love seat, and we presented a united front to Young and Lacey.

"Our lawyer is right next door," I remarked. "Do you think we should call Art in here, Tolliver?"

"Do you feel you need protection?" Detective Lacey asked quickly. "Have you received any unusual messages or phone calls? Do you feel threatened?"

I raised my eyebrows, looked at my brother. "You scared, Tolliver?"

"I don't think I am," he said, as if he were surprised by the discovery. "Seriously," he said to Detective Young, as if we'd just been playing up till then, "Has there been any kind of anti-Semitic demonstration against the Morgensterns? I guess I kind of thought society was past that. I love the South, don't get me wrong; but it does lag behind the times in social developments. I'm sure I could be mistaken." We waited for her to answer, but she just looked at us, an all-too-familiar expression of deep skepticism on her narrow face. Lacey looked more disgusted than anything else.

"Detectives," I said, getting tired of the dance, "let me point some things out." We were on the love seat the Morgensterns had used yesterday, and the two detectives were in the wing chairs we'd occupied. Though Brittany Young was at least ten years younger than Lacey, and a woman, at the moment her expression was identical to his. I took a deep breath. "The Morgensterns hired me after their daughter had been missing for several weeks. Though I'd read the newspaper stories about Tabitha, I'd never met Diane or Joel or any other member of the family. I had no idea they'd call me to work for them. I couldn't have had anything to do with her disappearance, it stands to reason."

I thought the atmosphere eased a little.

Detective Lacey took the lead. "Who, specifically, called you? Felicia Hart? Or Joel Morgenstern's brother, David? Or maybe Joel's father? None of them will claim responsibility."

The direct question stopped me short.

"Tolliver?" I never talked to clients directly until we got to the site. Tolliver thought it added to my mystique. I thought it made me very anxious.

"That was a while ago," Tolliver said. He went into his room, came back with a three-hole binder filled with computer printout pages. He'd been messing around with his computer more in the evenings, I'd noticed, and he'd designed some forms for our little business, Connelly Lang Recoveries. He'd been going back and entering all our past "cases" into the new format. This notebook was labeled "Case Files 2004" and the first page in each file (a green page) was headed "First Contact."

He scanned the page, refreshing his memory. "Okay. Mr. Morgenstern senior called us, at the request of his wife, Hannah Morgenstern. Mr. Morgenstern . . ." Tolliver read the page for a couple of minutes, then looked up to tell the cops that the older Mr. Morgenstern had told Tolliver about his missing granddaughter, and had asked Tolliver if he thought his sister could help.

"I explained what Harper does, and he got kind of angry and hung up," Tolliver said. "Then, the next day, the sister-in-law called."

"You're saying Felicia Hart called you?"

Tolliver checked the name on the page, quite unnecessarily. "Yes, that's who called me." He looked blank — deliberately blank. "She said no one else would face the truth, but she was sure that her niece was dead, and she wanted Harper to find Tabitha's body so the family could find some closure."

"And what did you think of that?"

"I thought she was probably right."

"In your experience, are families often willing to admit that they think their missing loved one is dead?" This was addressed to me. Detective Young seemed to be simply curious.

"This may surprise you, but yes. By the time they call me in, quite a few of them are. They have to have reached some kind of realistic place to even think about hiring me; because that's what I do, I find dead people. No point asking me to come if you think your loved one's alive. Call in the tracking dogs or the private detectives, not me." I lifted my shoulders. "That's common sense."

I can't say the detectives looked horrified. It would take a lot more than that to horrify a homicide detective, I would think. But they did look just that little bit harder around the eyes.

"Of course," Tolliver chimed in, "when people's loved ones are missing, most often the family isn't exactly navigating on common sense."

"Of course," I echoed, seeing that Tolliver

was trying to dilute the bad taste I'd put in their mouths.

"Don't you care?" Detective Young blurted. She leaned forward, her hands clasped, her elbows on her knees, her face intent.

That was a difficult question. "I feel a lot of different ways about finding a body," I said, trying to be truthful. "I'm always glad to find one I've been looking for, because I've done my job if I locate it."

"And then you get paid," said Detective Lacey, an edge to his voice.

"I like getting paid," I said. "I'm not ashamed of that. I deliver a service for the money. And I give the dead some relief." The two detectives looked blank. "They want to be found, you know."

It seemed so evident to me. But judging by their expressions, it didn't seem so obvious to Lacey and Young.

"You seem so normal, and then you say something just totally nuts," Young muttered, and her older partner gave her a stare that snapped her into the here-and-now.

"I beg your pardon," she said formally. "This is a subject I don't believe I've ever discussed with anyone, and it . . . strikes me as peculiar, I guess."

"It's not the first time I've heard that,

Detective," I said matter-of-factly.

"No, I guess not."

"We'll be going now," said Detective Lacey, running his hand over his short hair in an absent gesture, as if he were polishing a favorite ornament. "Oh, wait, I have one more question."

Tolliver and I looked up at him. Tolliver put his hand on my shoulder and exerted a slight pressure. But it wasn't necessary; I knew this was the crucial question.

"Have you talked to any family member since you were in Nashville to search for the Morgenstern girl? *Any* phone conversations?"

I didn't even have to think about it. "Not me," I said, and turned to look at Tolliver, fully expecting him to echo my words.

"Yeah, I talked to Felicia Hart a couple of times," he said, and I used all my self-control to keep my face and body still.

"So, you had conversations with Felicia Hart besides the initial one when she asked you to come to Nashville to look for her niece."

"Yes, I did."

I was going to kill him.

"What was the nature of these calls?"

"Personal," Tolliver said calmly.

"Is it true that you and Felicia Hart had a

relationship?"

"No," Tolliver said.

"Then why the phone calls?"

"We'd had sex," he said. "She's called a couple of times after that, while my sister and I were on the road."

I could feel my fingers curl into fists, and I made them straighten out, made my face remain calm. If it was also sort of fixed and rigid, well, I couldn't help that. I was doing my best.

Tolliver had a lot of appeal, and though we hadn't ever discussed it, he obviously enjoyed sex, judging from the way he tracked down opportunities to do it. I did, too, but I was *way* pickier than Tolliver when it came to selecting a partner. Tolliver viewed sex, as far as I could tell, as a sport he could play well, with any number of the people on his team. I thought of sex a little more personally. You revealed a lot of yourself during sex. I wasn't willing to let many people see that much of me, literally and figuratively.

Maybe these were typical male-versus-female attitudes about sex.

"So what did she want to talk about?" Detective Young asked. She had a narrow-eyed look that I didn't like, as if she felt she'd caught Tolliver out in a guilty secret.

"She wanted to blow off steam about the family situation, about Tabitha's being missing for so long, about how the stress was affecting Victor," Tolliver said easily, and I thought, *You're lying.* I looked down so my face wouldn't be so easy to read.

I thought of acting strange and making the detectives so nervous that they would leave, but I was really angry with Tolliver. He could make his way out of the tangle as best he could.

"What did she say in these conversations?"

He shrugged. "I don't recall specifics. After all, it's been months, and it wasn't that memorable." Aware he sounded less than gallant, Tolliver amended that to, "I didn't know I'd have to be telling anyone what she'd said. She was worried, of course, and not just about Victor. She was concerned about Diane and Joel, and about her own parents. After all, they're Victor's grandparents, even if they're not Joel's in-laws anymore. And — let's see — she said kids at school were accusing Victor of having something to do with Tabitha's disappearance, because a couple of times he'd mouthed off to his friends about his dad preferring Tabitha to him because Tabitha was Diane's daughter, and he wasn't Diane's son."

"What was your response?"

"I didn't have much of a response," Tolliver said. "I wasn't on the spot, and I didn't know the people involved that well. I felt she mainly wanted to vent to someone who didn't have a vested interest, and I happened to come along at the right time."

"Did she want you to return to Nashville?"

"We couldn't," Tolliver said. "We had a schedule to stick to, and any downtime we have we spend at our apartment in St. Louis. We're on the road pretty much year-round."

"You have that much business?" Detective Young said. He seemed startled.

I nodded. "We stay pretty busy," I said. I noticed that Tolliver had dodged answering their original question, but I sure wasn't going to point that out. I was ready for them to be on their way.

Lacey and Young gave each other a look, and a communication seemed to pass between them. The middle-aged man and the younger woman made good partners, somehow. They'd had a meeting of the minds somewhere back in their professional history, and they'd made it work for them. Until this moment, I'd thought Tolliver and

I had had the same thing working for us.

"We may need to ask a few more follow-up questions," Detective Lacey said, making an effort to sound pleasant and as though any further questions would be inconsequential — no problem, no sweat, don't worry, be happy.

"So, you'll be here?" Young asked, pointing at the floor to indicate she meant *right here at this hotel, don't leave town.*

"Yes, I suppose we will," I said.

"Of course, you'll want to go to the funeral," Young said, as if something she should have known was just now popping into her head.

"No," I said.

She cocked her head as if she couldn't have heard me correctly. "Say what?"

"I don't go to funerals," I said.

"Not ever?"

"Not ever."

"What about your mother's? We heard she died last year."

They'd been making phone calls. "I didn't go." I didn't want to feel her presence again, not ever, not even from the grave. "Goodbye," I said, standing and smiling at them. They were definitely disconcerted, now, and exchanged one of their glances again, without the certainty.

"So you'll stay in town until we contact you again," Detective Young said, tucking her hair behind her ear in a gesture oddly reminiscent of that of her partner.

"I think we've established that," I said, keeping my voice sweet and even.

"Of course we will," Tolliver said, without a trace of irony.

Six

After the departure of the police, the silence that fell was the noisiest silence we'd ever shared. I didn't even want to look at my brother, much less discuss what had just happened. We didn't move. Finally, I threw my hands up in the air, made a sound that came out "Arrrr," and stomped into my bedroom, slamming the door behind me. It immediately opened, and Tolliver strode in.

"All right, what did you want me to say?" he said. "Did you want me to lie?"

I'd thrown myself down on my bed, and Tolliver chose to loom over me, his hands on his hips.

"I didn't want you to say anything," I said, in as neutral a voice as I could manage. But then I bounced to my feet to glare at him. "I didn't want you to say *anything* today. What I would have wanted, if I could have had it, was for you to have shown a little discretion, a little common sense, months ago! What were you thinking? Was your upper brain involved in this process at all?"

"You just . . . can't you cut me some slack?"

"No! No! A waitress here or there, well, ick, but okay! You meet someone in a bar, well, okay! We all have needs. But to have a relationship with a client, someone involved in a case . . . come *on,* Tolliver. You should keep your pants zipped! Or can you?"

Since Tolliver was so in the wrong, he got even angrier. "She was just a woman. She isn't even a member of the family, at least not the direct family!"

"Just a woman. Okay, I'm seeing it now. Just a hole for you to sink into, is that what you're saying? So much for being selective. So much for thinking every time you have sex, 'Is this the woman I choose to have a baby with?' Because that's what it means, Tolliver!"

"Was that what you were thinking when you screwed that cop in Sarne? How you wanted to have his baby?"

There was another silence, this one charged with other tensions.

"Hey," he said, "I'm sorry I said that." The anger drained away.

"I don't know if I'm sorry or not," I said.

"You know you did a wrong thing. Can't you just say it? Do you have to justify it?"

"Do you have to ask me to?"

"Yes, I think I do. Because this wasn't only personal, this was business, too. You've never done that before." Okay, at least I didn't think he had.

"Felicia wasn't paying us. She's not really a member of the family."

"But still."

"Yeah, yeah," he said, crumbling at last. "You're right. She was too close to the action. I shouldn't have." He smiled, that rare, radiant smile that almost made me smile in return. Almost. "But she made a real pass at me, and I guess I was too weak to turn it down. She was offering, she was pretty, and I couldn't think of a real reason why not."

I tried to think of something to say, but I couldn't. Actually, why not? Exactly for this reason, that's why not — because this time, Tolliver's sex life had backfired on us. I thought we were in even more trouble than we'd been before, and that hadn't been inconsiderable.

Tolliver hugged me. "I'm sorry," he said, and his voice was quiet and sincere. I hugged him back, inhaling the familiar smell of him, laying my cheek against his hard chest. We stood like that for a long minute, with the dust motes floating in the sun coming through the hotel window. Then his arms loosened, and I stepped back.

"This is what the detectives should have asked you: who called you about the cemetery?" I asked.

"Dr. Nunley. And in Detective Lacey's defense, he did ask me that at the station."

"Did Nunley say who'd asked him to call? Or did you get the impression it was just his idea?" I went back out into the living room area to get a drink. Tolliver trailed after me, lost in thought.

"I thought someone had drawn you to his attention, because he asked a lot of questions. If he'd been the one who'd originated the invitation, he would have known more about you. That's my opinion."

"Okay. So we need to talk to him." I sympathized when Tolliver made a face. "Yeah, me, too. He's a jerk, all right." Tolliver pulled his cell phone out of his pocket and checked a number on a folded piece of paper. Tolliver always has bits of paper in his pockets, and if he didn't do his own laundry I'd have to be searching his pants all the time. He finally found the right piece of paper and the right number and punched it in. From his stance, I could see that he was listening to the phone ringing on the other end. Finally, a recorded message came on, and when the beep sounded, Tolliver left a message. "Dr. Nunley, this is Tolliver Lang," he said briskly. "Harper and I need to talk to you. There are some things left unresolved after yesterday's unexpected discoveries. You have my cell number."

"Now he'll think we want our money."

Tolliver considered this. "Yes, and he'll call back about that," he said finally. "Come to think of it, if he doesn't pay us, we won't get anything for this. I can't help but be glad we're getting the Morgenstern reward money."

"I don't really want to have earned it, you know?" He patted me on the shoulder; he knew exactly what I meant. Of course, he also knew that we would take it. We sure deserved it. "I can't help feeling that we've been yanked into this. I just hope we haven't been shoved right under a ladder or some other bad luck thing. I'm scared we might end up taking someone else's fall for this."

"Not if I can help it," Tolliver said. "I know I've slipped up, but you can be sure I'll do everything in my power from now on out to make sure no one can connect us with the Morgensterns' mess. And it's a simple fact that we didn't take Tabitha, a provable fact. In fact, what date was she taken?" We looked it up on the Internet. Tolliver checked our previous year's schedule. God bless computers. "We were in Schenectady then," he said, relief in his voice, and I laughed.

"That's plenty far enough," I said. "I'm glad you keep such good records. I guess we've got receipts to back that up?"

"Yes, on file at the apartment," he said.

"Not just another pretty face," I said, and cupped his chin in my hand for a second to hold him still while I gave him a kiss on the cheek. But my happy moment didn't last longer than a few seconds. "Tolliver, who could have done this? Killed the girl, and put her there? Can it possibly be true that it's a massive coincidence?"

He shook his head. "I don't think that's even remotely likely."

"You and I both know that massive coincidences usually aren't. But I just can't imagine a conspiracy so elaborate."

"I can't either," he said.

Oddly enough, the next person we heard from was Xylda Bernardo.

We'd just finished lunch. It was an uneasy meal. Art had shared it with us, and since he ate a completely different kind of meal from us (he had a major lunch, and we like a light lunch), and he liked to talk business while he ate, I can't say we enjoyed it a whole lot. Art was about to catch a flight back to Atlanta, since he couldn't think of anything else to do in Memphis. The police weren't prepared to charge us with anything that he could discover; and he'd made many, many phone calls to everyone he knew in the justice system in Memphis to try to find out. We'd basically paid a whole hell of a lot for Art to fly over here first class to stay at a great hotel, make a lot of phone calls, and hold one press conference; but we'd known it had been a gamble when we'd called him.

Our lawyer was downing a huge salad, garlic bread, and veal ravioli, while Tolliver and I were having soup and salad on a smaller scale. I was watching Art chew hunks of bread and trying to remember my CPR lessons. Art was explaining what we should expect.

"You'll probably need to produce a record of your travels during the time since you met the Morgensterns," Art said.

I glanced at Tolliver and he nodded. We were covered on all that. During the years we'd been traveling, Tolliver and I had learned to keep every single receipt, every single credit card slip, every single piece of paper that crossed our paths. This past year, we'd been especially diligent. We had a cheap accordion file that was always on hand in the back seat of the car, and the laptop; we kept good records. We sent off regular packets to our accountant, Sandy Dierdoff, who was based in St. Louis. She was a broadly curvy blonde in her forties. She'd only raised her eyebrows and given a bark of laughter when we'd explained what we did for a living. She'd seemed to enjoy our unusual lifestyle. In fact, she'd given us more good advice in our meetings with her than Art had ever even thought of sharing. Sandy had already emailed us about making our annual appointment; fall was fast turning into winter.

I was thinking about Sandy, and by extension our apartment in St. Louis, while I said goodbye to Art. We saw him leave with a mutual feeling of relief. Art was kind of proud of having us as clients, as if we were show business people; but at the same time, he wasn't at his easiest or most relaxed when he was alone with us.

After he left, and the staff had removed the lunch things, I asked Tolliver if he thought we could go out for a walk. I still hadn't forgiven Tolliver his huge error in judgment, but I was willing to put it on the back burner until I'd calmed down. A good walk might restore our sense of companion-ship.

Tolliver was shaking his head before the sentence even got out of my mouth. "We ran this morning in the gym," he reminded me. "I know you don't want to be cooped up in this hotel, but if we go anywhere, someone'll spot us and want a statement."

I called down to the front desk to ask if there were still reporters waiting outside the hotel. The deskman replied that he couldn't be sure, but that he suspected some of the people loitering in the coffee shop across the street were members of the press. I hung up.

"Crap," I said.

"Listen, put on your dark glasses and a hat and we'll go to the movies," he said. He found the complimentary *Commercial Appeal* we'd gotten that morning and looked up movie times. I found myself looking at my own picture on the front page of the Metro section. I'd only looked at the front section this morning, on purpose. There I was: thin, dark-headed, with big deep-set eyes and an erect posture, arms wrapped across each other under my breasts. I thought the picture made me look quite a bit more than twenty-four and that made me a little shivery. Tolliver, right beside me in the photo, was taller, darker, and more solid.

We both looked desperately troubled. We looked like refugees from middle Europe, refugees who'd fled some kind of persecution, leaving behind all they held of value.

"Want to read it?" Tolliver asked, extending the paper. He knew I didn't like reading the few stories in the press about us, but since I'd been staring at the picture, he offered it to me.

I put out my own hand in a "stop" gesture.

He handed me the movie section instead, and I began scanning the ads. We liked space movies and action movies. We liked movies with happy families. If they got threatened with danger, we liked them to get out of it more or less intact, maybe shooting a couple of bad guys in the process. We didn't like movies about miserable people who became more miserable, no matter how brilliant they were. We didn't like chick flicks. We didn't like foreign movies. I didn't want to go to the movies to learn a damn thing about human nature or the state of the world. I knew as much as I wanted to know about both those things.

There was a movie that fit our profile, which wasn't too surprising, I guess.

I put on a knit cap and my jacket and my dark glasses, and Tolliver bundled up, too. We got the doorman to call a cab instead of bringing our car around. We actually got a silent cab driver, my favorite kind. He could drive well, too, and he got us to the multiplex in time to buy our tickets and walk right in.

I love going to big multiplexes. I love the anonymity, and all the possibilities. I loved the teenagers who kept it clean, in their bright matching shirts and silly hats. Tolliver had had a night job in such a place in Texarkana, and he used to slip me in so I could hide in the darkened theater for a while, forgetting what waited for me at our home.

When the previews started running, I was as content as I could be. We sat together in the dark, passing the popcorn (no butter, light on the salt) back and forth.

We watched our pretty-pathologist-in-danger movie quite happily, knowing that everything would be okay in the end (more or less). We poked each other in the ribs when she was having a lot of trouble determining the cause of death of a very handsome guy. "You could have told her in a second," Tolliver said, in a whisper only someone as close as I could have deciphered. The theater wasn't empty, but there was plenty of room at this weekday afternoon showing. No one was talking out loud, and no child was crying, so it was a good experience.

When the movie was over, the bad guy killed several different ways after we thought he was dead initially, we strolled outside, chatting about the special effects and the probable future of the main characters. That was our favorite game. What would happen to them after the action of the movie was over?

"She'll go back to work, even if she said she wouldn't," I told Tolliver. "Staying at home will be too boring after all that shooting and chasing. After all, she bashed that guy in the head with her iron."

"Nah, I think she'll marry the cop, stay home, and devote herself to making her family supper every single night," Tolliver said. "She'll never order Chinese takeout again. Remember, she tore down the menu that was tacked to the wall by the phone?"

"She'll probably just order pizza instead."

He laughed and fished the receipt from the cab out of his pocket so he could call for another one to take us back to the hotel.

Suddenly, my left arm was seized in a strong grip. To say I got a scare would be a large understatement. I turned to stare at a woman holding me. She was wearing a voluminous coat with a loud plaid pattern. She had dyed red hair pulled up on one side of her head to cascade over to the other side in a waterfall of curls. Her lipstick was not exactly within the lines of her actual lips, and her earrings were huge chandeliers with glittery stones that caught the afternoon sun.

Tolliver had swung around and his free hand was heading for her throat.

"I just have to talk to you," she said, in a hurried, abstracted way.

"Hi, Xylda," I said, trying for that calm, level voice you use when you're talking to someone you know is over the edge.

"Xylda," Tolliver said, almost in a growl. He'd been ready for action, and now he had to be tolerant. With more force than necessary, he shoved his phone back into his pocket. "What can we do for you today? How'd you come to be here?"

"You're in such danger," she said. "Such terrible danger. I felt I had to warn you. You're so young, dear. You can't know how terrible this world can be."

Actually, I thought I had a pretty good idea. "Tolliver and I aren't young in experience, Xylda," I said, trying to keep my voice gentle. "Look, there's a restaurant over there. Shall we go have a cup of hot chocolate, or some coffee? Maybe they have tea?"

"That would be good, really good," she said. Xylda was as different from me as she could be: shorter, bulkier, and at least thirty years older. She'd been in the psychic business ever since she'd quit prostitution, which had been her first profession. Xylda's husband, Robert, had been her handler, and his death the year before had thrown Xylda for a real loop. I didn't know how she was going to survive unless someone else took her in hand. She sure didn't look or behave like someone I'd want to employ if I were in the market for a psychic. Then again, maybe I was overestimating the public. Some clients actually believed that Xylda's odd manner and dress reinforced the fact that she was a living, breathing psychic.

I disagreed. I knew that a lot of psychics, both real and fake, were also emotionally unstable or out-and-out mentally ill. If you're born psychic, you're going to pay a price, a high one. It's a terrible gift.

Only two of the psychics I'd met managed to live just like ordinary people, but those two were exceptions. And neither of them was Xylda, of course.

Looking gloomy but resigned, Tolliver led

Xylda into the cafe and helped her take her awful coat off. He left to get our drinks, while I settled Xylda in at a little table as far from other patrons as I could manage, given that the coffee shop wasn't a large business. I took a deep breath and tried to fix an understanding smile on my face.

Xylda clutched my hand, and I had to bite my lower lip to keep from yanking it away. Casual touching is not comfortable for me, and she'd already held onto me twice; but I reminded myself that Xylda must have a reason for the deliberate contact. As I knew from her own account at a previous meeting, Xylda was being bombarded with images from me. She'd explained it to me once when she'd been having a good day, back when Robert had been alive. "It's like watching a very fast slide show," she'd said. "I see pictures, pictures of the life of the person I'm touching, some from the past and some from the future and some . . ." She'd fallen silent and shaken her head.

"Do they all come true?" I'd asked.

"I have no way of knowing. I know they *might* come true."

Xylda looked at me now, and her blue eyes really saw me. "In the time of ice, you'll be so happy," she said.

"Good," I said, having no idea what she

was talking about. But that was the way of conversations with Xylda, if you could call this a conversation.

"You can't keep lying," Xylda said gently. "You have to stop doing that. It won't hurt anyone."

"I think I'm truthful," I said, surprised. Many things I could be accused of, and my accuser would be right. But not this.

"Oh, you're truthful about the things that don't matter."

"Did someone come to Memphis with you, Xylda?"

"Yes, Manfred did."

"Where is Manfred?" I wasn't completely sure who Manfred was, but learning someone had charge of Xylda was a relief.

"He's parking the car. There wasn't a space."

"Oh, good," I said, relieved to hear such a prosaic explanation. Tolliver arrived at the table with our drinks. Xylda seemed glad to get the coffee, which was redolent of vanilla and sugar, and she swirled in even more sugar with the little brown plastic stirrer. Mine was regular coffee, and Tolliver had gotten hot chocolate. "Tolliver, Xylda says Manfred is with her."

He raised his eyebrows in query, so he didn't know who that was, either. I shrugged. "She says he's out parking the car."

Tolliver stood and stared out the glass windows, then began waving vigorously to someone. "I think I spotted him," he said, sinking back into his chair. "He's coming in." Tolliver was smiling broadly.

"He's a good boy," Xylda said. She smiled at us. "Listen, I hear you found the Morgenstern girl." Suddenly, she sounded completely practical and all present and accounted for, mentally.

"Yes," I said.

"You know, they called me in."

"Yeah?"

"It wasn't the boy," Xylda said. "There was passion involved. But there was no sex with the little girl."

"Okay," I said. "Then why was she killed?"

"I don't know," Xylda said. She looked down into her coffee cup.

See what I mean about psychics being very little help?

"But I know you'll find out," Xylda said, and she looked up at me very sharply. "I won't be there to see it, but you'll find out."

"Are you going to a different city? Have you got another booking?"

"Yes," she said quite definitely. "I have another booking. You know, I'm the real

134

thing, and people know that when they meet me."

"Yes, they do," Tolliver agreed, and then a thin young man came up to us, dressed all in black. This was Manfred, I assumed.

"I saw her surprise you," Manfred said cheerfully. "Sorry about that. Are you her friends? She said she had to meet some friends here."

Amazing. Xylda's psychic ability had led her to meet with us outside a Cineplex. Manfred was a narrow-shouldered young man in his late teens or early twenties. He had a narrow face and slicked-back peroxided hair, a matching goatee, and at least one tattoo visible on the side of his neck. He had a face decorated with many piercings and his hands were covered with silver rings.

He matched Xylda, in an odd sort of way.

"I'm Tolliver Lang and this is Harper Connelly," Tolliver said. "Are you related to Xylda?"

"This is my grandson," Xylda said proudly.

I was willing to bet that few grandmothers would be able to look at Manfred's extreme facial embellishment without wincing, much less with Xylda's simple pride. There was much to Manfred that met the eye, and

135

quite a lot that didn't — and his grandmother was certainly psychic enough to
sense that.

We told the young man we were pleased
to meet him, and we explained that we
crossed paths with Xylda professionally
from time to time.

"She jumped up this morning, right at the
breakfast table," Manfred said. "She said
we had to go to Memphis. So we got in the
car, and here we are." He seemed proud of
having taken his grandmother so seriously,
of having gotten her here on time to keep
her self-appointed rendezvous.

"You know the body was found," I said to
Xylda, who'd finished her coffee before the
rest of us had begun to sip at ours.

"Yes, and I knew it was going to be found
in a graveyard," Xylda said. "I just didn't
know which one. I'm glad you found the
girl. She's been dead a long time."

"Since the day she vanished?" I asked.

"No, not quite," Xylda said. "She lived a
few hours. Not more than that."

I was actually relieved to hear this. "That's
what I thought. Thanks for telling me," I
said. I wondered if I should relay this bit of
information to the police or to Tabitha's
family. After a moment's consideration, I
realized that was a very bad idea. If it had

been hard for the police to believe me, it would be impossible for them to give Xylda any credence. If you could say *anyone* looked like an ex-hooker turned professional psychic, Xylda would be the picture you'd come up with. Police aren't inclined to trust either one, and Xylda reinforced that distrust with every sentence she uttered.

"I Saw it," Xylda said. I could hear the capital letter in her voice. Her grandson Manfred smiled at his grandmother, the epitome of pride. It was obvious Manfred simply didn't care that almost everyone in the shop had taken a moment or two to stare at our little group. I thought that was extraordinary, especially for a young man hardly out of his teens, if indeed he was. I realized that Manfred and Victor Morgenstern were very close in age. I wondered what the two would make of each other, and found the idea of their conversation almost unimaginable.

"Xylda, have you caught a glimpse of who took her?" Tolliver asked. He spoke very quietly, almost inaudibly, because there was no doubt people were listening.

"It was for love," Xylda said. "For love!" Xylda spoke right out.

She smiled at each of us, a distinct and separate look, and then she told Manfred it was time for her nap.

"Sure, Granny," he said. He stood and pulled her chair back for her. I hadn't seen a man do that in years. As Xylda picked up her purse and began to shuffle toward the door, the fascinated gaze of the other patrons following the progress of the enormous plaid coat, Manfred bent to take my hand. "A pleasure to see you," he said, and he suddenly sounded older than his years. "If you ever need a buddy to hang with, Harper, I'm willing to jump in there."

The look in his eyes told me that no matter how old Manfred was chronologically, biologically he was a fully developed male. Suddenly I felt very self-conscious and ridiculously flattered.

"I hear you," I said, and Manfred kissed my hand. Because of the piercings, the effect was strange. I felt a little tongue, a little brush of soft hair from the goatee, and surely a cold metallic touch from a stud in his mouth. I didn't know whether to laugh, or shriek, or pant.

"Just think of the kids we would have," Manfred said, and I opted for smiling.

"That's a step too far, there," I said. "You were doing great, up until the kids."

"I'll remember," he said, smiling back. "Next time I won't make the same mistake."

When they left, I turned to Tolliver to ask him what he'd gotten out of Xylda's tangled contribution. Tolliver was staring after Manfred with no friendly face.

"Oh, get real," I said. "Tolliver! He's years younger than me!"

"Right, maybe three," Tolliver said, and I remembered that Tolliver was three years older. "He's got balls, I'll give him that."

"Probably pierced ones," I said, and Tolliver gave me a startled look and an unwilling laugh.

"What would you say if I got a tattoo and a ring through my eyebrow?" he said.

"I'd definitely want to watch," I said. "And it would be interesting to see what kind of tattoo you picked." I looked at him for a moment, trying to imagine Tolliver with a silver hoop in his eyebrow or nostril, and I grinned. "And where you put it."

"Oh, if I ever got one, I'd get it on my lower back," he said. "So I could cover it up almost all the time."

"You've put thought into this."

"Yeah. A little."

"Hmmm. You've picked out the tattoo?"

"Sure."

"What?"

"A lightning bolt," he said, and I couldn't tell if he was serious or not.

SEVEN

During our cab ride back from the suburban Cineplex to the downtown hotel, I had a little time to think. Xylda was nuts, but she was a true psychic. If she said Tabitha had lived a few hours after the abduction, I believed her. I should have asked different questions, I realized. I should have asked Xylda *why* Tabitha's abductor had kept her alive for that long. A sexual reason? Some other purpose?

"Did it seem to you that Xylda was nuttier than usual?" Tolliver asked, echoing my thoughts to an eerie degree.

"Yes," I said. "The kind of nutty that made me wonder how old she really is."

"She couldn't be over sixty, right?"

"I would have said younger, but today . . ."

"She looked okay."

"As okay as Xylda ever looks."

"True. But she seemed to walk just fine, and maneuver all right physically."

"But mentally, she was quite a bit more off . . . so vague. 'In the time of ice, you'll be happy.' What the hell does that mean?"

"Yeah, that was weird. And the part about being truthful."

I nodded. " 'The time of ice.' She could have told us things that would have been a hell of a lot more to the point. Maybe it's the loss of Robert that's thrown her for such a loop? Not that she was ever Miss Stability. At least Manfred seems to be taking good care of her, and he respects her talent."

"Think we should mention that guy we met in San Francisco to the Morgensterns? Think they'd be open to a clairvoyant?"

"Nah," I said instantly. "Tom will make something up if he doesn't get a genuine reading."

"So would Xylda."

"But only when it didn't matter, Tolliver." He looked at me as if he couldn't see the difference.

"Like if it was some teenager visiting her on a dare, wanting to know if she'd be happy in the future, Xylda might make up stuff so the kid would leave confident and cheerful. That kind of thing, that can't hurt. But if a lot depended on it, if the client took her seriously, Xylda wouldn't say, 'Oh yes, your missing son is really alive,' unless she got a true vision. Tom will tell you something under any circumstances, whether or not he really knows anything. He'll just make it up."

"Then I won't mention him," Tolliver said, though he sounded a little huffy. "I was trying to think of some way to help them get through this, and I think the only way they're going to come out the other side of it is to find out who did kill Tabitha. That is, if it really *wasn't* one of them."

"I know," I said, surprised at his irritation.

"What did you get from her yesterday? When you were standing on the grave?"

I was very reluctant to return to that moment. But then I thought of the faces of Diane and Joel Morgenstern, and the cloud of suspicion surrounding them, and I knew I had to return to Tabitha's last resting place.

"You think we could go back to the site?" I asked. "I know there's no physical remains there, but it might help."

Tolliver never questioned my professional judgment. "Then we'll go," he said. "But I think we better go tonight, so no one'll follow us. We won't want to be in a cab for that."

I agreed, especially after I caught our current cabbie's curious look in the rearview mirror.

"You want him to drop us off on Beale?" Tolliver asked. "Maybe we could go listen to some music before supper?"

I glanced at my watch. It seemed unlikely that there would be good blues playing at five in the afternoon. "Why don't you go?" I suggested. "I'll go back to the hotel and take a nap."

So Tolliver got out at B.B. King's Blues Club on legendary Beale Street, and reminded the cabbie where he was to drop me off. The cabbie made a face, said, "Sure, man, I remember," and drove me right to the Cleveland. "He's a little on the protective side," the man said when I was paying him. "Your man is a worrier."

"Yes," I said. "My brother."

"Your *brother?*" The cabbie looked at me, half-smiling, sure I was pulling his leg.

I told him to keep the change because I was kind of rattled, and I scrambled out of the cab and into the hotel without looking around me, which was stupid.

For the second time that day, someone seized hold of me. But this time it was a man, an angry man. He grabbed me as I walked into the lobby, and he marched me over to a chair before I could even be sure who he was.

Dr. Clyde Nunley was slightly better dressed than he had been the morning before. This afternoon he looked like a typical college professor in his sport jacket and dark slacks. His shoes needed shining.

"How'd you do it?" he asked me, still gripping my arm.

"What?"

"You've made a fool out of me. I was standing right there. Those records were sealed. I watched over them. No one else had read them. How did you do it? You make me look like an idiot in front of the students, and then your damn pimp calls me to ask me for my money."

I was disgusted, and I realized Dr. Nunley had been drinking.

I tried to yank my arm away. He'd scared me, so now I was proportionately angrier.

"Drop my arm and stand away from me," I said, and I said it sharply and loudly.

Out of the corner of my eye, I saw that the three (very young) staff members at the counter were buzzing around nervously, unsure of what to do. I was so glad when someone else stepped forward and clamped a hand on Dr. Nunley's shoulder.

"Let go of the lady," said the man who'd been in the class the day before. He had that stillness about him that says, "I know what I'm doing and no one messes with me."

"What?" Clyde Nunley was very confused by the interruption of his bullying session. His grip on me didn't loosen. I had a wild impulse to grab the arm of Mr. Student, so we'd all be standing there holding on to one another. We must look ridiculous.

"Dr. Nunley, let go of me or I'll break your fucking fingers," I said, and that worked like a charm. He looked startled, as if I'd finally become a real person to him. Mr. Student kept hold of the inebriated professor, and his mouth moved in a very small smile.

By that time, one of the staff members had hustled around the desk and was striding over to us, trying to hurry without looking like he was hurrying. It was the pleasant-faced man in his twenties who'd checked us in. "Problem, Ms. Connelly?"

"Don't say a word," hissed Dr. Nunley, as though that would be sure to shut me up. He must normally deal with the well-mannered children of the privileged.

"Yes, there is a problem," I said to the young man, and Clyde Nunley's face twisted with surprise. He just didn't think I'd complain about him; I don't know why.

"This man grabbed me when I came into the lobby, and he won't leave me alone. If this gentleman hadn't helped me out, he might have hit me." Of course, I didn't know that, but Dr. Nunley had definitely been spoiling for a confrontation, and if he thought I was going to forget he'd called my brother a pimp, he had another thought coming.

"Do you know him, Ms. Connelly?"

"I don't know him," I said firmly. In an existential sense, this was the truth. Do any of us know each other, really? I was sure the staff would back me up with no qualms if they thought Dr. Nunley was a stranger off the street, out to harass me. The minute I said the words "Doctor" and "Bingham College" I'd lose some of my own stature as a wronged female.

My new assistant, Mr. Student, said, "In that case, mister, I think you should leave. And in view of the fact that you seem drunk, I'd call a cab if I were you."

The clerk made a courteous gesture toward the door, as if Dr. Nunley were an honored guest. "One of our bellmen will be happy to call a cab for you," the clerk said in a sunny voice. "Right this way."

And before Dr. Nunley could regroup, he was out onto the sidewalk and under the watchful eye of the two bellmen who stood there waiting for cars to pull up.

"Thanks," I said to Mr. Student. "I didn't get your name yesterday."

"Rick Goldman."

"Harper Connelly," I said, with a little nod. I shook his hand, though my own was not steady. "How did you come to be on the right spot at the right moment, Mr. Goldman?"

"Rick, please. 'Mr. Goldman' makes me feel even older than I am. Would you care to sit and talk for a minute?" There were two brocaded wing chairs at a comfortable angle and distance for conversation.

I hesitated, tempted. I wasn't as calm and steady as I was making out. In fact, I was still shaking. I'd been taken by surprise, and in a bad kind of way. "For a minute," I said carefully, and sank down as gracefully as I could manage. I didn't want Rick Goldman to know exactly how shaky I was.

He sat opposite me, his square dark face carefully blank. "I'm an alumnus of Bingham," he said.

That told me absolutely nothing. "So are lots of other people, but I don't see them here now," I said. "What's your point?"

"I was a cop on the Memphis force for years. Now I'm a private investigator."

"Okay." I wished he'd cut the circling around and arrive at the point.

"The board of trustees is pretty sharply divided right now," Rick Goldman said. Okay, I was getting bored. I raised my eyebrows and nodded encouragingly.

"There's a liberal majority and a conservative minority. That minority is very concerned with Bingham's public profile. When that conservative faction of the board found out what Clyde was doing in his class, they asked if I would oversee the visiting speakers."

"Keep your fingers on the pulse," I said.

"Keep my ear to the ground," he confirmed.

He seemed quite serious. I had a feeling Rick Goldman was a serious kind of guy. "Clyde didn't suspect you?"

"I paid my money and signed up for the class," Rick Goldman said. "Nothing he could do about it."

"The older lady in the class, she a monitor, too?"

"Nah, she just likes to take anthropology classes."

I thought about this for a second. "So, you just happened to be standing in the lobby here this evening?"

"No, not exactly."

149

"Following Clyde, were you?"

"No. He's boring. You're a lot more interesting."

I wasn't exactly sure how the private detective meant that.

"So have you been following me and my brother?"

"No. But I have been waiting here for you. I wanted to ask you some questions, after watching you in action yesterday."

I owed him the Q&A, after his timely intervention in the Clyde Nunley incident. "I'll listen," I said, which was more than I usually did.

"How'd you do it?" He leaned forward, his eyes fixed on my face. If the circumstances had been different it might have been a flattering moment. But I was afraid I knew what he meant, and that wasn't flattering at all.

I looked back at him with the same intensity. "You know I couldn't have learned any of that ahead of time," I said. "You *know* that, right?"

"Were you in cahoots with Clyde? And now you've had a falling out?"

"No, Mr. Goldman. I'm not in cahoots with anyone. I don't think I've ever heard anyone even say that phrase out loud, by the way." I broke eye contact, sighed. "I'm the real thing. You may not want to believe it, but eventually you'll have to. Thanks again." I got up and walked very carefully over to the elevators. My leg was still not steady, and it would be too embarrassing if I fell down.

I punched the up button with a quick stab of my finger. The elevator obligingly opened, and I stepped in, punching our floor number with a quick sideways motion of my hand. I stood with my back to the door so I wouldn't have to see him again.

I was ashamed that I had needed help. If I were as tough as I wanted to be, I could have thrown Clyde Nunley to the floor and kicked him. But that might have been a slight overreaction. I found myself smiling at the back wall of the elevator. I guess I'm the kind of woman who smiles when she thinks about kicking a man when he's down; at least, that man.

I told myself to stiffen my spine. After all, I'd handled that okay. I hadn't screamed or cried or lost my dignity. *I'm not a weak person,* I told myself. *I just get rattled sometimes.* And then there was the physical stuff left over from the lightning strike. One of those symptoms struck now, a headache so vicious I had trouble fitting my plastic key into the slot and getting into my room.

I opened my medicine bag and took a handful of Advil, and then I yanked off my shoes. I knew from experience how comfortable the bed was, and I knew in ten minutes I would feel better. I promised myself that. Actually, it took more like twenty minutes before the pain subsided to a bearable level, and then I looked at the ceiling and thought about Dr. Nunley and his temper until I fell asleep.

Tolliver woke me up a couple of hours later. "Hey," he said gently. "How are you? They told me when I came in that you'd had a problem with a man in the lobby, and some knight in corduroy had shown up to rescue you."

"Yeah." It was taking me a minute to gather up my senses. Tolliver had turned on my bathroom light, and he was a silhouette sitting on the edge of my mattress. "Nunley was waiting for me, and he was all 'How did you do this, you imp of Satan?' and so on. Well, he didn't go into the evil stuff so much. He just thought I was dishonest. But he clearly thought I was a big fraud, and he was mad you'd called him, and he wasn't nice about it."

"Did he hurt you?"

"Nah, grabbed my arm, but that's all. You

remember that older man in the class, the one we were wondering about? He was in the lobby, too, waiting for me to come back. He stopped Nunley, and the guy from the desk sent him on his way. Then he told me some interesting information. The only thing is, after that I got a hell of a headache, so I took some medicine and dropped."

"How's the leg?"

One problem often triggered another. We'd been to maybe ten doctors, and they all said that my problems were psychological — whether or not we told them about the body-finding thing. "The effects of a lightning strike are over when you leave the hospital afterward," one particularly pompous jackass had told me. "There are no well-documented long-term effects." Sadly, the problems I had with the medical community were common among lightning strike survivors. Very few doctors knew what to do with us. For some of us it was much harder — the ones who couldn't go back to work and were trying to get workmen's comp or disability payments, for example.

At least I didn't have tinnitus, which affected so many survivors, and at least I hadn't lost my sense of taste, another common problem.

"The leg's a little shaky," I admitted, feeling the muscle weakness as I tried to achieve a leg lift. Only the left leg rose. The right one just quivered with the effort. Tolliver began to massage it, as he often did on the bad days.

"So, tell me the interesting information about the man from the class."

"He's a private detective," I began, and Tolliver's hands stopped moving for second.

"Not good," he said. "At least, depending on his goal."

I tried to recall everything Rick Goldman had said to me, and Tolliver listened to it all with absolute attention.

"I don't think this really has anything to do with us," Tolliver said. "He may not believe you're a genuine talent, but since when did that matter? Lots of people don't. He just hasn't needed you yet. As far as the board of trustees, or whatever, you've already been paid a retainer by the college. It wasn't much, anyway. This was more for the good buzz than anything else."

"So you don't think Goldman can hurt us?"

"No. And why would he?"

"He didn't seem really angry or upset," I admitted. "But he might think we were defrauding the college."

"So, what's he gonna do about it? He's

not the guy who writes the checks. We were hired to do something, we did it."

I felt a little better about Rick Goldman after that, and I decided not to think about Clyde Nunley any more, though I knew Tolliver had a slow burn going about the professor being rough with me. Maybe we wouldn't run into him again. To change the subject, I asked Tolliver how his Beale Street jaunt had gone.

While his long fingers worked on my leg muscles, he told me about Beale Street, and his conversation with a bartender about the famous people who'd come to the bar to hear the blues. I grew more relaxed by the moment, and I was laughing when there was a knock at the door. Tolliver looked at me, surprised, and I shrugged. I wasn't expecting anything or anyone.

A bellman was there, holding a vase of flowers. "These came for you, Ms. Connelly," he said.

Who doesn't like to get flowers? "Put them on the table, please," I said, and glanced at Tolliver to see if he had the tip. He fished out his wallet, gave me a nod, and handed the bellman some bills. The flowers were snapdragons, and I didn't think anyone had ever sent me snapdragons. Actually, I didn't think anyone had ever sent me flowers before, unless you counted a corsage or two when I was in high school. I said as much to Tolliver. He pulled the little envelope from the plastic prongs in the foliage and handed it to me, no expression on his face.

The card read, "You have given us peace," and it was signed "Joel and Diane Morgenstern."

"They're very pretty," I said. I touched one blossom lightly.

"Nice of Diane to think of them," Tolliver said.

"No, this was Joel's idea."

"Why do you say that?"

"He's the kind of man who thinks of flowers," I said positively. "And she's the kind of woman who doesn't."

Tolliver thought this was foolishness.

"Really, Tolliver, you've got to take my word on this," I said. "Joel is the kind of guy who *thinks* about women."

"I think about women. I think about them all the time."

"No, that's not what I mean." I tried to think of how to put it. "He doesn't just think about wanting to fuck women, when he looks at them. I'm not saying he's gay," I added hastily, since Tolliver was looking incredulous. "I'm saying that he thinks about what women like." That still wasn't quite it, but it was as close as I could come. "He likes to please women," I said, but that wasn't exactly right, either.

The phone rang and Tolliver picked it up. "Yes," he said. "Hello, Diane. Harper just got the flowers; she says she loves them. You really shouldn't have done it. Oh, he did? Well, thank him, then." Tolliver made a face at me, and I grinned. He listened for a few moments. "Tomorrow? Oh, no thanks, we'd feel like we were intruding . . ." Tolliver looked acutely uncomfortable. "That's too much trouble," he said next. His tone was carefully patient. He listened. "Then, all right," he said reluctantly. "We'll be there."

He hung up and made a face. "The Morgensterns want us to come to their house tomorrow for lunch," he said. "They've had a lot of people bringing food by, they can't eat it all, and they're feeling guilty that we're stuck in Memphis because of them. There'll be other people there," he assured me when he saw my face. "The focus won't be on us."

"Okay, good. That would have crossed a line, after the flowers. There's such a thing as overdoing the gratitude. After all, it was an accident. And we're getting the reward. Joel said so. You should have asked me before you said yes. I really don't want to do that."

"But you see that we pretty much have to."

"Yes, I see that," I said, trying not to sound resentful. I thought that my brother wanted to see Felicia Hart again.

Tolliver nodded, a sharp gesture to close the subject. I wasn't quite sure I was through whining, but he was right. No point in discussing it any longer. "You ready to go back to the cemetery?" he asked.

"Yes. How cold is it?" I stood up, experimentally stretched the leg. Better.

"The temperature's dropping."

When we were all bundled up, I called downstairs to have our car brought around. A few minutes later, we were making our way back to St. Margaret's. The weekday nighttime traffic in downtown Memphis was not heavy. Nothing was going on at the Pyramid, and Ellis Auditorium looked dark, too. We drove east through depressed areas, shopping areas, and old residential areas until we got to the streets around Bingham College. The few people on foot were bundled up like urban mummies.

I began to recognize a few landmarks from the morning before. This time we didn't take the main drive through the college, as we had previously. Tolliver drove around the campus to reach a small road at the back of the college property. It had those white barriers that you pull back across the entrance, and yesterday they'd been pulled shut but unlocked, he'd noticed.

The same was true tonight. Rick Goldman, private eye, should tell Bingham their security had a few holes in it.

We passed between the open barriers. The crunch of gravel under our tires sounded especially loud. After a short stretch of landscaped lawn all around us, we entered the wooded corner of the campus. Though the city lay all around us, it felt like we were miles from nowhere. We drove slowly through the trees surrounding the old site, our headlights catching on the branches and trunks as we passed. Nothing moved in the cold stillness. We reached the clearing of the church and its yard. In the small graveled parking lot, we drove up to the low posts connected with wire that kept cars from pulling onto the grass. There was a security light on a high pole at the rear of the church, and one on the far side. They provided just enough light to make the shadow of the dilapidated iron-railing fence obscure the graveyard.

"If this was a horror movie, one of us

would be a goner," I commented.

Tolliver didn't respond, but he wasn't looking any too happy. "I thought the lighting would be better than this," he said. We made sure our coats were buttoned and zipped, gloves on, flashlights ready. Tolliver loaded some extra batteries into his pockets, and I did, too.

There was not even a night-light on in the old church.

When we shut the car doors behind us, the slams sounded loud as gunshots. Tolliver shone his flashlight on the wire so I could step over it, and I returned the favor. Then we opened the gate, which creaked loudly in approved horror-movie fashion.

"Just great," Tolliver muttered. I found myself smiling.

The ground, which had seemed fairly level in the daylight, was rough walking at night. At least, it was for me. I negotiated it slowly, worried about my faltering right leg. But I didn't ask Tolliver for help. I could manage.

From the entrance gate, we needed to work our way southeast to reach the secluded corner where I'd found Tabitha in Josiah Poundstone's grave. Of course, that was the darkest place in the whole cemetery.

"It feels bigger tonight," Tolliver said. His voice was just one step up from whispering.

160

I almost asked him why. Then I realized I didn't want to talk out loud, either. As we neared the open grave, I wondered if they'd dug up poor Josiah, too — and if so, what they'd done with him. The familiar vibrations of the dead began to sound louder and louder in my head.

"Have we ever been to a cemetery at night?" I asked, trying to shake off the uneasy, prickling feeling that was riding my shoulders. There was no definite reason for me to feel anxious. In fact, I usually felt alive, alert, and happy in graveyards.

Certainly, no one else was around. The cemetery was surrounded on two sides by thick stands of trees, on the third side by the parking area (beyond which were more trees), and on the fourth by the old church. It wasn't too far off a busy, modern street, but I'd noticed on our previous visit how isolated the graveyard felt. Bugs and birds had sense enough to keep silent and lay low.

"There was that time the couple in Wisconsin wanted you to do a reading at midnight on their son's grave," Tolliver said in my ear. It had been so long since I'd spoken, I had to recall the question I'd asked.

I was immediately sorry to be reminded about Wisconsin. I'd been trying to forget, to stuff that night into the closet where I kept horrors. Just to add to the weirdness of the couple and their request, they'd requested Halloween night. Plus, they'd invited about thirty best friends. I guess they'd figured if they were going to pay us that much money, they were going to get some mileage out of the event. They'd been mistaken about what I could do, though I'd never tried to mislead them. Right out there, in front of all their friends, I'd blurted out what had really happened to the child. I shuddered, remembering. Then I made myself shake off the memory. *Focus on this night, this dead girl, this grave,* I told myself. I took a deep breath, let it out. Then another.

"I know the body is gone," I said, almost in a whisper. "The body's always been my connection, but I'm going to try to recreate what I got from her yesterday."

"We're in an isolated graveyard in the dark," Tolliver muttered. "At least you're not wearing a long white nightgown, and at least we're together. And believe me, my cell phone battery is fully charged."

I almost smiled. Usually, I felt most comfortable in a cemetery; but not this one, not this night. I stumbled again. Cemeteries are tricky going, especially the older ones. So many of the new ones have the flat headstones. But in the older ones, there are broken headstones in the grass, which is often uneven and tufted with weeds. In more secluded cemeteries, the living often leave trash on top of the dead — broken liquor bottles and crushed beer cans, condoms, food wrappers, all kinds of stuff. I can't count the times I've found underpants suitable to both sexes, and once I found a top hat set jauntily upright on a stone.

St. Margaret's graveyard was free from debris of that sort. It had been mowed and trimmed at the end of the summer, so the grass was fairly low. Our flashlights bobbed through the darkness like playful fireflies, sometimes crossing their beams and then floating away.

The still air was cold, a cold that bit through my gloves and made me shiver. I had on a knit cap and scarf, but my nose felt especially chilled. Tolliver, some steps ahead of me and to my left, made the beam of his flashlight dance as he rubbed his hands together.

The night had a thick, waiting quality that made the hair on the back of my neck prickle. I tried to identify the swoosh of the traffic on the road off through the trees, but there was an absolute silence. I felt a stab of alarm. Surely, at night, I should be able to see the lights of those cars, even through the trees? I slowed down, feeling suddenly disoriented. The flashlight beams seemed dimmer. I was very close to the right spot, but somehow I couldn't pick it out. The buzzing of the bodies around me seemed extraordinarily clear and strong for such old corpses. I started to say my brother's name, but I couldn't speak. Suddenly, Tolliver gripped my lower arm with both hands, very tightly, bringing me to a complete standstill. "Look at your feet," he said in a very strange voice. I shone the light directly downward.

In one more step I would have fallen into the open grave.

"Ohmygod. That was close. Thank you. Do you hear anything?" I whispered. One hand slid down to mine, squeezed it, and released it. There was something odd about the feel of that bony hand.

And then I realized Tolliver's flashlight was shining at me from the other side of the grave, with Tolliver holding it.

My heart pounded so fast I thought the vibrations might tear my chest apart. I sank down to my knees on the soft, freshly turned earth.

"See?" said the voice, though I couldn't

have said where it had come from. With an increasing sense of dread, I directed my flashlight down into the grave.

There was another body in it.

EIGHT

Tolliver didn't seem to be able to move from his side of the open grave, and we both shone our flashlights down at the body.

"At least I didn't fall in," I managed to say, and my voice sounded hoarse and strange to my own ears.

"He stopped you," Tolliver said.

"You saw him? Clearly?"

"Just his silhouette," he said, and even Tolliver's voice was strained and breathless. "A small man. With a beard."

This was the first time such a thing had happened to us. It was like being an accountant for five years, and then suddenly being presented with a set of alien numerals that had to be balanced in five minutes.

Tolliver stumbled around the grave to kneel beside me, put both his arms around me, and we held each other fiercely. We were shivering, shivering intensely — not from the cold, but from the nearness of the unknown. I made a little noise that was horribly like a whimper. Tolliver said, "Don't be scared," and I turned my head a little to tell him I wasn't any more scared than he was; which was to say, quite a lot. He kissed me, and I was glad for his warmth.

I said, "This is a thin place."

"What's that?"

"A place where the other world is very close to this world, separated only by a thin membrane."

"You've been reading Stephen King again."

"It felt strange from the moment we got here tonight."

"Did you feel anything different when we were here the first time? Yesterday?"

"The old ones always feel a little different from the new ones. Maybe I saw the dead more clearly, with more detail." I held him tighter. Now that I'd gotten over my startled reaction to the ghost, I had plenty of other fears to cope with. We had a situation on our hands. "What will we do about the body, Tolliver? We shouldn't call the police, right? We're already under enough suspicion."

My feelings about the law were, at best, ambiguous. I couldn't blame the Texarkana PD for not knowing what was going on in our household when I was a teenager. After all, we'd struggled so hard to conceal it. I hardly blamed them for not finding Cameron; I, of all people, knew how hard it could be to find a dead person. But now that I was grown, the thing I valued most was the ability to shape my life as I wanted. The law could take that away from me in a New York minute.

"No one knows we came here," Tolliver said, as if thinking out loud. "No one's come out here since we got here. I bet we could leave and not get caught. But someone's got to get this body out of the grave. We can't just leave him."

I was beginning to feel calmer. "Who is it?" I asked, and my voice was steadier. After all, bodies were my area of expertise. I was not at all worried about being this close to a corpse. I was worried about the police suspecting I'd made him a corpse.

"I'm not sure." Tolliver sounded a little surprised, as if he should have known who was in the hole from the brief glimpse we'd had.

"Let's look again," I said practically. I was feeling a little more like myself.

We pulled apart then, and deployed our flashlights.

If my heart could sink any lower, it did.

Since the body was on its stomach, I couldn't identify its face, but the clothes were familiar.

"Crap. It's Dr. Nunley," I said. "He's still wearing the clothes he had on when he grabbed me at the hotel." I pressed the button on my watch, and the dial illuminated. It looked as though I had a fairy perched on my wrist. "It's been three hours since that happened. Just three hours. The lobby staff had to talk to Dr. Nunley to get him to leave, and they'll remember it. This couldn't be worse."

"Not for him, anyway," my brother said, his voice dry. But he had a slight smile on his face. I could just see the edge of his mouth in the cast-back light. I felt like punching him in the arm, but I wasn't sure I had enough muscle control to manage it. "And it's not so good for us, you're right," Tolliver admitted.

"Have we left footprints? Has it rained since we got here yesterday?"

"No, but the dirt here around the grave has been turned over, and I'm sure we've left traces somewhere. On the other hand, so many people have come through the cemetery since you found Tabitha . . . and we're both wearing the same shoes we wore out here yesterday."

"But there wasn't this loose dirt then. I don't know how we would explain coming out here tonight. Oh, I'm so sorry I got you into this."

"Bullshit," he said briskly. "We were doing what we do. You wanted to see if you could get some other bit of information from the grave. Well, we found out more than we wanted to know, huh? But it's not your fault." He hesitated. "Do you want to try to talk to him, the — the ghost? And what about getting a reading from the body?"

Tolliver's suggestion was as bracing as that brisk slap detectives give hysterical women in old movies. "Yes," I said. "Sure." Of course, I should have thought of that. I had to calm myself first, and center myself. Not too easy, since I was already buzzing like crazy just from being so close to a fresh body.

The closest I could get to Clyde Nunley's corpse without climbing down into the grave — which might have destroyed or damaged evidence — was to hang over the edge with my hand extended to him. I lay down on the ground and wriggled forward. Tolliver held on to my legs. The hole wasn't so deep, and I managed to touch the shirt on Dr. Nunley's back.

His death was so recent it was like a

continuous droning in my head, almost drowning my reason, and I had to wait for that to subside before I got a sense of his passing. "Hit on the head," I mumbled, caught up in the sheer astonishment he'd felt. "On the back of the head. So surprised." The shock of it was still lingering around him. He absolutely had not expected the attack.

"Here?"

"Yes," I said, straining to extract the pictures of the end of his life. He was so fresh, so recently translated into this lump of flesh that could neither act nor reason. I saw the darkness around him, the tombstones, everything like it was now: the cold, the rough ground, the upturned earth. "Oh, it hurts! Oh, it hurts! My head!" And the hole coming at me, couldn't throw out my hands to take the fall, grayness . . . blackness.

I was close to that blackness myself when Tolliver hauled me up and braced me against him.

"Here, open your mouth," he said, and then he repeated it. "Open!"

I parted my lips, and he pushed a piece of peppermint into my mouth.

"Come on, you have to have some sugar,"

he said, and his voice was sharp and commanding.

He was right. We'd found that out, by trial and error. I made myself suck on the candy, and in a few minutes I felt better. Next came a butterscotch.

"It's never been this bad," I said, my voice weak. "I guess it's because he's so new." I was worried I couldn't make it across the cemetery back to our car without a lot of help from Tolliver.

"He's absolutely gone, right? That . . . who stopped you — wasn't him? I did think I saw a beard."

Every now and then, we'd found a soul attached to a body. That was rare, and until this night I had thought that would be the eeriest thing we could find. Now we knew there was more.

"Clyde Nunley's soul's gone," I said, not willing to commit myself further than that. "And we should be, too." I gathered myself to make the attempt.

"Yeah," Tolliver said. "We got to get out of here."

I paused, halfway to my feet. "But we'll be leaving him by himself."

"He's been by himself for a hundred years," Tolliver said, not pretending he didn't understand. "He'll have to be by himself for a while longer. For all we know, maybe he's got company."

"Does this qualify as the strangest conversation we've ever had?"

"I think so."

"I couldn't have anyone else but you here, no one else would understand," I said. "I'm so glad you saw him, too."

"And that's never happened before, right? You've never mentioned anything like that."

"Never. I've known when souls were still attached to the body, and I've wondered if those would be ghosts if they didn't detach. I've always wondered if I would see a ghost sometime. I've always been a little disappointed that I haven't, in a way. Oh my God, Tolliver. He saved me from falling right into that grave on top of the corpse. The first time I see a ghost, and he saved me."

"Were you scared?"

"Not that he would hurt me. But I was afraid because it was spooky and I didn't know what to do for him. I don't know why he can't or won't go on, I don't know how he experiences time, I don't know his purpose. And now all his people are gone, I guess. No one could visit him or . . ." I shut up, afraid of sounding maudlin.

They all want to be found, you know.

That's all they want. Not vengeance, or forgiveness. They want to be found. At least, that's what I'd always thought.

But Josiah Poundstone — I was sure he was the ghost — had been firmly located since the moment of his death. Someone had erected the "Beloved Brother" headstone. And someone had murdered him, if that was part of his awareness. When I'd stood on his grave in the daylight, I'd felt only the faintest flutter from him, so overwhelmed had I been with the thrumming from the most recent corpse. I'd assumed Josiah Poundstone was gone for good.

Apparently, I'd been wrong.

NINE

We made our way back to the car, taking our time. I had to hold on to Tolliver here and there, and I don't think he was sorry to hold onto me. We dusted dirt off my jacket, and stomped our feet to remove bits of soil.

"If there were an emergency room for psychological shocks, we could go there," he said, unlocking the car.

"I've never left a body unreported," I said, remembering how proud I'd been of that fact only a day before. "Never." I shuddered. "I wish I could put my brain in a warm bath of something scented," I said. "And give my nervous system some aromatherapy."

"That mental picture is just disgusting," Tolliver said.

He was right, but that didn't stop me from wanting some way to soothe my emotional self. I took a deep breath and tried to put the frivolous thoughts on the back burner.

We still had decisions to make, and they wouldn't be easy ones.

"Did you get anything from the . . . did you get anything?" Tolliver asked.

"Yeah," I said. "Yeah, Dr. Nunley was really taken by surprise. I don't know why he was out there, but he never expected the person with him had any evil intent."

"Do ordinary people expect to be attacked, ever?" Tolliver asked reasonably.

I gave him a disgusted look. "No, they don't, smart aleck, and that's not what I meant. What I mean is — he wasn't with a stranger. He was with someone he knew, and he had no idea that the other guy wished him ill."

"You just using 'guy' for the ease of it?"

"Right."

"We can't tell the police."

"Sure we can, but they won't believe us. I don't know what else we can do. And I absolutely don't think we should tell them we were at the grave site again."

We argued back and forth all the way to the hotel — and with time out for discretion in front of the staff, resumed our argument when we were alone in the elevator.

When we stepped out, we were struck speechless to see Agent Seth Koenig waiting outside our room.

If the management had cast glances at us on our way through the lobby, we'd been too engrossed in our own problems to pick up on it. *Certainly not a psychic,* I thought ruefully. *If I ever claim to be one, strike me dead.* We were completely taken by surprise.

As one, we stopped in our tracks and stared at him.

We weren't alone in the staring department. He was laying one on us.

"What have you two been up to?" he asked.

"I don't believe we need to talk to you," Tolliver said. "My sister tells me you're an FBI agent, and we don't know anything of interest to you."

"Where have you been?" Koenig asked, as though we would be compelled to tell him.

"We went to the movies," I said.

"Just now," he said. "Where were you just now?"

Tolliver took my hand and led me past the agent, who was surely persistent.

I repeated what Tolliver had said. "We don't have to talk to you."

"If it was anything to do with Tabitha Morgenstern, I need to know it." His voice was rough and hard.

"Fuck off," I said. Tolliver gave me a startled look. That's not my usual style. But

177

I wanted to get away from this guy. Tolliver got the door unlocked and whisked me inside at top speed. We slammed the door behind us.

"He's obsessed with his failure," I said, as I began to shed all my outerwear. I noticed my shoes were stained with dirt from the cemetery, despite my efforts. I reminded myself that I had to clean them later. At the moment, I couldn't summon the energy. I felt awful: exhausted, weak, upset. "I have to shower and go to bed. I'm sorry I'm not more help."

"Don't say that," Tolliver said. He hated it when I apologized.

I often thought, and sometimes said, that Tolliver would be better off if he hadn't undertaken the role of my backbone. But when I tried to imagine myself going on the road alone, I felt a huge hole in my middle that refused to fill with anything. I tried to keep myself fit and did everything I could to ensure my health, but the fact remained that sometimes I was just overcome by the physical problems that plagued me. And the job itself drained me, though I loved it.

What Tolliver got out of accompanying me, I wasn't able to figure. But he did seem to want to do it, and he accused me of self-pity when I tried to get him to do something he might find more fulfilling.

In the meantime, we shared everything: the money was our money, and the car was our car, and the planning and execution of the itinerary was ours.

"Come on," Tolliver said, putting an arm around me helping me to my room. "Hold up your arms." Like a child, I held my arms up and he pulled off my sweater. "Sit on the bed." I did, and he pulled off my shoes and socks. I stood, and he unzipped my jeans.

"I'm good," I said. "I got it from here."

"Sure? Need candy? Need a drink?"

"No, just a shower and bed. I'll be okay after some sleep."

Tolliver said, "Call if you need me," and went back out to the living room. I heard him turn on the television. I couldn't even remember what night it was, so I didn't know if one of his shows was on. We could never count on being able to keep up with episodes, and we'd discussed learning more about TiVo for the set in our apartment.

I thought I heard Tolliver's cell phone ring while I was in the tub, but I simply didn't care who was calling. I soaked in hot, scented water, then scrubbed myself bright pink. After I dried off and put on my pajamas, I was disgusted to find out I still hadn't unwound enough to sleep. I turned on my own television to have background noise while I painted my nails. I decided on a nice dark red, which looked autumnal, and I had a lovely peaceful half hour to myself. You can't be said to have any worries if your fingernails are the center of your universe, and it gave me time to decompress.

I couldn't settle down to read when that was done, though Tolliver had brought a box of paperbacks up with us. We pick them up here and there, and leave them for other people when we're done. We love secondhand bookstores, and we'll go a mile or two out of our way if we've heard of a good one in the area. I'd been reading a biography of Catherine the Great, who may have become an empress but also managed to have a messy life. Maybe all empresses did. I just couldn't get into her tonight, and I was still jangling too much inside to get in the bed. I wandered into the common living room to see what Tolliver was up to.

He was fuming; there was no other word for it.

"The TV screen is going to break if you keep glaring at it like that," I said. "What's up?" Tolliver didn't do a lot of brooding and mulling, so I never thought twice about asking.

"Personal," snapped Tolliver.

I was shocked for a minute, and then gave myself a piece of good advice. Treat this casually, and don't get all tearful and hurt.

"Okay," I said calmly. "What's the score in the game?" Tolliver was watching football, which I couldn't care less about, but the question did knock him out of his funk and redirect his irritation. He was off and running on the failure of his favorite team, the Miami Dolphins, to get a first down. Since I know about as much about football as I do about quantum physics, I tried to look sympathetic while keeping my mouth shut. Sleep was out of the question until this was resolved, one way or another.

"We could use some food," I said, and called room service. I got a hamburger for Tolliver, and a grilled chicken sandwich for me.

By the time I'd done that, Tolliver had calmed down and was wearing his usual expression of good humor. "That phone call was from Felicia Hart," he said.

I tried to keep my face still and receptive. I tried very hard not to twitch.

"I've told you I'm sorry for being . . . for starting something with her," he said. "I'm not going to say it again."

"I didn't ask you to," I pointed out.

"Right." He shook his head. "Residual guilt," he said, by way of explanation. "She wants to see me again. I said it wasn't a good time."

"She saw you today, and she was reminded of how fine you are," I said, careful to be smiling when I said that. "I bet she wants to start up again."

He shook his head. "That seems really unlikely."

"I wonder if she'll be at the lunch tomorrow," I said, trying to sound innocent. "I'll run interference for you if you need me to. She'll probably try to get you by yourself."

"I don't think so," he said, refusing to be drawn.

"She's very protective of Victor," he said after a long pause. I wondered if he'd seen any of the action on the television screen. "Do you remember what Victor's alibi was when Tabitha was abducted?"

"Well, it was spring break, so he wouldn't have been at school," I said. "Nope, I don't recall. Why don't we look it up?"

Tolliver set up his laptop and hooked up to the hotel's Internet service. We began to do a little research into the crime that had led to us being in this room at this moment.

I sat by Tolliver, my arm around his shoulders, as he brought up the familiar story and the images from eighteen months ago. I had forgotten some of the details, and now that I knew all of the people involved, the pictures had much more impact.

What I noticed, first of all, was how many pictures included Agent Seth Koenig. He was in the background of most of the pictures that had appeared in relation to the disappearance. In all of the pictures, whether he was in the foreground or talking to someone in the background, his face was absolutely serious. He was a man absorbed in his mission.

It was shocking to see how much the Morgensterns had aged since Tabitha's abduction. Even Victor looked more adult now — though at his age, that was maybe only to be expected. In the pictures, Diane looked more like five years younger, and Joel looked . . . lighter. He was still charismatic and handsome now, but he walked more heavily, as if he were carrying a burden on his shoulders. I hated to sound all corny about it — but it was true.

We combed through the stories, refreshing our memories.

On that warm spring morning in Nashville, only Diane had been home with

Tabitha. Joel had gone to work two hours before. Spring is always a busy time for accountants, and Joel went in most Saturdays until after the tax deadline. That Saturday, he'd gotten in to work so early that no one had seen him arrive. Joel told the police that several other accountants had come into the office after he'd been there an hour. Though he hadn't been under continuous surveillance from the time the other workers had begun arriving until after Tabitha's abduction, he'd been seen at fairly frequent intervals. That time frame made it seem unlikely he could have managed the crime, but it was a possibility.

As for Diane, she'd told us what she'd been doing — arguing with her daughter, talking on the phone, getting ready to go to the store. She'd been unobserved for most of that time.

So much for the parents.

Tabitha's stepbrother Victor had also gotten up early that morning. Victor had driven to his tennis club for an 8:00 A.M. lesson, which had lasted an hour. And then, Victor said, he'd just stayed around the tennis courts to bat some balls against the wall and talk to some of his friends. The friends, apparently, had remembered seeing Victor, but they weren't sure what time that had been. After that, Victor said, he'd stopped at a gas station to fill his car and buy a Gatorade. The gas station cashier had verified the episode. Victor had arrived home about 11:00 A.M. to find his house exploding with the beginnings of panic. Again, there was no way to pin down times more accurately. If Victor had planned ahead, he could have abducted his half sister.

According to one of his friends, Victor hadn't been especially fond of Tabitha. But this "friend" couldn't think of anything specific Victor had ever said about Tabitha, just that Victor thought she was a spoiled brat.

That seemed like a perfectly ordinary thing for a big brother to say about his sister, whether she was his full sister or his half sister. On the other hand, Victor was at a volatile age.

Were there other suspects? Sure. The articles we read brought up the fact that Joel was a CPA for Huff Taichert Killough, a firm that handled accounts for lots of music industry people. This fact opened the door to vague allusions to shady record company accounting, as if Joel was possibly mixed up in some dubious financial dealings that might have earned him some enemies. But no facts were ever produced to back up that intriguing possibility. And, in fact, Joel continued to work for the same firm. Now he worked for the Memphis branch instead of the Nashville branch, but of course the newspapers didn't specify whether the change of locale had included a change of job description, or not. If some money-laundering scheme had become an investigative reality, I was sure the reporters would have caught wind of it, since they were all over the abduction like white on rice.

I studied the pictures that had been included with the articles: Victor, looking sullen and lost; Diane, looking wasted; Joel, his face bleached of feeling. There was Felicia, looking angry and fierce, her arm around Victor, and by her side was Seth Koenig, the FBI agent who'd been waiting in the hall for us this evening. Hmmm. He was saying something to her in the picture, caught forever in mid-sentence, his face serious behind a pair of dark glasses. The caption read, "Felicia Hart, aunt of the missing girl, comforts her nephew, Victor Morgenstern, as she discusses the case with an FBI agent. The FBI offered their lab facilities or any other assistance the local police might deem necessary."

"Look," said Tolliver, sounding amused.

The next picture was one of us. We both had on dark glasses, too, and I had my head turned away. That was a habit of mine when I saw cameras. I don't mind being photographed, but that doesn't mean I like it, either.

There was a brother of Joel's, too, a near-clone but a bit older, named David. I didn't recall seeing him at the Morgenstern house, but maybe by the time we'd been called in, he'd returned to his work and his life. People had started drifting back into their normal orbits about that time, when it seemed as if the situation was not going to be resolved quickly.

"I don't think we know a damn thing more," I complained.

"No, probably not," Tolliver said. "We haven't called the police, either."

"They'll find out it's us calling, if we do," I said. "They'll find him. He'll be missed soon. I don't think we can risk it." Okay, that might seem the last word in callousness from me, and believe me, I wasn't happy about it. I was very aware that Clyde Nunley was lying out there dead in the dark and the cold. But you know, the dead don't feel a thing. They're just waiting.

If he wasn't found the next day, maybe I could "find" him a second time. No one would be surprised if we happened to go out to the old cemetery the next day, I figured. It was our choosing to go there in the middle of the night that would seem extraordinary; and now that I came to think of it, it *had* been an extraordinary thing to do. And foolish, too.

But now we were stuck with it, and we'd have to take the consequences if our presence was discovered.

As I climbed into my bed that night, I was more confused about what had happened to Tabitha Morgenstern than I'd been before I found her bones. And the presence of the ghost at the grave site was forcing me to rethink all my suppositions about the dead. I had plenty to worry about; but my body was exhausted, and before I knew it, I was asleep.

I don't dream much, but that night I dreamed of holding hands that had been reduced to bones. I wasn't frightened in my dream. But I knew it wasn't right.

The next morning, there was a knocking at the door while Tolliver and I sat over breakfast, reading the morning paper. Tolliver was working the crossword. I'd reread everything I could find on the abduction of Tabitha, and I'd worked my way up chronologically to the new articles about the recovery of a body that might be hers. I'd reached the stories that were wringing the dregs out of the discovery of the child's body. This included an article on the main subject — the very tentative positive identification based on dental work — plus a rehash of the abduction, the family's plans for a memorial service the following week, quotes from the grieving grandparents; a companion story about Memphis's "hidden" cemeteries; and an article about child abduction in general, with statistics on the number of children found alive, the number found dead, and the number of those who were never found. Cameron had plenty of company.

There's not much that's more frightening than the idea of a child vanishing, gone for good. I thought of my little sisters, and shivered. Mariella and Gracie were pretty formidable kids when I'd lived with them in the trailer. I didn't know what they were like now, since my aunt and her husband kept telling us the girls didn't want to see us. That might or might not be true, but if it was so, Iona and Hank had been feeding them a load of untruths about us that I wanted a chance to rectify. The girls might not love me, but I loved them.

My mind had wandered, but the knock recalled me to the here and now.

We looked at each other. Tolliver rose. He looked through the peephole.

"It's the FBI guy again," he said.

"Shit," I murmured. I was wearing a hotel bathrobe and nothing else, since I'd showered again this morning after doing my time on the hotel treadmill.

"You'd better let me in, I've got news for you," the voice on the other side of the door said.

Tolliver glanced back at me.

We considered.

"Okay," I said. "Better find out what he wants."

Tolliver opened the door, and Seth Koenig stepped in at once and closed the door. His eyes flashed to my legs, and then away. "I taped the news this morning, since I thought you two might not have seen it," he said. He waited for us to respond, and we both shook our heads. We don't turn on the television as a matter of course. From the expression on his face, I felt pretty bad about what was coming.

He strode over to our television and popped the tape in the hotel player. He used the remote to turn on the set. After a moment of sports scores, Shellie Quail filled the camera. She looked resplendent in a bright fall suit and her usual gleaming makeup. Shellie had on her sober newscaster face. Clearly, she was going to deliver Grim Tidings.

"A groundskeeper at Bingham College made a shocking discovery early this morning. Dennis Cuthbert was sent to the site of the old St. Margaret's church and cemetery to make sure the garbage had been picked up after the discovery, two days ago, of Tabitha Morgenstern's remains interred in an ancient grave in the cemetery. What Cuthbert found was just as shocking. Inside that same grave, he found *another* body."

They sure did love the word "shocking."

The camera cut to a husky black man wearing a dark blue uniform. Dennis Cuthbert looked mighty upset. "I got here, and I see the car parked in the parking lot," he said. "Wasn't anyone supposed to be here, so I began looking around a little."

"Did you think at that point that there was anything *wrong?*" Shellie asked, her face in a sober mask.

"Yeah, I did wonder," said Dennis Cuthbert. "Anyway, I started walking around, and soon I notice that the grave look a little different."

"How?"

"The edge look a little collapsed. So I go over there and look down, and there he was."

Good. He'd walked over the area where I'd lain to touch the corpse.

The camera swung back to Shellie, who said, "Inside that grave, Cuthbert found the body of a man, tentatively identified as Bingham College professor Dr. Clyde Nunley. Dr. Nunley was *dead.*"

Switch to the outside of an older home probably dating from the 1940s, the kind yuppies bought and restored. "Dr. Nunley's wife, Anne, told the police that her husband had left their home for the second time between six and seven o'clock last night to check something out, he said. He didn't give any details. When he hadn't returned home at his usual time, she went to bed. When she woke this morning and found him still missing from the home, she called police."

Evidently, Anne Nunley had declined to be interviewed, because she didn't appear on the screen. Smart woman.

Close-up of the gleaming Shellie. "Police aren't saying *how* Dr. Nunley died. But a source close to the investigation said his death could have been an accident, or could have been *murder.* Apparently suicide has been ruled out. Back to you, Chip."

The picture turned into gray lint right after that.

I didn't dare to look at Tolliver. I didn't want to look at Seth Koenig, either. He stepped forward to turn off the machine, and then he faced me. "What do you make of that, Miss Connelly?"

"I think it's very strange, Agent Koenig."

"Please call me Seth." He waited a beat to see if I'd return the courtesy, but I didn't. I wondered what to do now. I wanted the agent to leave with a fervent desperation, because I needed to discuss this very puzzling development with Tolliver.

"The groundskeeper noticed a car in the parking lot," Seth Koenig said. He waited for us to respond.

"That's what the reporter said," Tolliver said. He sounded as cool as ice. I envied my brother his composure and wished I could match it.

Of course, there'd been no other car there when we'd parked in the parking lot. Dr. Nunley hadn't committed suicide, and he hadn't died by accident. He'd been murdered. We knew it without a doubt.

"There were rocks in the grave," Seth Koenig said.

I did look up then, and met his eyes.

"What kind of rocks?" I said.

"Big ones. They'd been aimed at his head."

"But . . ." My voice trailed off as I thought that through. Granted, we hadn't had sunlight or much time or inclination to examine the inside of the grave. But I was sure the "big rocks" hadn't been there. This might be a clumsy attempt to make the death look accidental; the scenario would be that Dr. Nunley somehow slipped and fell into the open grave, hitting his head on the rocks that lay in the bottom. The killer wanted the police to think it was such an accident; or in an alternative version, that Dr. Nunley had indeed been murdered, but there at the site, by someone who got him to climb down into the grave and then pelted him with large rocks until he expired. Oh, *that* sounded likely.

Seth Koenig sat on the coffee table in front of me. His eyes met mine. His were a peaty brown, warm with a golden undertone. His whole face was craggy and lined and attractive, and right at the moment, he was concentrated on me.

"I don't know what kind of person you are," he said. "But I know you have a gift. Right now, I want you to use that gift. I want you to go see Clyde Nunley's body in

194

the morgue, and I want you to tell me what happened to him. Something tells me you'll let me know."

Now here was a poser. What could I say?

"Why are you here?" Tolliver said. He stood behind me, leaning over so his elbows were resting on the back of the couch right by my head. "What is your involvement with this case? I know the FBI is no longer actively involved. But you're offering your lab facilities to the police, right?"

"Right," Koenig said. His eyes had turned their high-beam stare on Tolliver, which was a relief to me. "But I'm also here to lend whatever help and support they need, and I'm staying until . . ."

He couldn't finish the sentence.

"You were called in at the beginning," I said, making my voice gentle. "You were in Nashville."

He took a deep breath. "Yes, I was. Our paths never crossed there, but I was sent there when Tabitha was first missing. I talked to the mother, the father, the brother, the aunt, the uncle, the grandparents. I talked to the crossing guard who'd admonished Tabitha about jaywalking, I talked to the teacher who'd threatened to send a note to her parents about Tabitha's talking in class, and I talked to the lawn man who'd

195

told her dad that Tabitha was going to grow up to be real pretty." He took a deep breath. "I went with the police to talk to the moms who drove in the car pool with Diane, I talked to Victor and his friends, I talked to Victor's ex-girlfriend who'd sworn she was going to get even with him, and I talked to the maid who said Tabitha hated to pick up her room." He sat silent for a long moment. "I never learned a thing from any of them. I never discovered a single reason anyone would want the girl out of the way. She wasn't perfect. Even people who loved her had a problem with her every now and then. So, Tabitha wasn't all sweetness and light. No kid is, especially no kid in that in-between age. But as far as I can tell, her mom and dad loved her no matter what she did or said. As far as I can tell, they were trying hard to be good parents. As far as I can tell, they didn't deserve what happened to them because of Tabitha's disappearance."

"Why Tabitha? Why are you so wrapped up in this? You must have investigated other disappearances," I said. "Some of them children, I'm sure."

He rubbed his face with both hands, hard, like he wanted to erase some of the lines in his flesh. "Lots of sevens," he said. "Too many."

Tolliver and I glanced at each other. Tolliver didn't understand the reference, either.

"Sevens?" I tried to keep my voice very quiet. This man was going through a lot, and I didn't want to sway his balance.

"Kidnapping. That's the program designation for kidnapping," Koenig said.

"There was never a ransom demand for Tabitha," Tolliver said. He was leaning forward, his elbows on his knees. "The FBI can come in even when there's no crossing of state lines? When there's no ransom demand?"

The agent nodded.

"Any suspicious disappearance of a child under eleven," he said. "We've offered all our facilities to the Nashville police and the Memphis police. We've got forensic experts examining the body. Our guys already went over the grave. Thank God whoever killed Nunley didn't dump him there before our team had finished. And the same team has been all over the grave this morning since the body was found."

I shut my eyes and leaned back in my chair.

"Of course, Nunley was here last night grabbing you by the arm, Ms. Connelly. But we know he left after that. He wouldn't let the hotel staff call him a cab. They saw him get in his car and leave. Did he contact you again last night?"

"No," I said. "He didn't."

"Why was he so angry?"

"He thought I'd cheated somehow. He was having trouble accepting my ability as real. He was trying to find a rational explanation for something that's just unexplainable." I wondered if I needed to call Art Barfield.

Seth Koenig looked thoughtful, as if he was making a very large mental note.

"And where were you, Mr. Lang?" Koenig asked.

"I was walking down Beale Street, trying to find some good blues to listen to. Doing a tourist thing."

"What time did you get back to the hotel?"

"About seven, I think. Harper had been asleep."

"I was upset after the little scene with Dr. Nunley," I explained. "I had a terrible headache. I took some medicine and lay down."

"Did anyone see you here during that time?"

"I didn't have room service, and no one called." Dammit.

"And you, Mr. Lang?"

"It's possible someone will remember me in some of the places I stopped in on Beale." Tolliver listed the places he'd visited, and told Agent Koenig he'd had a beer at one bar. "It's also possible no one will recall me. The street wasn't crammed with people, but it was busy enough."

"And you were on foot?"

"Yes, we took a cab to the movies."

"You saw what movie?"

We went all through our afternoon, including our meeting with Xylda Bernardo and her grandson Manfred.

"I've met Ms. Bernardo," Koenig said, a slight smile on his lips. It was the first time I'd seen him smile, and it looked good on him.

He stayed another hour, taking us over the afternoon and evening over and over. Just when I was beginning to think we were home free, Koenig said, "And now we come to an interesting point. Who was the man in the lobby with you last night, the man who sent Dr. Nunley on his way?"

I'd wondered when he was going to get around to Rick Goldman. "His name is Rick Goldman. He's a private detective, he told me," I said carefully. "He was in the class at the cemetery, so he was there two mornings ago. According to him, he signed up for Occult Studies because the — well, a faction of the governing board, whatever it's called — was a little uneasy about Dr. Nunley's class. According to him, they'd asked him to take the courses, observe what happened, and report back to them."

"You got his card?"

"We aren't on those terms."

Koenig snorted. He'd taken a couple of notes. Now he put his little notebook back into his pocket. I was a bit surprised that he didn't use something higher-tech, like a BlackBerry.

"One more question," he said, wanting me to relax so he could spring something on me. I refused to take his unspoken invitation to breathe easier. "When you two went out last night, why'd you return to the St. Margaret's cemetery?"

TEN

I'd been waiting, like a cartoon character with a piano hoisted over its head, for the big collapse of the conversation, and here it was.

Tolliver and I glanced at each other. We had a choice to make. Did Koenig know we'd been there because he had solid evidence of our presence? Was this sheer conjecture, a stab in the dark to see if he hit a nerve? Or did he only know we'd taken our car out?

Tolliver tilted his head slightly. *Up to you,* he was saying.

"We went for a long drive. We had cabin fever," I said. "We just looked at Memphis. We've never been here before. But we avoided anywhere we might be recognized. We don't want any more media attention. We want to be out of here, and out of the public eye."

"You're one of the few people I could hear

say those words without wanting to laugh in their face," Koenig said. He passed a hand over his crisp dark hair. "And I can't impress on you how lucky you are that it's me investigating this case, instead of . . ."

"One of your colleagues who wouldn't believe I can do what I can do?" I said.

His mouth snapped shut. After a second, he nodded.

"No one knows, right? Where you work? That you're a believer."

He nodded again.

"How long have you realized there's more to this world?"

"My grandmother could see spirits," he said.

"You have a big advantage over people whose minds are closed," Tolliver said.

"Most days I don't think so," the agent admitted. "Most days, I'd be happy to be like the other people I work with. Then I could just dismiss you people, all of you. But I believe you have exceptional abilities. That being said, I don't think you're telling me the truth. In fact, I think you're lying." Koenig looked at us with a kind of profound disappointment. I almost felt guilty.

"We didn't kill him," I said. That was the important truth. "We don't know who killed him, or why."

"Do you think the Morgensterns killed Clyde Nunley? Do you think they killed their daughter?"

"I don't know," I said. "I hope to God they didn't." I hadn't realized how much I hoped that the Morgensterns were innocent of their daughter's death. And if they hadn't killed Tabitha, I couldn't imagine why they would kill Clyde Nunley. I was assuming that the same person or persons had killed both victims.

That assumption might not be true. "Tolliver and I have been invited to their home for lunch today," I said, just to change the subject. "We'll see more of the family then, I guess."

"Do you want to see what you can get from the body?" Koenig asked as casually as if I'd been a fiber expert or a pathologist. "That is, if I can arrange it."

This was kind of exciting, being taken seriously by a law enforcement professional.

"I'll do Nunley if you let me do Tabitha," I said.

He looked genuinely surprised. "But you've already, uh, 'done' Tabitha."

I didn't really want to review Nunley. Been there, done that. I'd do it, though, if I could have another chance at the little girl. "That day, I was so upset and shocked when

I realized there really were two sets of bones in the grave. Maybe I could get more."

"It may take some time, but I'll see what I can do," Koenig said. I couldn't help but notice his eyes flicked over my bare legs again. Well, he was a male, after all. I didn't think Koenig was particularly interested in the person who used those legs.

"It drains her to touch a body," Tolliver said, trying to force Agent Koenig to acknowledge that I was making a generous offer.

"Interesting," he said, and that was his only comment. "Let me know when you return from the Morgensterns' house, would you? Maybe you'll pick up some impressions from someone there."

"Hey, once again, not psychic. The only time I get impressions is when I touch a corpse, and I'm not planning on there being any at the Morgensterns' house. In fact, I'd just as soon this case get solved so quickly I wouldn't have to locate another body until we travel to our next job."

"Assuming you get to," Koenig said pleasantly.

There was a significant pause, while Tolliver and I absorbed the threat.

"If push comes to shove, we once did a favor for the governor," I said, very quietly.

I was very willing to shove.

I loved the expression on Koenig's face. I'd really surprised him, and that was a true pleasure. Childish, I know, but I never said I was adult all the way through. I don't ever reveal who my clients have been, but in this case, I felt that I had to take a stand.

"You mean you can call the governor of this state, maybe get him to come down on me or on the Memphis police, let you leave Memphis?"

I didn't say anything. I let what I'd said reverberate a bit.

"That's an unexpected threat," Koenig said. His face had gotten colder and harder. "Of course, any threat from you two is unexpected. I kind of think you won't be ringing that bell."

We looked at each other. "You'd be surprised what we'll do," I said. Tolliver nodded.

Koenig gave us his best tough-guy stare.

"Whose car was it?" Tolliver asked.

It took Koenig a second to change mental gears.

"Whose car? You mean, the car left at St. Margaret's?"

Tolliver nodded.

"Why should I tell you?"

"After all we've shared, and you're not

going to let us know?" My tone may have been a wee bit mocking.

"I think we can take it that the car was Dr. Nunley's own vehicle," Tolliver said. "Just a guess on my part."

"Yeah," Koenig admitted. "It was Nunley's car. It wasn't there at nine last night, but it was there early this morning."

We tried not to look too startled. We'd been there earlier; the body had been in the grave, but the car hadn't been there, for sure.

"How do you know that?" I asked, and was proud that I sounded so unconcerned.

"The campus police take a turn back there every night about nine, and no one was parked in the St. Margaret's parking lot. Since they're campus cops, they just cruise through the lot. They don't even get out of the car, much less check the inside of every grave. The strange thing is, Nunley was probably in the open grave already. The time of death was way earlier than that. He couldn't have died after nine. The body temperature indicates he was dead by seven at the latest, and the stomach contents tend to bear that out. Of course, the lab results aren't back, and there's a lot more to be learned from the body."

Tolliver and I exchanged a glance. It took

all my self-control to keep from covering my eyes with my hand. We hadn't known how lucky we were. If the campus police had caught us there with the corpse, no way in hell would anyone have believed we were innocent.

"So, Agent Koenig, why do you think the killer drove the car away and brought it back?" I asked. "Let me put on my thinking cap." I held a finger to my cheek in a parody of concentration.

Actually, I already had a pretty good idea. Or rather, three ideas. One, the killer wanted to get the car cleaned to erase any forensic traces. Two, the killer had to fetch something and take it back to the cemetery to complete the picture he was trying to paint. Three, the killer heard us coming and wanted to get the car out of there while we were approaching, so we wouldn't see who was driving.

Seth Koenig looked from me to Tolliver with a stony face, not amused in the least. He said. "That man is dead. If you can't take that seriously, you're just not human."

"Playing the not-human card," I said to Tolliver.

"As if we hadn't heard that one before," he said.

"I know what you're doing," the agent

said. "And you're good at it, I'll give you that. Were the rocks in the grave when you saw the body?"

"We didn't see the body," I said flatly.

"They were big rocks. Big enough to crack a skull," Koenig said. "I think that's why the killer had to come and go. He had to go get a couple of big rocks. He threw them down in the grave so they'd land on Nunley's head — might have taken a couple of tries. The killer wanted the scene to look as though Nunley might have tripped and fallen into the open grave. But we're pretty sure that just didn't happen. Dr. Nunley was almost certainly murdered."

"Dum-dum-*dum*," I said.

"I know you're not laughing inside about this," Koenig said. "I know you want me to leave so you can talk about it. I'm letting you know I'm available for further conversation. And if you remember anything, you're smart enough to realize we need to know about it." He rose, in an easy motion that made me envious.

"We understand," Tolliver said, getting up at the same time. He stood between Koenig and me. "We'll be talking to you." He hesitated. "I appreciate that you're doing your best with this case. It's bothered Harper a lot, too." He looked back at me, and I nodded. Though we were ready, past ready, for Koenig to leave, this had been a much more amicable interview than we usually had with anyone who carried a badge.

When the door shut behind Koenig, Tolliver didn't move for a long moment. Then he turned to me with raised brows.

"That was different," I agreed.

"The bad thing about him being halfway nice is that I almost don't like lying to him," my brother said. "The good thing is, he gave us a lot of useful information." His face darkened. "Like the time of death."

I nodded. "That's pretty scary, huh? That we got there at just the right moment not to run into the murderer?"

"I wonder if we were that lucky. I wonder if the murderer wasn't parked somewhere, watching us — to see if we'd find the body and call the cops. If we didn't, he'd know he needed to do something different, because there'd be no point in bringing the car back if there'd be a police officer standing there saying, 'And what are you doing in the deceased's automobile?' "

I shivered, picturing someone lurking in the dark coldness of the old graveyard, someone watching and waiting to see what we made of our discovery. I'm no good at detecting the presence of living people. But the awful image faded after a moment. That didn't hang together.

"No, no one was there," I said. "Because someone did bring the rocks — thought it *was* of use to try to cover up the murder. So it stands to reason that the killer didn't know we'd found the body in the meantime, that we could testify that there wasn't anything in the grave but the corpse when we saw it."

Tolliver thought that over, nodded. It made sense. "Assuming we tell anyone. Assuming people believe us," he muttered.

"Yes, always assuming that." I stood and stretched. Because of my bad leg, I couldn't stand as smoothly as the FBI agent, who was way older. I tried not to resent that. I moved carefully, loosening the muscles. "And we just missed the campus cop patrol. We thought it was so deserted out there! They should put in a traffic light." There was a lot more thinking to do about what Seth Koenig had told us, but we had a social engagement I was dreading. "I'm going to get ready for the lunch. I guess we have to go."

Tolliver blew out a deep breath. He was as reluctant as I was, and he had the added complication of Felicia Hart's probable presence. "I think the Morgensterns feel guilty because we can't leave Memphis," he said. "They feel kind of like they're our host and hostess."

"But their daughter is dead, and they should be free to think about that, concentrate on that."

"Harper, maybe they don't want to. Maybe we're a welcome distraction."

I shrugged. "Then at least we're serving some useful purpose." But I couldn't even feel good about that. "I think this is a bad idea."

"I'm not exactly looking forward to it myself. But we have to do it."

I held up my hand, because his tone was definitely on the testy side. "I get that. And I'll stop sulking in a minute. Okay, you shower. I'll get dressed." I glanced at my watch. "We've got an hour and a half. Do we have directions?"

"Yeah, I got them over the phone from Joel. I'm sure Felicia is going to be there." He gave me a stern look. "Do I have to ask you to be nice?"

"Of course I will be." I gave him just enough of a smile to make him anxious. We didn't talk much during the long drive across the city. I drove, Tolliver navigated.

The Memphis home of the Morgenstern

family was not unlike their Nashville home, though it was located in a somewhat more modest neighborhood. Diane and Joel liked upscale suburbs, not old city neighborhoods. They liked the kind of place where the trees are only partially grown and the lawns were rolled out in strips, where people jog in the early morning and the late evening and there are always service trucks circling the houses like remoras seeking sustenance from sharks.

The Morgenstern house was pale brick with dark red shutters and doors, a yard that would be beautiful in the spring, and a curving doublewide driveway that already contained a few shining cars, including a pearly Lexus, a dark red Buick, a green Navigator, and a candy-apple red Mustang. We parked and got out. I don't know about Tolliver, but I felt I was on alien ground. There were Thanksgiving decorations out at some of the homes, and Diane had put a couple of hay bales in the front yard, topping them with pumpkins and squash and cornstalks and other fall paraphernalia.

Maybe, when we have a house, I'll do the same thing, I thought, and knew right away that was total bullshit. I'd just been trying to tell myself I could live in as nice a place as the Morgensterns and not feel strange and out of place.

Tolliver smiled at me over the top of the car. "You ready?" he asked. "You look great today, you know."

I was wearing a rust-colored long-sleeved sweater over dark brown corduroys and leather high-heeled boots. I had a dark brown suede jacket on. At the last minute, I'd thought about jewelry and added a plain gold chain. I seldom wear jewelry, but this had seemed a good time to add a little gleam. Tolliver had stretched himself to wear a button-up shirt and khakis. I wondered if he had dressed for Felicia Hart's benefit. He said he didn't want her attentions, didn't understand her . . . but I wondered.

I went up the sidewalk, picking up my feet with an effort. I felt more like dragging them. As I rang the doorbell, I noticed a sort of decorated plaque hanging by the right side of the door, brass and turquoise and shiny stones combined in a really interesting way, with etched symbols of doves and Stars of David. I thought it looked as though it was a door, and the depth of the case indicated there might be something inside. I raised my eyebrows at Tolliver, who shrugged. He didn't know what it was, either.

Diane answered the door. She wasn't looking good; I guess that was to be expected. Her pregnancy was laying into her hard, giving her large rings under her eyes, and she'd lost all grace, moving heavily and with ponderous deliberation. But she'd fixed a hostess smile on her face, and she said she was happy we'd come. Joel came next, and shook our hands. He looked in my eyes and told me how glad he was to see me.

Even a non–Joel fan like myself could feel a twinge. And yet, I didn't think there was anything behind his personalization of a commonplace greeting; I didn't imagine he wanted to have an affair with me. It was just his way.

"We're in the family room," Diane said, her voice limp. "It's been the nicest quiet morning, with the telephones turned off and the computers shut down. No one's even watched the television." Her face crumpled for a moment, then came back with a pleasant social smile. "Come say hello to everyone."

"Everyone" turned out to be Felicia and her father, Joel's parents, Victor, and Joel's brother, David. Also on hand were a couple of friends of Diane's from Nashville, who'd driven over for the day. The two women were named Samantha and Esther; they were about Diane's age and extremely well groomed, which made me feel sorry for Diane. There was a little conversation going on, of the low-level and subdued variety. Joel waved a hand to gather everyone's attention.

"For those of you who don't know her yet, this is the woman who found Tabitha," Joel said, and the faces all went absolutely blank.

This was a very strange reaction, one I hadn't foreseen. I'd never been announced like this. The introduction was odd enough; especially considering the dad of the murder victim was doing the introducing. And it was like I'd done them a great and grand favor, instead of being paid for a service that (as far as I was concerned) had borne fruit months too late. Naturally, when I'd worked for them in Nashville, the Morgensterns had paid me for my time. I had a sudden notion: maybe I should turn down the reward money, or donate it to charity, since I'd taken their money before and not given them back the location of their daughter. I put that away to mull over later, but my initial reaction was "Hell, no." I never promised anyone I'd find anything; only that if I did, my COD (cause of death) would be accurate. I'd spent days of my time and lots of my energy searching for Tabitha; she just hadn't been there to be found.

I realized another thing as I stood there in the unwanted spotlight. No one in this house knew about the body in the grave in St. Margaret's cemetery; the newest body, that is. They'd been incommunicado all morning, by Diane's own testimony. I opened my mouth to share the news, and then I shut it. They would find out soon enough. I glanced at Tolliver, and he nodded. He'd arrived at the same point.

The older Morgensterns, who were only in their mid-fifties, rose to their feet and slowly made their way to me. Mrs. Morgenstern was the one needing the help; she had Parkinson's, I could see. Mr. Morgenstern looked as strong as his sons, and his handshake was firm. In fact, if he'd been single and he'd asked me out, I'd have thought about accepting, because Mr. Morgenstern was as good-looking as his sons, too. "We're so grateful that we can finally take care of Tabitha," Mrs. Morgenstern said. "You've performed a great service for our family. Now that they've learned for sure about their girl, maybe Diane and Joel can welcome the little one to come with a clear mind. My name's Judy, and my husband's name is Ben."

"This is my brother Tolliver," I said, in

turn, having shaken hands with the couple.

"This is Felicia's dad, Victor's grandfather, Fred Hart," Ben said. Fred Hart didn't look as hale and hearty as Ben Morgenstern, but again, for a man in his fifties, he looked good: a bit thick around the waist and gray on top, but still a man you'd reckon with. He had a drink in his hand. I was pretty sure it wasn't soda or tea.

"Good to meet you, Fred," I said, and he shook my hand without comment. Fred Hart's square face was set in an expression I thought must be habitual. He was serious and grim, and his mouth was a compressed flat line that seldom curved in a smile. Of course, he'd lost his daughter to cancer, and he had probably gone through another emotional wringer when his step-granddaughter had been taken. He took another sip from the glass in his hand, and his gaze returned to his living daughter. Maybe he thought she would vanish, too.

The three grandparents were standing in front of built-in shelves that were clogged with framed family pictures and other memorabilia.

"Look, they still have Tabitha's menorah up," Judy said, pointing to a candlestick. I did recognize that particular symbol of Judaism. There was another menorah right by Tabitha's, but it was radically different in concept.

"Each kid has their own?" I guessed.

"Some families do that," Judy said in her gentle voice. She pointed with a trembling hand. "There's Victor's. Of course, his had to be different." She gave me a conspiratorial smile that said all teenagers were difficult. Victor's menorah was like a little stage or shelf with the eight small candles on it, behind it a little backdrop, a mirror topped with an elaborately worked brass header. If both menorahs hadn't been designed to hold candles, I wouldn't have recognized them as the same religious object.

Fred Hart reached out to point at a picture. His finger was shaking. "My daughter," he said, and I obediently looked at the snapshot, which was a happy one. A very attractive woman with short auburn hair and big brown eyes had been photographed sitting on a white-painted wrought iron chair in a garden at the height of its beauty, probably in May, I thought. She was holding a baby on her lap that must be Victor, a little boy in a sailor suit. His hair was fiery, too — not too surprising, with both parents being red-headed — and he was grinning at the camera. I figured he was about two years old, though I'm not good at pegging baby ages. Mr. Hart touched the frame of the photo with a kind of stern tenderness, and then he silently turned away to stand at the window, looking out.

Judy and Ben took me over to meet their other son, Joel's brother, David, a slighter, less magnetic version of his brother. I'd seen David in pictures, but the man in the flesh made little impression. David had the same reddish coloring and blue eyes as Joel, but he was built along sleeker lines and his eyes didn't have the draw of Joel's. David Morgenstern didn't seem particularly glad to meet me. From the distant way he touched my hand instead of actually shaking it, I gathered that he couldn't fathom why Tolliver and I should be invited guests in his brother's home.

I was kind of wondering the same thing, so I didn't blame him for his coolness. Oddly enough, on our previous job we'd also been invited to the client's home for a lunch. But that was hardly the normal procedure. Normally, we were in and out of the town as quickly as we could manage. I didn't like this social fraternizing with clients; it seemed to lead to deeper involvement in their problems, and that meant trouble. I promised myself on the spot that I wouldn't do it again.

Though Fred Hart remained aloof from the little crowd, the older Morgensterns had decided I was in their charge. Since Ben and Judy were persistently dragging me (and Tolliver, too) around the room from guest to guest, there was no way I could dodge the next person on the route.

"This is our son Joel's former sister-in-law, Felicia Hart," Judy said, and her voice had taken on a distinctly cool tone. "Fred's daughter."

"Joel's first wife, Whitney, was just a dear," Ben said, which was one way of saying Whitney's sister was not. There was definitely some bad blood there. I wondered what could have happened to make the older Morgensterns dislike Felicia so heartily.

I said, "We know Felicia," at the same moment Felicia said, "Of course, I saw Tolliver and Harper the other day at their hotel," and shook hands with us both with perfect aplomb. But her eyes weren't as neutral as her manner. I hadn't expected her to care about seeing me today, but I had expected her to have a strong reaction when she saw Tolliver. I'd expected that it would be a pleasurable reaction.

I'd have to classify it more as smoldering, or maybe volcanic.

Not "take me in your arms and let's jump

into the volcano of love," but more "let me push you into the molten lava."

I began a slow burn. What was up with her? Maybe she imagined Tolliver would refer to their past relationship in front of her father, or maybe, like David, she didn't think we belonged at a family gathering (though surely she didn't have that much claim on Joel's present family). If that was the case, shame on her. If Tolliver was good enough to be her bed partner, he was good enough to break bread with her nearest and dearest. But just as I was tensing up and looking for a moment to say something barbed, Tolliver squeezed my hand. I relaxed. He was sending me a clear message that Felicia was his problem.

After I'd chatted for a brief moment with Diane's friends Esther and Samantha, I tried to find a spot to hole up. Not only were the emotional crosscurrents a little draining, but my leg was hurting. It tingled and felt weak, as though it might decide to give way on a whim.

I found an empty chair right by that of another person who seemed to be feeling like an outsider: Victor, Joel's son by his first marriage. The boy — the young man — was hunched in a chair in a corner, defiantly apart from the rest, and he eyed me with apprehension as I walked over and sank down in the soft chair beside his. Victor gave me a brief look of acknowledgement, then fixed his gaze on his hands.

I was sure that Victor, like me, was remembering our encounter in another living room, in Nashville, and how he'd lost all his restraint and wept on my shoulder. It had made me feel good, actually, to be trusted like that.

For all I knew, Victor was recalling his breakdown with profound regret.

What I *could* be sure of was that Victor thought this gathering sucked. He was trying to get as far away from the grown-ups as he could. He'd had good manners ingrained in his character, and he'd gotten taller and more mature in the past few months — but he was still a teenager; a teenager who would far rather be out with his buds than hanging around with his family on this dismal occasion.

I didn't blame Victor for that, either.

So the room was full of people who didn't particularly want us there; some of them were pretending to be pleased, some of them weren't. Even our host and hostess were acting sheerly out of an imagined obligation.

I could see their point of view. I could even share it. Yet here we were, with no graceful way to get out of this uncomfortable situation. The only exit laid through a blatantly transparent excuse, such as a sudden illness, a phone call summoning us elsewhere, or something equally lame. I couldn't think of how to arrange such a thing without causing even more unhappiness.

In silence, Victor and I watched Samantha carry a glass of iced tea to Joel, watched him accept it with a pleasant nod, watched the woman's eyes as she stood by him hoping for another crumb of his attention.

Victor looked at me and snorted. "My dad, the babe magnet," he said derisively, including me in his age bracket so it would be okay to talk to me. Victor didn't sound envious, which I thought would be the case with most teenage boys. He sounded like the babes were the objects of his scorn, right along with his father. Now that he'd overcome his reluctance to speak, he seemed to feel we'd renewed our bond. He leaned closer. Victor said, "You're not Jewish, are you?"

"No," I said. That was easy.

"Victor, honey!" Judy Morgenstern called. "Go out to the Buick and get my cane, please." The boy looked at me intently. I wondered if there was something specific he wanted to say to me. He gave me a dark glance as he heaved himself up out of his chair and strode off to fetch the cane. I thought I might have a little recovery time, but no. To my surprise, Felicia took his place. I have to admit, I was curious. Not only did I wonder what she wanted to talk about, after her chilly greeting earlier, but also I wanted to discover why Tolliver had ever been attracted to this woman.

At the moment, my brother was talking to David, and he shot me a questioning glance, a little on the concerned side, when Felicia seated herself beside me. But he was too far away to hear our conversation, so I could say what I liked.

"You live here in Memphis, also?" I asked politely. I rubbed my right leg, which was aching, then forced my hand to be still.

"Yes, I have a condo in midtown," she said. "Of course, you have to have security there. My dad had a cow when I bought in the Towers. 'It's midtown, you're going to get attacked and mugged!' " She smiled at me in a conspiratorial way, as if the concern of one's parent was a silly thing. "The parking garage is completely enclosed; you can only get in if you have a sticker. And there's no pedestrian walk-in; entrance only through the building. There's a guard at the car exit, twenty-four/seven. It's expensive, but I couldn't live with my father anymore. Way past the age to move away." Her dad had a fresh drink in his hands; I'd watched him disappear into the kitchen and return with it. He resumed staring out the window. Felicia followed my gaze and flushed.

"You're very security conscious," I said, to deflect the moment.

"You have to be, when you're by yourself," she said. "Joel is always trying to get me to move out to east Memphis somewhere." She shook her head with a smile, inviting me to share her amusement with Joel's concern. The implication was that she and Joel were close; I got that. "And my dad would like me to move back with him. He lives in this huge house, all alone." Again, message received; her background was stuffed with money. "But as this family's situation proves, you can be in much more danger in the suburbs than you have to be in midtown, if you take precautions."

"Of course, they were in Nashville then," I said.

"Same difference. Everyone feels too safe in the suburbs. They take security for granted."

Diane, Samantha, and Esther left the room, and I figured they were heading to the kitchen for food preparation. I wondered if I should volunteer, but I decided they'd be much more comfortable with each other if I wasn't there. I turned back to Felicia.

"I'm sure they don't take security for granted anymore," I said, very quietly, and a shadow crossed Felicia's narrow, elegant face.

"No, not anymore. I'm afraid they'll always be looking over their shoulders, with this baby that's coming. Victor is old enough to take care of himself, at least to some extent. Vic is a typical teenager." She shook her head, smiling. Typical teenagers, evidently, were stupid. "They think they're immortal."

"Victor, of all teenagers, should know that's not true."

Felicia looked abashed. But she plowed ahead with the conversation. "It's strange; Victor's physically healthy as a horse, like I am. His mom — my sister, Whitney — she was the sickly one in our family. Whitney had all these allergies when we were kids. My parents would have to sit up with her all night, she'd be wheezing and coughing." Felicia's face looked grim. I wondered what kind of nurturing Felicia had gotten while

Whitney's heath crises were front and center in the Hart household. "She got pneumonia when we were in junior high, and mono, and tonsillitis, and when she was in college she had a ruptured appendix, after she'd started dating Joel. I've never been in a hospital." She looked over at her former brother-in-law. "You should have seen the care Joel took of her. He'd hardly let anyone else in the room during the final stages of her last illness. He wanted her all to himself. Second in hovering was my dad." She looked across the room at Fred Hart, who'd suddenly decided to talk to Joel. I didn't know what the conversation covered, but Joel was looking politely bored.

"I guess Victor was too young to visit the hospital much."

"Yeah, we didn't want him to remember Whitney like she looked toward the end. I stayed at their house and took care of Victor. He was so little, so cute."

"He's a handsome young man," I said politely.

"I still keep an eye on him for my sister's sake. It's been great, having them here in Memphis. Victor stays with me sometimes if things get too tense at home."

She was dying for me to ask her why things would be tense at home. Surely, the abduction and disappearance of a little girl was reason enough? "He's lucky to have such a conscientious aunt," I said, selecting the least weighted of responses.

"I saw your brother a couple of times," Felicia said suddenly, as though tossing a pebble into a pool to see what happened.

"That's what he told me," I told her in a completely neutral voice.

She seemed stymied when I didn't continue. After a pause, Felicia said, "I think he took it a bit hard when the distances between us made me think we'd be better off apart."

I had no response to that, but I was angry, you can bet on it. This was totally not the story Tolliver had told me. So, of course, she was lying.

"It must be difficult to find someone to date, when you're at that in-between age," I said.

Her eyes narrowed.

"I mean," I continued, "men are either married, or they're on their first divorce, and they may have kids and all kinds of entanglements."

"I haven't found that a problem," she said through clenched teeth. "But I suppose since you travel all the time, it's very hard to meet *eligible* men."

Oh, ouch — not. If she thought it would bother me to be reminded that I was always in Tolliver's company, she was wrong. Besides, why should I cross swords with this woman? Tolliver was an adult, and he could handle her mixed signals, all on his own.

"Do you know Clyde Nunley?" I said, looking anywhere but at her face.

"Well, we went to Bingham together," she said, which gave me a jolt. I'd been so sure she'd say she'd never met him. "He's a couple of years older, but we know each other. Clyde and David are actually fraternity brothers."

She nodded at David. He looked questioning, and when she smiled at him, he came over, though a bit reluctantly. David Morgenstern would not want to be president of my fan club. But he shook my hand civilly, and when Felicia said, "Harper was asking about Clyde Nunley."

David rolled his eyes. "What an asshole," he said. "He was a wild guy in college, lots of fun, but he decided he was the establishment as soon as he became a professor. Smarter than mere mortals, cooler than dry ice. I don't see him socially, but I do catch a glimpse of him at alumni meetings."

Not any more.

"Look, Diane wants us to come into the

229

dining room," Felicia said, and I rose to follow the others. David excused himself and went down the hall to a door I assumed was a bathroom's. Tolliver was having a serious talk with the older Morgensterns, but from the few words I caught, he was talking about the Memphis city government. I thought they looked a little relieved, maybe glad not to have to be talking about Tabitha, just for a few minutes. I trailed in the direction Felicia indicated. We were both glad to have an end to our tête-à-tête, I think. I didn't know what Felicia had thought she needed to convey to me, but I'd missed it. "Why'd you ask about Clyde?" Felicia asked suddenly.

"He came to our hotel last night, kind of irate," I said, after a moment.

She looked astonished. "What on earth about?"

"I don't know," I said, not wanting to talk about it any longer.

Diane had simply made a buffet out of all the food the neighbors had brought over. She and her two Nashville friends had arranged the dishes on a long counter in the spotless kitchen. There was an eat-in area at one end of the room, and the gray winter sky loomed through the large windows around that table in an unpleasant way.

There was also a breakfast bar with high stools forming a right angle to one end of the counter, and I'd passed through a formal dining room. This house was focused on eating.

Some of the dishes were hot, some were cold, and there were a lot of casseroles. Some of the flowers and plants the family had received were arranged in with the food and on the two dining tables, formal and informal. This attractive presentation was a talent of Diane's I hadn't expected. I wondered if her friends had done it all, and then chided myself for not giving her enough credit. I'd never seen the un-stressed side of the woman.

While the guests were milling around, I eyed the room. The kitchen was simply beautiful, like something that could be photographed for a magazine. White cabinets, dark marble counters, a center island. Beautiful china stacked at the beginning of the spread, and shining silver. The sinks and appliances gleamed with stainless steel — not a fingerprint in sight. If the Morgensterns had a maid, she was invisible. Maybe Diane was the kind of woman who cleaned when she got upset.

At Diane's urging, Joel's parents went through the line first, with Diane herself holding Mrs. Morgenstern's plate while the older woman selected what she wanted to eat. Diane got them settled at the table in the formal dining room and told the rest of us to please go ahead. I lined up behind Felicia and David.

As I waited, I watched Fred Hart shake his head when Diane urged him to get in line. Felicia observed the encounter with a curiously blank face, as if she had no emotion left for her father. After a long moment, she went over to him and said something to him in a low voice. He flinched away from her and left the room. As I picked up a plate and silverware, I wondered if I should go out searching for a happy family. Maybe it was my line of work that threw me in the path of so many unhappy ones.

Esther attracted my attention with a little wave of her hand. It was my turn to begin serving myself, and I'd been standing immobile, holding up the line. I gave myself a mental shake.

Some generous soul had brought a thinly sliced roast, but I passed it by, and instead got some broccoli, a fruit casserole baked in some kind of curry sauce, a roll, and a cold three-bean salad. There was the dining table in the dining room, a set of barstools at the kitchen counter, an informal family table, or we could go back in the living room, Diane told us. I got my utensils (rolled up in a bright napkin) and sat at the kitchen counter, since I was spry enough to climb up onto the high stool. When I'd been settled there approximately ten seconds, Esther put a glass of tea by my plate, her bright toothy smile as ferocious as a shark's. "Unsweetened," she said. "Okay?" Her voice hinted that it better be.

"Good, thanks," I said, and she swam away.

To my surprise, Victor sat beside me. I assumed he'd gotten his grandmother's cane and delivered it. His plate was invisible beneath a truly amazing array of food, very little of it involving vegetables, I noted. He had a can of Coke that he popped open with a defiant hiss.

"So, what you do, it's just weird, right?" was his opening conversational gambit.

"Yes, it is."

Maybe he'd meant to offend me. If so, my matter-of-fact reply took him off base. I was actually glad to get a dose of sincerity.

"So, you travel all the time?"

"Yeah."

"Cool."

"Sometimes. Sometimes I wish I had a nice house like this."

He glanced around him contemptuously. He could dismiss the value of a beautiful and cared-for home, since he'd never lacked it. "Yeah, it's okay. But no house is good when you're not happy."

An interesting and true observation — though in my experience, comfort never hurt whether you were depressed or whether you were cheerful.

"And you're not happy."

"Not much."

This was a pretty intense conversation to be having with someone I didn't know at all.

"Because of Tabitha's death?" Since we were being blunt.

"Yeah, and because no one here is happy."

"Now that she's been found and she can be buried, don't you think things will get better?"

He shook his head doubtfully. He was eating all the while we were having this incredibly doleful conversation. At least he shut his mouth when he chewed. Suddenly I realized I was closer in age to this boy than anyone else in the house, and I knew that was why he'd sought me out.

"Maybe," he said grudgingly. "But then we gotta get ready for the baby to come, and it'll cry all night. Tabitha did," he added, almost inaudibly.

"You really were fond of her," I said.

"Yeah, she was okay. She bugged me. But she was okay."

"The police gave you a hard time when she was taken."

"Oh, yeah. It was intense. They questioned me, Dad had to get me a lawyer." He was a little proud of that. "They couldn't get that I wouldn't have anywhere to put her. Why would I take her? Where would I take her? We fought, but even real brothers and sisters fight. You fight with your brother, right?"

"We grew up in the same house," I said, "but he's not really my brother. My mom married his dad." I was surprised at my own words. Sentences just kept coming out of my mouth.

"That would be freaking weird, living in the house with someone your own age you weren't even related to. Especially if you're not the same, you know, sex."

"It took some getting used to," I admitted. It hadn't taken long before Cameron and I and Mike and Tolliver had bonded against the common enemy. I took a deep breath. "Our parents used drugs," I said. "They used a lot of cocaine. Weed. Vicodin. Hydros. Whatever they could buy. They used alcohol to fill in the cracks. Did your parents ever have a problem like that?"

His mouth literally dropped open. Not as sophisticated as he'd thought himself, Victor. "Geez," he said. "That's awful. Kids use drugs, not parents."

If that wasn't the most naïve thing I'd ever heard, it was pretty damn close. But it was kind of nice, too, that he still had illusions like that. I waited for a direct answer.

"No," he said, having gathered himself. "My folks would never. Never. Use drugs. I mean, they hardly even drink."

"That's good," I said. "I wish all parents were like that."

"Yeah, Dad and Mom are okay," he said, trying to sound tough and careless. But he'd been shaken. "I mean, you can't tell them stuff. They don't know anything. But they're there when you need them."

He even called Diane "Mom," and that reminded me how young Victor had been when Diane had married Joel.

"You've been around a lot," Victor said, running a hand through his auburn hair. "You've had a real life."

"I've had more than my share of real life," I said.

"But you would know . . ." His voice trailed off, just when the dialogue was turning in an interesting direction.

I didn't try to prod Victor to pick up the conversational thread. I'd covered all the bases I could with this kid, without getting into the realm of questions too strange to ask him. I hadn't initiated this conversation, but I'd learned a lot from it. I knew, as I watched Victor check out the dishes left on the kitchen counter that he hadn't yet sampled, that this boy had a secret. It might be a big secret, it might be a small one, but I needed to know it, too. I thought maybe he would come to me with it; though teenagers could spin on an emotional dime.

The kitchen had one of those little televisions mounted below the cabinet, presumably so the cook could watch *Ellen* or *Oprah* while she did her job. Though Diane had boasted that televisions were off and phones were off the hook, someone had turned this one on, maybe to catch the weather or some sports scores.

Though the sound was turned down in deference to the occasion, something caught Victor's attention, and he stood squarely in front of it, plate still in hand. The expression on his face grew startled, puzzled, alarmed, all at once.

It wasn't hard to figure out what he was seeing.

Well, we'd known the news would reach the Morgensterns sooner or later, and the moment was now.

"Dad!" said Victor, in a voice that brought his father to his side at a good pace. "Dad! They found that college guy dead, in Tabitha's grave!"

I sighed, and looked down at my plate. I hadn't thought of it quite that way. After all, it had been Josiah Poundstone's for much longer. It was a much-used grave.

Quite a hubbub ensued, with the big television in the family room getting switched on, and everyone gathering in front, plates still in hand or discarded where the eater had been perching. I consulted Tolliver silently. He looked at the food regretfully, so I guess he hadn't filled up while he could. He nodded. We needed to be gone.

So as not to be hopelessly rude, we quietly thanked Diane, who hardly knew we were speaking to her. That done, we let ourselves out of the house. I wondered if they even realized we'd slipped out.

"If we go back to the hotel, someone'll want to come talk to us," Tolliver predicted gloomily.

"Let's go to the river."

I don't know why moving water is soothing, but it is, even on a cold day in November in Tennessee. We went to a riverfront park, and even though I was wearing my high-heeled boots, we enjoyed strolling through the nearly empty area. The Mississippi flowed silently past the Memphis bluffs, as it would do long after the city crumbled, I supposed — if the world didn't get destroyed altogether. Tolliver put his arm around me because it was so chilly, and we didn't talk.

It was good to be silent. It was good to be away from the crowd at the Morgenstern house, and alone with Tolliver. I discounted the two middle-aged homeless guys that passed a bottle back and forth when they didn't think we were looking. They were as happy avoiding us as we were avoiding them.

"That was a strange interlude," Tolliver said, his voice careful and precise.

"Yes. Pretty house. I loved the kitchen," I said.

"I had a talk with Fred. He's got an outstanding lease on the Lexus." Tolliver is jonesing for a new car. Ours is only three years old, but it does have a lot of miles on it. "Saw you talking to Felicia," he continued.

"Felicia brought up the fact she'd seen

you socially," I said, which was the nicest way I could put it. "She seemed to think you all had had a conversation about not seeing each other."

"Interesting, since she keeps calling me," he said, after a moment. "I can't figure her out. No house in the burbs for us."

Though his voice was light and ironical, I realized he'd been at least taken aback. A woman he'd been to bed with, a woman who'd actively pursued him, had shown no desire to speak to him when she was with her family. Yeah, that would make anyone feel pretty bad, whether or not the relationship was desirable. My ill feeling against Felicia Hart began to congeal into something quite solid. I changed the subject.

"Victor has a secret," I said.

"Maybe he's got jerk-off magazines under his bed. Babes with big boobs."

"I don't think that's his secret. At least, not the secret that interests me."

We walked a moment in silence.

"I think he knows something about one of his family members, something he's trying *not* to connect to the murders."

"Okay, confused."

"He's a pretty innocent kid, all things considered," I said. I was trying hard not to sound overly patient. "And he's had some

240

big blows in his life."

"Working hard not to draw parallels, here."

"Me, too. But the point is, I think Victor can connect some member of that family to . . ."

"What, exactly? His half sister's death? Clyde Nunley?"

"Okay, I don't know. Not exactly. I'm just saying, he knows something, and that's not healthy for him."

"So what can we do about it? They won't let him hang around with us. They won't believe us. And if he's not talking . . . besides, what if the subject of the secret is one of his parents?"

Another silence, this one a little huffy.

"Speaking of Joel," Tolliver said, "how come you're not panting like all the other women?"

"All the other women are panting?"

"Didn't you notice that the woman detective practically drooled whenever she said his name?"

"No," I said, quite surprised.

"Didn't you see the doe eyes his wife makes at him?"

"Ah . . . no."

"Even Felicia sits up and takes notice when he speaks. And his own mom looks at him about twice as much as she looks at her other son, David."

"So, I gather you've been watching Joel pretty closely," I said cautiously. Understatement.

"Not so much Joel himself, as the way people react to him. Except you."

"I see that he's a man that women like to be around," I said, by way of acknowledgment. "But he doesn't really do anything for me. The snapdragons, I knew those were his idea, and I did tell you then that he was the kind of man who noticed women, who knew how to please them. But I don't think he's really interested in anyone but Diane. I don't think he really understands his own magnetism, to tell you the truth. Or maybe he just accepts it as part of his world, like if he had green eyes or a great singing voice, or something."

"So, he's got charisma for women that he doesn't use," Tolliver said.

"More or less."

"And you're saying it doesn't affect you, like it does other women." Mr. Skeptical.

"I'm saying . . . yes, that's what I'm saying."

"If he weren't married to Diane, if he asked you out, you wouldn't jump at the chance?"

I gave that more thought than it deserved.
"I don't think so."

"You're impervious?"

"It's not that. It's that I don't trust men who don't have to work for what they get."

Tolliver stopped, and turned me to him with a hand on my arm. "That's ridiculous," he said. "You mean a man should have to work for the love of a woman?"

"Maybe," I said. "Maybe I'm saying that Joel has probably come to accept this automatic king position as the norm, as his due. Without working for it."

"You don't think he's a virtuous man?"

"I think he is. I don't think he's a crook, or a secret addict, or a cheater."

"So, your sole objection is that he doesn't have to work for love?"

"I'm saying, there's something wrong about getting so much invested in you without setting out to earn it."

Tolliver shrugged. "I'm still not sure I understand," he said.

I couldn't explain it any better. I'm not real good at explaining things, especially emotional things. But I knew what I meant. And I didn't entirely trust Joel Morgenstern.

Eleven

When we got back to the hotel, Rick Goldman was waiting for us, sitting in the same chair in the lobby he'd used before.

"I should've figured he'd show up, considering the scene last night," I told Tolliver. "I wonder if he's told the cops yet."

I introduced Rick to Tolliver as politely as if Rick had come to ask us to tea. But there was a muscle jumping in the private detective's jaw, and his whole body was tense.

"Can we have this talk somewhere a little more private?" he growled at me.

Tolliver said, "That would be best, I think. Come with us."

The ride up in the elevator was silent and ominous.

The maids had been in, and the room looked clean and welcoming, I was glad to see. There's something kind of seedy in having guests in your hotel room when the evidence of your stay is strewn all around you in disorderly heaps; room service cart, crumpled newspapers, discarded books, a shoe here and there. I'd been enjoying having a sitting room at this hotel, though I never forgot I was paying for it through the nose.

"You didn't have to kill Nunley," Rick Goldman said. "I know he was an obnoxious drunk, but he didn't hurt you." He switched his level gaze to Tolliver. "Or were you so angry he manhandled your sister that you tracked him down after I left?"

"I might just as well suspect you," I retorted, not a little pissed off. "You're the one laid hands on him. You can leave right now if you're going to sit there and accuse us of stuff without having the slightest bit of evidence that we ever saw the man again."

I took my jacket off and walked over to the door of my room, tossing it inside. Tolliver unbuttoned his more slowly. "I take it you've been to the police already with your little story about what happened in the lobby," he said.

"Of course," said Rick. "Clyde Nunley was an asshole, but he was a professor at Bingham. He had a family. He deserves to have his murder solved."

"I saw he was married, on the news," I said. "Though, come to think of it, he didn't wear a wedding ring."

"Lots of men don't," Rick said.

"Not in my experience," I said, surprised.

"He had a metal allergy," Rick said.

"You knew him a little better than I thought."

"I read his personnel file," the private detective admitted.

"I'm betting the weird content of Clyde Nunley's classes wasn't the only reason he was being investigated," Tolliver said. "I'm betting he had some affairs, maybe with a student or two? And the college decided they'd better check him out. Am I right?"

"There was a certain amount of talk on campus."

"His wife wasn't so amazed when he didn't come home at night," I said. "She didn't even call the police until the next morning." I sat on the couch and crossed my legs, lacing my fingers together in my lap. Tolliver was still hovering around the room, too restless to perch. Our guest had thrown himself down into one of the wing chairs without waiting for us to ask him to be seated.

"Rick, do you still have a lot of friends on the force?" Tolliver asked.

"Sure."

"So you won't mind when they ask the

staff what they saw last night?"

"Of course not."

"Even when they tell your former colleagues that they watched you throw a guy out of the lobby, while my sister was absolutely passive?"

I made my eyes look all big and tearful. I look frail anyway, no matter how tough I actually can be.

"I wonder who they'll remember being violent and forceful, you or Harper?"

"Damn. And I was helping her out." Rick Goldman looked at us as if he could not believe people like us were walking the earth unjudged. "You people!"

"I did appreciate your helping me, right up until the time you insulted me," I said. "But Clyde Nunley was a pest, not a danger. Now he's dead, and I had nothing to do with it. We were just over at the Morgensterns', and they heard the news while we were there. Pretty upsetting."

"They asked you to their house?" This, again, got a big reaction.

I said, "Some people don't treat us as if we were frauds and murderers."

He threw up his hands, as if I'd stepped over a dearly held boundary. "I give up," he said.

A little drama on the part of the old Rick-ster.

"You two are no better than scam artists," he said. "It makes me crazy that I can't figure out how you do it. You were right on the money about those deaths, right on the money. How'd you get the documents ahead of time? I really want to know how you did it!"

There's no convincing someone who's not open to reason, or to anything else, for that matter.

"You're not going to believe I'm the real thing, anytime soon," I said. "There's no point in talking to you. Besides, the police will be coming, and I want to shower before they get here." That wasn't true. I'd already showered. I just wanted Rick Goldman to leave, right away.

TWELVE

Manfred Bernardo called us from the lobby about three o'clock, asking if he could come up. I smiled when I imagined what the staff was making of Manfred, with his metallic face.

"I wonder what happens when he goes through airport security detectors?" I said to Tolliver. He'd been reading a Robert Crais mystery, one of the earlier ones featuring Elvis Cole, and he'd been smiling to himself from time to time.

"I don't think that's a problem Manfred confronts often," Tolliver said, but not as if he cared one way or another.

Manfred enjoyed touching people. When I answered the door, I observed that he was perhaps only an inch or two taller than I, but even as I was registering that, he leaned over to give me a kiss on the cheek.

I didn't give him one in return, because casual kissing's not my way. But I think I was smiling as I showed him into the room.

"Hello, Tolliver," he said, as Tolliver rose to shake his hand. Tolliver just goggled at Manfred for a second. Manfred was wearing all black again; this time he was encased in leather pants, a sheer black T-shirt, and a leather jacket. He was wearing heavy boots and a small fortune in silver on his hands, face, and neck. His platinum hair had been touched up, and his goatee matched. I wondered if all this was for my benefit, or if Manfred just loved looking remarkable for its own sake.

"Please, have a seat. I hope your grandmother's well?" I asked. I sat on the love seat, expecting Manfred to take the wing chair next to Tolliver's, but he sat down beside me.

"She's not doing real good," Manfred said. His smile faded, and I could see he was worried. "She's having bad dreams about people in graves they weren't supposed to be in."

"Have you been watching the news? I don't know how close you live to Memphis, but you get the Memphis news in the evening?"

"We don't watch television," Manfred said simply. "Grandma thinks it interferes with her brain waves. If I want to catch a program, I go over to a friend's."

"Then let us show you what an FBI agent brought us today," Tolliver suggested, and after he turned on the television, he ran the tape.

Manfred watched silently. He had taken hold of my hand, which was odd, but it didn't seem sexual. It seemed as if he was trying to connect with some emanation I was giving off. The Bernardo family must have some very interesting family reunions if they were all as sensitive as Xylda and Manfred.

"No, we're the only ones," Manfred said absently, still focused on the television. His many silver rings were just now warming to room temperature after his walk into the hotel.

My eyes widened for a moment, and Tolliver glanced at me as if to ask me what was wrong, but I shook my head. He looked at Manfred's hand on mine, and raised his eyebrows to ask if I was uncomfortable. I shook my head, letting him know it wasn't a problem.

After the tape had run, Manfred said, "The man in the grave was the man who asked you to come here to do the reading?"

"Yes," I said.

"So there was an old burial first, when the

church was still open, am I right?"

I nodded. Manfred's eyes were very blue, and though they were focused on me, they weren't seeing me.

"And then the little girl was in there?"

"Right."

"Then you found the man last night, when you were in the cemetery?"

I jumped, but Manfred's hand kept mine prisoner, gently but firmly.

"Yes," said Tolliver slowly. "We found him last night."

"My grandmother was doing a reading for you, at the time you found him, and she knows you saw the visitor," Manfred said. I had the uncomfortable feeling his eyes were looking right through me.

"Visitor?" I asked.

"That's what she calls ghosts," Manfred said, and suddenly he was just a very young man again, holding hands with a woman he thought was cute, and giving her a big grin. The stud in his tongue winked at me. "Grandma uses a lot of her own terminology."

This was a most interesting boy. He seemed not to have had much experience of the world, and yet he knew some unexpected things. I had the feeling Manfred would not be overawed or even impressed

252

by riches or sophistication.

"Not a boy," he said, smiling, looking directly into my eyes. The sexual tone was back with a roar. "I'm definitely a man."

I didn't know if I was a bit excited, or if I wanted to run screaming into my room. I smiled at him.

"Grandma wanted me to tell you you'll see Tabitha's first grave," he said. "I didn't understand when she gave me the message. Her hip is acting up too bad for her to leave home today, so she asked me to come see you. She likes you a lot, you know. She wanted to warn you. Watch out for that grave."

As he had in the coffee shop, he bent and kissed my hand, making sure I got the gamut of sensations for the second time. He looked up at me from his bent posture. "Makes you think, doesn't it?" he said softly.

"Thinking isn't doing," I said practically.

"Not yet," he said. He stood, shook Tolliver's hand, and left as suddenly as he'd arrived.

"What was all that about?" Tolliver said, looking distinctly suspicious.

"Evidently, when he's touching you, he can read your mind, sort of," I said, feeling a little uncomfortable that some of my thoughts had been fairly graphic. "I don't

253

know if that applies to the populace in general, or to people who have some kind of psychic talent, or what."

"But Xylda is the only one who makes predictions," Tolliver said. "And she's added to them today. You'll be happy in the time of ice, whatever that means, and you'll see Tabitha's original grave."

"I don't think I want to hang around Xylda anymore," I said. "And if she reads the cards for me, I don't want to know about it. It just creeps me out."

"What about Manfred? You want to hang around him?" At least Tolliver was smiling when he said it.

"Oh," I said deprecatingly. "You know, he's more than a little different. I mean, you can't help but wonder, when you see someone so extreme . . ." Then I couldn't figure out how to finish the sentence.

Tolliver had mercy on me. "If I knew a girl with that many piercings, I'd wonder, too," he said.

"Well, it's already mid-afternoon, and we've had a helluva day. What could we do next that would make it just one round of fun?"

"I could balance the checkbook."

"Big whoop."

"We could see what the in-room movie

service has to show."

"I'm sick of this room, and I'm ready to do something a little more active than watch a movie."

"You got an idea?"

"Yeah. Let's go down to the riverfront park to run."

"What about the reporter?"

"We'll sneak out the back."

"It's cold and it looks like rain."

"Then we better run fast."

THIRTEEN

We avoided the reporters, but not the Memphis police. Detectives Young and Lacey were less than thrilled at our choice of activity when they tracked us down. I'd been wondering when we'd be hearing from them. I was only surprised they hadn't called the hotel and told us to get our asses down to the station.

They had on their London Fogs, their gloves, and their scarves. Lacey looked morose but resigned. Young looked resentful. Come to find out when we jogged over to them, Young had a cold. In the middle of her narrow face, her reddened nose stood out like a reindeer's, and she had a tissue clutched in the hand not occupied with an umbrella.

"Are you nuts?" she snarled. "Out here in your skintight whatevers, when it's freezing!" She made a vague gesture toward my running pants. I ran in place for a minute, slowing down gradually. I felt cold and wet, but I also felt exhilarated, as if the chilly damp air had blown away some of the cobwebs in my head.

"I guess you want to talk to us about something?" Tolliver was doing some stretching, and I saw that Detective Young's eyes had strayed to his ass. Lacey said quickly, "Yes, ma'am, we sure do. Do you two want to come down to the station with us? At least it's dry and warm."

"I definitely don't want to go to the station," I said. "Isn't there a coffee shop somewhere close? Unless you're going to arrest us, going to a cafe would be a lot nicer. Maybe they'd have hot chocolate?" I was deliberately tempting poor Young, who sneezed twice in succession and applied her damp wad of tissues to her raw nose.

"There's that place on Poplar," she said to her partner, who looked indecisive. "Remember how good their pie is?" she said, in a heavy-handed attempt at a bribe.

It worked like a charm.

Thirty minutes later we were in a restaurant so warm that the windows were steamy, with coffee in front of the men, hot chocolate in front of Detective Young and me. Lacey was happy as a pig in a wallow with a piece of pecan pie with whipped topping on a plate in front of him, and Young was almost weeping with relief at being indoors.

"Agent Koenig tells us you've heard the news about Clyde Nunley," she said, her voice sounding nasal but at least human.

We nodded. "He came by our room this morning and told us," I said, wanting to be as honest as possible. I always try.

"Rick Goldman came by the station, too," Young said, after he swallowed. He looked blissful. "Rick was telling us that he had a run-in with Nunley in the lobby of your hotel, Ms. Connelly."

"Yes, that's true. He ended up propelling Dr. Nunley out the door. Truthfully, I think Dr. Nunley was drunk. He was very belligerent." I hoped I looked as frank and open as I was trying to be.

"You're not the only person who's commented on that. We'll find out what his blood alcohol level was. What beef did he have with you?" Young asked. Maybe her cold medication was making her blunt, or maybe she was just tired of do-si-doing around.

"He thought that somehow, despite all his precautions, I'd gotten into his precious private records and memorized the COD on all the burials. Goldman accused me of the same thing."

"And did you do that?"

"No, I don't need to. I'm the real deal."

There was a moment of silence, while the detectives either thought that over, or dismissed it as another piece of chicanery on my part.

"Did you two go out again last night?" asked Young directly. "After Mr. Lang here came back from wandering Beale Street?" Detective Lacey put down his fork and gave us a look that might have penetrated steel.

"Yes, we did," Tolliver said. After all, we'd gotten the car from the valet. There was no way we could deny it.

"Where did you go?"

"We drove down to look at Graceland," Tolliver said. I blinked. What a good lie. Almost any tourist in Memphis would want to at least drive by Elvis's home. And since we'd just told Koenig we'd been looking at the sights of Memphis, this tied right in. Actually, we'd looked up Graceland on the laptop this morning after Koenig had left, so we'd at least have an idea what we were supposed to have seen.

"At night?"

"Yeah, we didn't have anything else to do. And we weren't sure if we'd ever be back this way again. So we drove down to White-haven, and we took a couple of passes in front of it. That's some place. You gotta love the gates."

"And you're not going to go back and see it in the daylight, tour the house?"

"He's buried on-site, right?" I asked.

"Uh . . . yeah. And Vernon and Gladys, his mom and dad, and Minnie May, his grandma."

"No." I shook my head definitely. "I really, really, wouldn't want to do that."

Detective Young sucked at her teeth. She looked as though she were feeling a bit better, now that she was warm and had finished her hot chocolate. Her short brown hair still looked lank and tired, but her eyes were showing a spark of spirit. Her partner had that happy look that sugar-loving men get after they've had something especially rich. But the pie hadn't made him smarter.

"Why not?" he asked now. "Why not go see the place they're buried?"

"You know, I connect with bodies. It might kind of ruin the Graceland experience for me." On the other hand, it might answer a few questions. Tolliver was looking amused.

"So you see why we just drove by," Tolliver said, picking up the thread of the narrative. "We'd already cruised around the Pyramid and Beale Street. So, we went back to our hotel."

I was glad I'd washed my shoes off this morning, and that the hotel laundry had our jeans.

"And the Fibbie came to see you first thing this morning," Detective Young said. I was glad we'd mentioned it, since it seemed Young already knew about Koenig's visit.

"Yes. He wanted us to know right away about the body found in the grave. I'm guessing he wanted to get our first reaction."

"And what reaction did he get?"

"Well, of course, we were sorry Clyde Nunley had been killed, or had fallen into the grave and hit his head, or whatever really happened to him. It's never good to hear someone's dead." Though with some people it's less bad than with others. "But it's not like we had any reason to want him dead."

"You might have been a little upset, Mr. Lang, him manhandling Ms. Connelly like that. Specially in a public place. Specially since someone else had to help her, since you weren't there."

Oooh. Low blow. But I thought Tolliver could stand up to it, and he seemed to be coping, if his slight smile was any indicator. "Harper can take care of herself," he said,

261

which pleased me. "Even if Goldman hadn't been there, she would have been okay."

Since that hadn't worked, Lacey tried something else. "Agent Koenig says he wants your reading of Nunley's body, and that you would like access to Tabitha's body."

"That's not exactly what I said," I told him. "It wasn't my idea. He thought I might get more of a reading if I tried again, and I agreed that might be so. Of course I don't want to be around the child's body again — but if you have any idea I'd be a help, I have to make myself do that."

"I have no idea what to believe about you," Lacey said, his small blue eyes examining me again for maybe the twenty-fifth time. "I never met anyone like you, and I swear I don't know if you're a fraud or a — I just don't know what you are."

"Lots of people feel that way," I said, because he seemed so uncomfortable. "Don't worry about it. I'm used to it."

"You two have kids?" Detective Young asked suddenly.

Tolliver and I stared at her blankly.

"Us?" he said, after a long pause.

She seemed to realize she'd put her foot in it. "Sorry, I just assumed you two . . ."

"We've lived together since we were teen-

262

agers," I said. "Tolliver's dad married my mother. He's like my . . . brother." For the first time, I hesitated before I said those words.

"I have two," she said, obviously wanting to get off the subject as quickly as possible. "I have a boy and a girl. If my child went missing, I'd want every stone turned to find that child. I'd deal with the devil if I had to. I'll ask the Morgensterns how they feel about you . . . visiting Tabitha's body again. We'll see what they say."

I wondered what the two cops would say if I told them I'd talked to a ghost the night before. I wondered how fast they'd write us off as charlatans. I thought again of the hard hand gripping my arm, and I had to close my eyes for a minute. How could it be that Josiah Poundstone's ghost was there? I had thought I had the whole thing straight in my mind, the whole life-after-death procedure, but now I stood on shaky ground.

I noticed the traffic outside was getting heavier, and the sky was getting darker. As we sat in the diner with the two detectives, the afternoon had drawn to a close. I had an almost irresistible urge to go back to the cemetery, to see if the ghost was still there, what it was up to. What did ghosts do? Were they there when a human wasn't there to react to them? Did they materialize when they wanted to communicate, or were they always . . .

"Harper," Tolliver said gently. "Are you ready to go?"

"Oh, sure," I said, hastily pulling my jacket back on. The detectives were standing, their coats zipped and buttoned, and from their expressions, they'd been waiting for me to respond for some time.

"Daydreaming," I said. "Sorry." I did my best to look alert and normal, but that's not always my best thing anyway, and I don't think I was very successful. "Maybe our run tired me more than I thought."

Given a valid-sounding reason for my distracted state, the two cops looked a bit happier, though Lacey would never be my best friend. "You need to go back to the hotel and get some rest," he said. "Don't go getting into any more trouble while you're here in Memphis. We'll get back with you after we've talked to the Morgensterns."

"Right, thanks," Tolliver said. After their car had left, we paid our part of the bill and left the diner. "What was that all about?" Tolliver asked when we were in the car and trying to make a left turn into traffic to go back to the Cleveland.

I told him the questions I'd been asking myself.

"I can see where that's interesting, and I would like to know the answers, too," he said. "But from now on, you should have your thinking sessions when you're safe in bed, or something. You had a pretty strange expression on your face."

"Did I look weird?" I asked, oddly hurt.

"Not strange-ugly," he said instantly. "Strange, as in, 'not there.' "

"Oh," I said.

Finally, he took advantage of a hole in the ever-swelling traffic going out of downtown. We were headed back toward the river before I spoke again. "You know who I'd like to talk to again?"

"Who?"

"Victor. But you talk about peculiar, it would seem real peculiar if we called him and asked him to come to see us."

"Yeah. No way we can do that."

"You think since they treated us to a meal, we could invite them to a meal at a restaurant?"

Tolliver thought it over. "They're in mourning right now, and they've probably got all kinds of arrangements to make. Plus, what reason would we give? Yeah, we could insist we owe them a meal, but what are we gonna talk about? The only connection we have is the death of their daughter. That's just not enough to carry an evening, Sis."

He hadn't called me that in a long time. I wondered if Young's comment had shaken him up, too.

"Maybe not," I admitted. "But as long as we're stuck here, and I guess we are . . . hey, I wonder what would happen if we left?" There was a moment of silence. "We'd probably get called right back," I concluded, "until they've decided what happened to Clyde Nunley. Why would he get killed? I just don't understand. The only thing he knew was — what could he have known?"

"What's the only connection between Clyde Nunley and Tabitha Morgenstern?" Tolliver asked. He was definitely guiding me to a conclusion. I hate it when he does that.

"They shared a grave."

"I mean, besides that."

"There was no connection."

"Yes, there was."

It was almost full dark now, and the mass of lights in the eastbound lanes was almost bumper-to-bumper. We had much easier going in the westbound lanes. It began to rain again, and Tolliver turned on our windshield wipers.

"Okay, I give." I threw up my hands in exasperation. "What was the connection?"

"You."

FOURTEEN

This hit me with an impact about equal to a bag of cement.

"So you're saying Clyde Nunley was murdered because he knew who had recommended me for this little gig at the college." I felt cold all over. I may be used to death, and I may know better than anyone how inevitable and ordinary a state it is, but that doesn't mean it's easy to feel you contributed to it. It's like sleet; you know if the atmospheric conditions warrant, there's going to be sleet, but you don't have to be happy about it.

"That's what I think — and I thought about this a lot, last night. I couldn't accept the giant coincidence that Tabitha's body was here. If it wasn't a coincidence, we were steered to find it. We were used. And the person who did that had to be the person who killed Tabitha. Clyde Nunley asked you to read this cemetery. So someone must have whispered your name in Clyde Nunley's ear. I don't know if that person held something over Clyde, or made a friendly suggestion. 'Hey, you're having this class about the occult, you have this cemetery just laying there, let's get a weird woman who specializes in finding the dead to come have a look.' "

"So, you think that Clyde balked when Tabitha's body was found?"

"I think he did. Or else he couldn't swallow the coincidence any more than we can, and he figured that whoever had talked him into inviting you to Memphis had to have some kind of inside knowledge about the girl's death. Just because he was a jerk doesn't mean he was dumb."

"True," I said absently. "Well, I guess that narrows down the field, right?"

"How do you figure that?"

"Couldn't be Victor."

"Why not? I'll bet he's pre-enrolled at Bingham. This is his senior year in high school, right?"

"Oh. Well, could be. That seems kind of thin, but okay. What I was thinking — both Felicia and David went to Bingham. And the older Morgensterns, Judy and Ben, would surely know a lot of people who went there, if they didn't themselves, since they live in the city and paid for David's tuition for four years. I bet the same holds true for Fred Hart."

After all, the older Morgensterns weren't so darn old. "Judy has Parkinson's too badly to have gotten Tabitha to the grave, but her husband is really fit," I said. "Fred Hart looks pretty strong, too."

"That would be awful, if it turned out be to the granddad," Tolliver said.

"It's going to be awful if it's *anybody*," I said. "No matter who. Anyone doing that to an eleven-year-old, that's beyond horrible." I paused to collect myself. "I was so shocked at finding her, I didn't take as long as I should have to . . . pick through the experience."

"So you do want to read the body again? If Seth Koenig gets it set up?"

"He wants me to read Clyde Nunley. Of course, he doesn't know that I already have. I don't want to touch Tabitha again. I don't even want to think about it. But I have to be sure I know everything she can tell me."

"You're a good person," he said, taking me by surprise.

"I don't think I'm especially good, and there are a lot of people who would argue the other way," I said, trying to conceal how pleased I was. I looked down at my watch and pressed the button to check the date. Something clicked inside my memory. "Oh, God, it's about time to call the girls."

Tolliver said something that would have made my ears turn red if I hadn't heard it a hundred times before. But he didn't protest tonight, though he often argued against this bi-weekly ordeal we put ourselves through.

We waited until we got to our room. I noted with satisfaction that there weren't any reporters outside at all, and no messages waiting. (The first day, there had been twenty or so, and we'd thrown them all away.)

To determine whose turn it would be to dial the number and talk to Iona, we did Rock, Scissors, Paper. As always, I made the wrong choice, which is pretty funny when you come to think of it. If I were actually psychic, as I'm so often accused of being, I think I could manage to win a simple game like that.

I speed-dialed Iona's number. Iona Gorham (née Howe) was my mother's only sister. She'd been married to Hank Gorham for twelve years, twelve long and childless and God-fearing years. She'd taken charge of Mariella and Gracie when my mother and stepfather went to jail, after the investigation into Cameron's abduction exposed some of their worst faults as parents. I'd had nothing to say about it, because I was underage then. I'd gone into a foster home myself. Iona and Hank hadn't wanted me, which was probably just as well, I guess. At seventeen, they thought my lifelong association with my mother would have irrevocably tainted me. I had a senior year in the high school I'd been attending, a year that was weirdly pleasant despite my shattered emotional system. For the first time since my childhood, I lived in a clean house with regular meals I didn't always have to cook myself. I could do my homework in peace. No one made suggestive comments, no one used drugs, and my foster parents were simple, nice, strict people. You knew where you were. They had two other foster kids, and we got along if we were very careful.

Tolliver, who was twenty then, moved in with his brother, Mark, so he was okay. He came by as often as he could, as often as the Goodmans would let him.

"Hello?" The man's voice yanked me back to the here and now.

"Hank, hello, it's Harper," I said, making sure that my voice was even and level and uninflected. You had to be Switzerland to talk to Iona and Hank. *Neutral,* I told myself repeatedly. *Neutral.*

"Hello," he said, with a total lack of welcome or enthusiasm. "Where are you, Harper?"

"I'm in Memphis, Hank, thanks for asking."

"I guess Tolliver's with you?"

"Oh, you bet," I said, cheerful as all get-out. "It's cold and wet here. How about in Dallas?"

"Oh, can't complain. In the fifties today."

"Sounds good. I'd like to talk to Mariella, if she's around, and then Gracie."

"Iona's gone to the store. I'll see if I can track the girls down."

What a stroke of luck. I held the phone to my chest while I told Tolliver, "The Wicked Witch isn't there." Iona had a deep fund of excuses to keep us from talking to the girls. Hank was not as resourceful, or as ruthless.

"Hey," said Mariella. She was nine now, and she was a lot of trouble. I never told myself she'd be an angel if she lived with us, because I knew better. For their first few years, Mariella and Gracie had never had the care and attention of parents who were in their right minds. I'm not saying my mother and stepfather didn't love their girls, but it wasn't the kind of love that would prompt them to become sober and responsible. At least we older kids had had that, once upon a time. We knew what was right and proper. We knew what parents should be like. We knew about fresh sheets and home-cooked meals and clothes that only we had worn.

"Mariella, it's your sister," I said, though of course Hank had told her who was on the phone. "What's happening with you?" I had tried so hard, and so had Cameron and Tolliver. Even Mark had stopped by with food from time to time, when he'd had extra money.

"I got on a basketball team," Mariella said, "at the Y."

"Oh, that's great!" Actually, it was. It was the first time Mariella had given me anything besides a sullen grunt. "Have you started playing yet, or are you still practicing?"

"We have our first game in a week," she said. "If you were here, you could come."

I widened my eyes at Tolliver to let him know this call was not going as usual. "We'd love to," I said. "We have to check our schedule, but we'd be really glad to watch you play. Is Gracie playing, too?"

"No, she says it's stupid to get out there and sweat like a pig. She says boys don't like girls who sweat. She says everyone will call me a lesbo."

I heard a shocked exclamation from Hank in the background.

"Gracie's wrong," I said immediately. "She just doesn't want to play basketball herself. Maybe you can play basketball a little better than Gracie, huh?"

"You bet," said Mariella proudly. "Gracie can't come within a mile of the hoop. I hit it twice last practice."

"I'm sure there's something Gracie can do that's special to her," I said, floundering to be diplomatic and yet reinforce the positive stuff that was going on with Mariella.

"Huh," said Mariella derisively. "Well, *anyway.*"

"Have you all had your school pictures taken this year?"

"Yeah. They should be back soon."

"You both save us two, you hear?" I said. "One for your brother Tolliver to carry in his wallet, and one for me to carry in mine."

"Okay," she said. "Hey, Gracie joined the chorus."

"No kidding? Is she around?"

"Yeah, she's coming in the kitchen right now." Sound of a scuffle.

"Yeah?" This was Gracie, all right. Gracie was deep into hating us.

"Gracie, I hear you're in the chorus at school."

"Yeah, so?"

"Are you a soprano or an alto?"

"I dunno. I sing the melody."

"Okay, probably a soprano. Listen, we were thinking of coming to one of Mariella's games. Do you think you could sit with us if we did?"

"Well, I might be there with my friends." Whom she saw at school, every day, and talked to on the phone half the night, if Iona was to be believed.

"I know that's important," I said, back to being Switzerland, "but we don't get to see you too often."

"Okay, I'll think about it," she said unenthusiastically. "Stupid basketball. When she runs down the court, her cheeks bounce up and down. Like a hound dog's."

"You need to be a good sister," I said, maybe not as neutrally as I could have wished. "You need to cheer for Mariella."

"Why should I?"

Okay, not neutral at all. "Because you're damn lucky to *have* a sister," I began, my voice hot, and then I heard myself and backed off. I took a deep breath. "You know why, Gracie? Because it's the right thing to do. Here's your brother." I handed the phone to Tolliver.

"Gracie, I want to hear you sing," Tolliver said. That was exactly the right thing to say, and Gracie promised to find out when the chorus would be singing for the first time so Tolliver and I could put the date on the calendar. Then Gracie evidently handed the phone off.

"Iona," said Tolliver, with the faintest pleasant intonation. "How are things going? Really? The school called again? Well, you know Gracie isn't stupid, so there must be some other problem. Okay. When's she going for testing? It's good the state's paying for it. But you know we'd . . ." He listened for a while. "Okay, call us with the results. You know we want to hear."

After a couple more minutes of listening to this broken conversation, I was delighted when Tolliver finally hung up. "What's going on?" I asked.

"A couple of things," he said, frowning. "That was almost a good conversation with Iona. Gracie's teacher thinks Gracie may have ADD. She recommended testing, and Iona's taking her this week. The state will pay for the testing, evidently."

"I don't know anything about that," I said, as if I could have been prepared for this.

"We'll have to look it up on the net."

"She would have to take the drugs if she's got it, Iona says."

"What are the side effects?"

"There are some, but Iona was more concentrating on the benefits. Evidently, Gracie's been pretty disruptive at school, and Iona wants some peace."

"Don't we all. But if the side effects . . ."

We spent the rest of the evening on the Internet, reading articles about Attention Deficit Disorder and the drugs used to treat it. If this seems excessive or odd, consider this: Tolliver and Cameron and I had raised those girls from birth. My mother had been roused to try to take care of them when they were infants, but if it hadn't been for us, Mariella and Gracie wouldn't have eaten, or been changed, or learned how to count, or been read to. When Cameron had been snatched, Mariella had been only three and Gracie had been five. They'd gone to a preschool together for a few mornings a week, because we'd enrolled them and then told my mother they had to go. We'd gotten them to the preschool before we went to our own school, and all Mom had to do was remember to pick them up, which she usually did if we left her a note.

Here I was remembering, when that was

the last thing in the world I wanted to do.

"Enough of this," Tolliver said after a while, when we felt we knew a little bit about the disorder and the drugs used to treat it. "We'll learn more when we know if she has it or not."

I felt like I was drowning. I'd had no idea there were so many things that could go wrong with a child's learning processes. What happened to kids in the years before all these things were identified, and a course of treatment laid out?

"I guess they were labeled slow or difficult," Tolliver said. "And that was the end of it."

That made me feel sad for all the kids who'd never had a fair shake, because their problems hadn't been understood. At the same time, we'd just read two articles about how parents were overmedicating their children for those same problems, so that even children who really did just have some disruptive personality traits were being dosed with drugs that shouldn't have been given them. It was just scary. I wondered if I'd ever have the nerve to have a baby myself. It didn't seem too likely. I'd have to trust my partner completely, to bring his child into the world. The only person I'd ever trusted that much was my brother Tolliver.

And the strangest thing happened as I had that thought. The world seemed to freeze for a minute.

It was like someone had thrown a giant switch in my head. Tolliver was turning away to go to his room, and I was getting up out of the chair I'd pulled over to the desk so I could read the screen on the laptop. I looked at Tolliver's back, and suddenly the world slid sideways and then realigned itself in a new configuration. I opened my mouth to say something, and then I closed it. I didn't know what I wanted to say to him. I didn't think I really wanted him to turn around.

He started to turn, and I bolted for my room.

I shut the door behind me and leaned against it.

"Harper? Is something wrong?" I heard his anxious voice on the other side of the door. I was in a total panic.

"No!"

"But you sound like something's wrong."

"No! Don't come in!"

Tolliver's voice was a lot chillier the next time he spoke. "All right." And he moved away, going to his own room, I supposed.

I sank down to the floor.

I didn't know what to say to myself, how to treat someone as idiotic as me. I was poised in a perfect position to ruin the only thing I had in my life. One word, one wrong act, and it would all be gone. I would be humiliated forever, and I would have nothing.

I had one black moment in which I wondered if I should just go on and kill myself and have done with it. But my strong survival instinct rejected the fleeting notion even as it ran across my brain. If I'd lived through being hit by lightning, I could live through this new knowledge.

He must never know. I crawled across the floor to the bed; pulled myself up, lay prone across it. I planned the next week of my life in a few painful minutes, appalled at my own monstrous selfishness as I did so. Keeping Tolliver with me for one more minute was an awful thing to do.

But I couldn't let go, I argued with myself. If I suddenly shooed him away, he'd suspect something as sure as shooting. I just couldn't do it. In a week or so, when I could figure out the right way. Until then, hold myself carefully; guard my every action.

Life, which had seemed like such a rich crazy quilt laid out before me, suddenly assumed a grayer prospect. I climbed into the hotel bed, as I had climbed into hundreds of hotel beds.

I stared at the ceiling, at the bar of light from somewhere below that crossed it, at the bright red eye of the smoke detector. For hours I tried to remap my life. But I didn't have a clue which direction to go.

Fifteen

I was more like a zombie than a person when I came out of my room the next day. Tolliver was eating breakfast, and he poured me a cup of coffee without a word. I went over to the table cautiously, sinking into my chair with as much relief as if I'd negotiated a minefield. He glanced up from his paper, gave me a horrified look.

"Are you sick?" he asked. "God, you look like something the cat dragged in!"

That actually made me feel much better. If he'd said something sweet, I'd have lost it then and there, grabbed hold of him, and sobbed all over his shirt front.

"I didn't have a good night," I said, very carefully. "I didn't sleep."

"No shit. I can kind of tell. You better get out your makeup."

"Thanks for the boost, Tolliver."

"Well, I'm just saying. We don't want the coroner mistaking you for the corpse."

"Okay, enough." Somehow, I felt much better after this exchange.

Tolliver had been reading the paper, and he shoved it over to me. He was not going to say anything about my strange behavior of the night before, apparently. "Not much about Tabitha today. I guess it's getting cold."

"About time." I picked up my coffee cup with a shaking hand, managed to get the edge of the cup to my lips without spilling anything. I took a long sip, set the cup down with just as much care. Tolliver had kept the sports section, and he was involved with a basketball story, so he didn't witness this embarrassing weakness. I exhaled, felt some relief, and took a steadier drink. Okay, caffeine was a good thing. I got a croissant out of the basket, knew I'd regret it later, and ate the whole thing in about forty-five seconds.

"Good," was Tolliver's only comment. "You could use some body fat."

"You're just a bundle of compliments this morning," I said tartly. I felt *much* better now. Suddenly I felt a surge of optimism, with even less ground than I'd felt my deep depression of the night before. I'd been overly dramatic, right? This was okay. We were all right. Everything would be the same.

I ate another croissant. I even buttered it.

"Are you going to run?" Tolliver asked mildly.

"No," I said.

"You're just a party animal today. Croissants and no running! How's the leg today?"

"Fine. Just fine."

There was a long pause.

"You were acting kind of weird last night," he said.

"Ah. Lot to think about," I said vaguely, waving the last piece of croissant in an arc to indicate the breadth of my thought.

"I hope that worked out for you," he said. "You scared me a little."

"Sorry," I said, trying to keep my voice light and airy. "A sudden attack of thoughtfulness will do that to you."

"Um-hum." He stared at me, his dark eyes full of his own thoughtfulness.

The cell phone rang when he'd gone back to his newspaper story, and I reached over to answer it. Somehow his hand was there before mine, and I wondered what was happening with him. We were sure being mysterious with each other, these days.

"Tolliver Lang," he said.

"All right," he said, after a moment.

"Where is that?" he asked next.

"All right, we'll be there in forty-five minutes," he said, before folding the phone shut.

He looked at me, somehow harder and sadder than before.

"The family gave permission," he said. "We can go see the body now."

I got up and walked into my room to get dressed without another word.

When I came out twenty minutes later, I was clean and my clothes were fresh, but that was about all I could say. Despite Tolliver's advice, I didn't fool with makeup, and I only ran a brush through my hair. I wore it short, since I couldn't have dealt with a lot of hair to arrange, some days; today was definitely one of those days. I'd pulled on the top sweater in my suitcase, which was cream-colored, and the top pair of jeans, and the top pair of socks. Luckily, I only carry things that can coordinate, because otherwise I would have looked like I'd dressed in the dark.

Tolliver was about on par with me sartorially, and he hugged me when I emerged, ready to go. I was so surprised that I hugged him back for a moment, feeling thankful and grateful for him, as I always did. Then I realized what I was doing, and I froze, every muscle in my body going tense. I could feel the change in him when he realized that something was wrong between us.

"What have I done?" he asked, pulling away, looking down at me. "What have I done to you?"

I couldn't meet his eyes. "Nothing," I muttered. "Let's just get this over with."

The car was full of an uneasy silence as we followed the directions Tolliver had been given. Before I had time to calm myself and prepare mentally, we were at the morgue. There were so many dead inside, and they were so fresh, that the vibrations gathered in intensity and strength. When I got out of the car, I was already feeling a little light on my feet. I know we went in, and I know we talked to a few people, but later I remembered nothing. By the time we walked down a corridor I was humming from my head to my toes. I could hardly note my physical surroundings as we followed the very heavy, very young woman leading us to the body we'd come to see. Her big rear swayed in front of me as she walked, and her lank dark hair switched from side to side. She hadn't bothered with makeup, and her clothes were strictly thrift shop. This must be a job that sucked the hope out of you.

The young woman knocked at a door that

looked no different from any of the other doors. She must have heard a reply, because she held the door open and we went inside. A sandy-haired man in a lab coat said, "Hi." He was standing against the wall. There were two gurneys in the room. The lump on one of them was far bigger than the lump on the other. Tolliver gasped and coughed from the smell. Even through the heavy plastic covering the bodies, the odor was pervasive.

I said, "Tolliver, you can go," but I knew he wouldn't.

I introduced myself and Tolliver.

"Dr. Lyle Hatton," the man said. He was very tall and gawky, and he had a way of looking down through his glasses that registered as contemptuous.

His dislike and scorn was something I could ignore in the face of the overwhelming thrumming.

I started to lift the plastic so I could touch Tabitha's body directly, but Lyle Hatton said, "Gloves!"

He was annoying. I had a mission here, and the vibrations were resounding so loudly that I could hardly comprehend what he wanted. It seemed my choice was either touching her through the plastic sheet, or putting on plastic gloves. I wasn't aware I'd ever thought about the barriers between me and a corpse, and classified them. Cotton would have been better than plastic for my purpose, I knew instinctively.

But I wasn't being given that option. So I lay my hand on the plastic sheet, over the area where her heart should have been; of course, the shape under the sheet was not a full shape anymore, not after eighteen months in the ground. Immediately, I fell into Tabitha's last moments: *woken from sleep, a nap. Seeing a blue cushion, descending. Feeling . . . betrayal, disbelief, horror, NO NO NO NO Mama save me save me save me.*

"Save me," I whispered. "Save me." I wasn't touching her anymore. Tolliver had his arms around me. Tears were streaming down my face.

I put my arms around Tolliver, too; a dangerous indulgence, but I needed him so much. I looked at the masked man in his medical scrubs. "You collected evidence from the body?" I asked.

"I was there," Dr. Hatton said guardedly.

"Did you find any threads in her nose and mouth? Blue, they would have been."

"Yes," he said, after a notable pause. "Yes, we did."

"Suffocated," I said. "But she fought all the way."

Dr. Hatton made a sudden movement with his hand, as if he was going to show me something, but then he stopped in mid-motion.

"What are you?" he asked, as if he was talking to some interesting hybrid.

"I'm just a woman who got hit by lightning," I said. "I wasn't born the way I am."

"Lightning either kills you or you get over it," Dr. Hatton said impatiently.

"I can tell you've never dealt with a live person who's had the experience," I said. "You get hit with a few thousand volts, a few months later you come talk to me about what your life is like."

"If that many volts hits you directly, you're dead," he said simply. "What people survive is the energy discharge from it hitting very nearby."

I couldn't believe this guy, arguing with me about what had happened to me while Tabitha's body was right here between us.

"Whatever," I said, and straightened up to show Tolliver I was ready to go. It was hard to pull my arms from around him, but I did it, and his arms loosened around me.

I went over to the second shape, the larger one. I closed my eyes and placed my hand over the body.

My eyes flew open and I glared at Dr. Hatton. "This isn't Clyde Nunley," I said. "This is some young man who died of knife wounds."

Dr. Hatton looked at me as though he were seeing a ghost. "You're right," he said, as if I weren't standing right there. "You're right, my God. Okay," he said, very carefully, as though I might pounce on him, "let me take you to Dr. Nunley."

Tolliver was furious with Lyle Hatton, and I wasn't far behind him in that. But I was determined to complete my errand. We followed the doctor down the hall to a larger room, a cold room, full of bodies. It was not orderly; the gurneys were not lined up in neat rows. Here and there a hand or foot protruded. The smell was unique, a *bouquet de la mort.* The vibrations in this place were overwhelming. All the dead waited for my attention, from an old woman who'd been murdered in her own home to a baby who'd died of SIDS. But I was only here to call on one corpse, and this time Lyle Hatton led me to him. I was dizzy from being surrounded with all the newly dead, and it took me a long minute to focus on Clyde; then I saw it all again: the surprise, the blow, the fall into the grave. I nodded sharply to Dr. Hatton when I was through, and I staggered as I turned away from my final contact with Dr. Clyde Nunley.

"You can walk?" Tolliver asked, very low.

"Yes," I said.

"Wait," Lyle Hatton said. I looked at him inquiringly. The overhead light winked on his gold-rimmed glasses. "Since you're here, can I ask you to do one more thing? You were right about the blue threads. You knew when I showed you the wrong body. Maybe you can help me with one more thing."

Everyone wants a freebie.

"What do you need?" I asked. I wasn't in the mood for finesse.

"This body here . . . I can't determine a cause of death for this woman. She was living at home with her son and daughter-in-law, and she developed stomach symptoms. She might have had any number of things wrong with her, but I've met the couple, and I suspect there's something hinky about her death. What do you think?"

Though Hatton was a jackass, I like to help the dead when I can.

"Tox screen didn't show anything, autopsy turned up nada," Hatton said coaxingly. "She lost a lot of weight and had various stomach symptoms before death — diar- rhea, nausea, and so on — but she hated going to the doctor and she didn't turn up at a hospital until it was too late."

"This one?" I asked. I could see a pale hand, though it was not the right color a hand ought to be. I closed my eyes and touched her hand with my finger, a bare contact Hatton made no attempt to block.

"Don't try this on me," I said, feeling exhausted. "This is a young woman who died of aplastic anemia."

Dr. Hatton stared at me as if I'd grown another head. He checked the toe-tag. "I'm sorry," he said, sounding sincere. "I really thought that was her. This is." He double- checked the tag on the body next to the poor young woman.

I sighed heavily. I touched the plastic wrapped around this body. I narrowed my eyes. If he wanted to play, I was up to it.

"Cleona Chatsworth," I moaned, "Come forth!"

Out of the corner of my eye, I caught Tol- liver ducking his head to hide his smile. Dr. Hatton was growing even paler than he'd been before, almost to the point of match- ing one of his clients. He gasped. I'd heard the name right. Luckily for me, Cleona Chatsworth wanted someone to know what had happened to her, wanted it very badly.

"Cleona was poisoned," I whispered, my free hand moving in a circle over the corpse. I thought Hatton was going to faint.

"What do I look for?" he croaked.

"Someone gave it to her in salad dressing," I crooned. "The selenium."

I opened my eyes and said, "This lady was poisoned."

Lyle Hatton stared at me with glassy eyes.

"We're going now," I told Tolliver, who was glaring at the doctor, his hands curled into fists.

So we left the room, and we went back down the long hall. The young woman had waited down the hall for us, and as silently as she'd escorted us there, she led us back to the door to the outside. I was profoundly glad to step out into the cold gray day and take a deep breath of air untainted by death. Tolliver and I stood watching the heavy traffic on Madison for maybe five minutes, inhaling and exhaling, happy to be out of the building. The humming had seemed very intense before I'd entered, but it had only been a shadow of what I'd felt when I was actually within the walls.

When I felt more like myself, I said, "It wasn't Diane who killed her. Tabitha was wanting her mother."

He absorbed that. "That's good, then," he said. "One down."

"Don't laugh at me," I said, though his mouth hadn't twitched. "I think at least it's a start."

"Sure," he said. "And I'm not doing any laughing." He gripped my arm so I'd look at him. "I don't know how you do it and stay sane. I really, really admire you."

Now was *so* not the time for Tolliver to be all real and sympathetic.

"I want them to name the murderer." I began walking across the parking lot to our car. "Usually, I'm more or less accepting of the fact that people murder other people. That's just part of the world, I guess. But I'm really mad about this. I'm really, really angry."

"You've had children before," Tolliver said, meaning that I had read their deaths before.

"Oh, sure, I've done children. But this is different. I don't know why. Maybe it's the family, still waiting to find out what happened to her, figuring it's one of them who did it. This has just gotten to me."

"That's not good. It's tearing you up. I don't want this to happen to you."

"Well, me either. But I can't seem to stop it, and I can't tell who did it from touching her. And we can't leave for a while, I guess."

"Do you want to leave?"

I was buckling my seat belt. "What does that mean?" The tone of his voice had put me on guard.

"You usually can hardly wait to get out of town after we finish up with a client, but you haven't said anything about leaving for a day or two. You want to be here? What's the attraction? Manfred Bernardo? Or Joel Morgenstern? Or Seth Koenig?" He turned the key in the ignition with unnecessary force. He was definitely not looking at me.

"Huh?" I stared at him as if he'd started speaking in Swedish.

Then, as his meaning sunk in, I laughed. It was just too ironic. The thing was, in past times there might have been some basis for his question. I might have been thinking about Manfred, or having secret fantasies about Seth Koenig, or Joel Morgenstern. His wrestler's body was fit and powerful, also good fuel for fantasies — *Ooooh, pin me to the mat, Joel!* But being pinned down was never a fantasy of mine.

And though our age difference was minimal, I regarded Manfred Bernardo as a boy.

"Tolliver, I meant it when I told you I'm not interested in Joel. Plus, he seems happy in his marriage and I've never wanted to be an adulterer. Now Manfred, mmmm." I smacked my lips. "That's different. You can't help but wonder what's under all the leather."

Tolliver gave me an incredulous glance, saw I was smiling, and had the good sense to look embarrassed. "Okay, okay, I'm sorry," he said. "The truth is, I'm in kind of my own situation."

"What?" I was instantly serious. "What's up?"

"Felicia has stepped up her phone calls," he said. We were at a stoplight, and he looked at me steadily.

"Despite the way she acted yesterday? Like she'd never seen you before?"

He nodded. "Yeah. She's called, like, four times since we left the hotel."

"You sure you don't want her to call?" I was kind of feeling my way through this, because I couldn't tell what Tolliver was leading up to.

"I definitely don't. You've told me before that sometimes you felt men were dating you because you were so — so different from other women?"

I nodded.

"Well, that's kind of the way I'm feeling." The light changed, and he turned his eyes to the road ahead. "We never seemed to have that much in common. She never acted affectionate, or like she wanted to get to know me better. I can't understand her constantly trying to hook up now, again. And then when she actually sees me, she acts like she never was with me. And then she calls me again."

"You did do the nasty with her. Maybe she really, ah, enjoyed that with you?" I was trying not to sound self-conscious. This was not a frequent topic of conversation between us. Neither of us were kiss-and-discuss types. It was tacky. Plus, not suitable.

"To tell the truth, it was only about average. It was just . . . sex," he said, with a shrug. He seemed to feel he had lacked gallantry toward a woman he'd bedded. "She's a pretty woman, and real intense. In fact, maybe a little too intense. And not all that interested in talking."

I groped for the right thing to say. "Like she was using you?" I said, making damn sure there wasn't a hint of smile anywhere in my vicinity.

"Exactly," he said. "So, I guess I know how women feel when a guy's just using them to masturbate inside."

Crudely put, but I understood exactly what he was saying. "And Felicia's calling you all the time, now?" It was hard to reconcile that with the self-contained and sleek young woman I'd met.

"Yeah, after not hearing from her for months and months, she's in a frenzy."

Maybe seeing Tolliver had reminded her of how good he'd been? Maybe it had been a long time since she'd had sex, and here was a sex partner whose excellence was a known factor, a sex partner who wouldn't entangle her in any relationship talk?

"How are you dealing with it?"

"At first, I thought about doing it," he said, looking really embarrassed. "I mean . . ."

"Sex is sex," I said, trying to sound understanding.

"But something about her puts me off," he said. "I can have sex with someone I don't, ah, have a relationship with, and enjoy it. But we have to at least *like* each other."

"She doesn't like you?" I was hesitant. I'd never heard Tolliver talk about a woman like this, and I have to say, I was a little worried.

"I don't know. I'm not sure I like her, now."

"Because she's eager?" I wasn't sure I liked the implication.

"No, no. I mean, that's flattering." He gave a frustrated shrug. "I'm not one of those guys who only likes women as long as they're hard to get. And I don't think women are sluts if they admit they want sex. It's because Felicia's so . . ." He floundered, looking for the right words. But he couldn't find them.

Finally he said, "She's too deep for me. It's like swimming in the ocean, when you're used to a pool."

That was brilliant, and I gazed at Tolliver with admiration and some surprise. He looked a little surprised, himself.

I didn't know what to say, so I took refuge in facetiousness. "It's all your fault, Tolliver," I said. He looked at me skeptically. "You're just so darn magnetic. They can't live without you."

He gave me an eye roll. "Cut it out," he said.

So the subject passed away, but I didn't forget it, and I thought about it while he watched a basketball game on ESPN. He would know I wasn't dismissing his concern, that I'd keep it under my skin until I had an idea about it. In the meantime, I felt like reading. I'd gotten heavily involved in an old mystery, Marjorie Allingham's *A Tiger in the Smoke,* and after a page or two I was in the England of decades ago.

When the room phone rang, I was simply

irritated at having to put down my book. I was closest, so I answered it.

A male voice said, "Hey, can we come up?"

"Who is this?"

"Um. Sorry. This is Victor, you know? Morgenstern?"

I could feel my face wrinkle in a frown. "Who is 'we'?"

"My friend Barney and me."

I covered the receiver and relayed the request to Tolliver. "This is weird. I want to talk to him, and here he arrives on our doorstep," I said. Tolliver was not so pleased. In fact, he looked mildly exasperated. "Oh, okay," he said. "I was thinking about going out for lunch, trying to get some barbecue as long as we're here in Memphis. But we'll see what he wants. You think he's just show-ing off to his friend or something?"

I shrugged, uncovered the receiver, and gave the boy our room number. After a few minutes, there was a tentative knock on the door.

Tolliver answered it, looking quite grim and intimidating. Actually, he was probably just aggravated at the interruption to his game watching, but Tolliver is a tough-looking guy, and when he's unhappy, he tends to look a little dangerous. If the two teenagers had been dogs, the ruffs on their necks would have been standing up. Like many teenagers, Victor and his friend Barney were strange combinations of tentative and aggressive.

Victor was wearing a tight knit shirt, which allowed us to see just how much he'd been hitting the gym. He didn't have his father's magnetism, but he did have a pair of big blue eyes that worked almost as well. His blond friend Barney was taller, narrower, but still a substantial hunk of immature male. Both were wearing school jackets, jeans, and Pumas. Victor's "Tommy" polo shirt was green-and-white striped, and Barney's Ralph Lauren was golden brown.

"So, uh, you doing okay?" Victor asked me. "This is my friend Barney."

"I'm fine, thank you," I said. "Barney, I'm Harper Connelly. This is my brother, Tolliver Lang."

"Hey," said Barney. He looked at us furtively, and then back down at his shoes. He and Victor were sitting close together on the love seat, while Tolliver and I were in the chairs.

"Can I get you anything to drink?" I asked politely.

"Oh, no, no thanks. We just had a Coke down in the car," Victor said.

There was a small, awkward silence.

"Look, dude, I want to talk to your sister," Victor told Tolliver. He had on the most manly face he could muster.

My mouth twitched, though I did my best to look neutral.

"Go right ahead," Tolliver said seriously. "Were you wanting me to leave the room?"

"No, dude," Victor said anxiously. He looked at his friend Barney, who shook his head, to reinforce Victor's denial. "No man, stay here."

The teenager turned his head to me. "You were in Nashville, so you know how bad that was," he said. "I mean, you know that was really awful."

I nodded.

"So my mom — my stepmom — flipped out for a while."

"Flipped out how?" I sat forward, focused my attention on the young man. Not completely to my surprise, Barney took Victor's hand. Victor looked startled, but not at having his hand held by another male. He was just surprised Barney felt it was okay to do that in front of us. They looked at each other for a moment, and then Victor squeezed Barney's fingers in a tight grip.

"She was all . . . using pills, you know? She got really strung out. Felicia was having to drive over to Nashville from Memphis all the time to make sure the house was running okay."

"That must have been really hard," I said, trying to sound both gentle and encouraging.

"It was," he said simply. "My grades went way down, and I was missing my sister, and it was really bad. My dad tried to keep going to work, and my mom would get up and try to clean the house or cook, or just have lunch with friends, but she was crying all the time."

"The loss of a family member causes all kinds of changes," I said, which was just about meaningless. It couldn't begin to cover the "changes" the sudden absence of a sister could cause, as I had good reason to realize. I had no idea where Victor was headed with this, but I found myself increasingly curious, curious enough to provide conversational lube to keep the talk going.

"Yeah," he said simply. "We sure had a bunch." He seemed to gather himself. "You know, that morning? The morning she was — gone."

"Um-hm," I said.

"My dad was in the neighborhood," he said in a rush. "I spotted his car a couple of blocks from the house."

I didn't sit upright and shriek, "Oh my God!" but it was definitely an effort to stay in my relaxed position. "He was?" I said, quite calmly.

"Yeah, because . . . I mean, I did go to tennis practice," Victor said. "But after that, my friend I had in Nashville; I mean, it wasn't anything like Barney, but I did, um, have a friend, and he and I hooked up, and then I needed a shower, so I thought I'd run home, but when I went past the house I saw Dad's car at the stoplight two blocks away, and I thought he might notice something. I mean, what was there to notice? But parents, you know." Victor shrugged. "So I just went back to the park and hit some balls, met some other friends who'd come to play. The courts were only ten minutes away from home and I even parked in the same spot when I went back, so it was pretty easy for me to say I'd never left."

We were both shaken by this little account.

"Of course, I couldn't say anything," Victor said.

"I can see that it would be hard to get into that," Tolliver said.

"Yeah, you know, one thing would lead to another, and then I'd have to tell them. About me."

And the world revolved around Victor, of course. "So they don't know yet," I said.

"Oh, God, no!" He and Barney rolled their eyes at each other. "Dad and Mom would freaking flip out."

"My mom is cool about it, which is awesome," Barney said. I was glad to confirm he had vocal abilities.

I'd meant that Victor's parents didn't yet know he'd seen the car, but of course Victor had interpreted my question his own way.

"You're sure it was your dad's car?" Tolliver asked. "Absolutely sure?"

"Yes, I'm sure," Victor said, as if he had his back against the wall and an army against him. "Of course, dude. I know my own dad's car."

I'd never heard anyone call Tolliver "dude" before, and even under the circumstances, I was kind of enjoying it. "What's he drive?" I asked Victor.

"He's got a Lexus hybrid," Victor said. "A bamboo pearl–colored Lexus with the ivory leather interior. We looked at the website for like a week before we ordered the car."

Okay, that was distinctive. It couldn't be confused with many other cars, for sure. I was conscious of a bitter disappointment, as if a show dog I'd become fond of had turned and bit me.

"And you never asked him about that," I said, and I couldn't keep the disbelief out of my voice. "You're saying your dad could have snatched your sister, and you've known that all along, and yet you've never said anything to anybody about it."

Victor turned a deep red. Barney looked at me with outright hostility.

"Because," I went on when they didn't speak, "you know you're telling us that your father lied about where he was, and you're saying he almost certainly grabbed your half sister, his daughter, and killed her."

He raised his head, and almost spoke; his mouth moved; and he was so young, so disturbed, it almost hurt to badger him like this, but I had to.

"Leave him alone," Barney said. His big hands, so smooth and unscarred, had fisted. "Vic's been through hell over this. He knows his dad couldn't do anything like that. But he saw the car, and he can't forget that. You don't know what it's like."

Actually, I did, pretty much.

"So, Victor, you gifted us with this information — why? So we could be disturbed, along with you?"

Victor's face couldn't have gotten any redder, and he obviously had to dredge for a reason he'd unburdened himself on us after more than a year of silence. "I thought," he said painfully, "I thought you'd know who killed her. I thought you'd be able to *see* it. I couldn't tell. I already said, then I'd have to say I was home when I said I wasn't, too . . . I was *scared*."

"How have you been able to live in the house with him for all these months?" I asked, out of sheer curiosity.

"I didn't see him." Victor struggled with what he wanted to say. "I saw the car. I didn't see his face, I didn't talk to him, I just saw the car. There are other Lexuses in the world, like my grandfather's. There are plenty in that neighborhood. We lived in pretty nice suburb."

"But you seem convinced that it was your father."

"Just because it was where it was. So close to our house. And at the time, I thought, 'There's Dad.' Because of course, Grand-dad was in Memphis, and we were in Nash-ville."

Tolliver sat back in his chair and gave me a quizzical look. What were we supposed to do with this? Something, some small thing, at the time had convinced this wretched boy that he was seeing his father in his father's car. He hadn't doubted it. Now, he was saying he hadn't actually seen the driver. There were other pearl-colored Lexuses — Lexi? — around, of course, as Victor had also pointed out. I almost hated the boy for giving us the burden of useless knowledge.

Victor, however, seemed to be feeling better now that he'd told us the story. I could see by the little gathering motions of his body that Victor was preparing to sweep out with his boyfriend in tow. I felt angry about that, but I struggled against it. After all, I didn't have any right to beat the boy to a pulp because he'd finally revealed a secret he should have told right off.

A sharp knock at the door made me jump. The two boys looked pretty anxious, and I knew for sure that no one in his family knew where Victor was. I was beginning to think that our suite was the home away from home for anyone remotely connected to the disappearance of Tabitha Morgenstern.

Tolliver looked out the peephole, not a normal precaution of his.

"David," he said briefly. Victor and Barney moved apart as if their inner attraction had suddenly been set on "repel." Instead of being a couple, they were transformed into a couple of guilty teenage buddies, caught somewhere they had no reason to be, by an adult who would surely scold them. "Should I let him in?"

"Why not?" I said, throwing my hands out.

David stepped into the room, his eyes flashing around to all the corners suspiciously. Vindication was written large on his face when he saw his nephew. "Victor, what the hell are you doing here?" he asked, righteous indignation practically dripping from his voice.

"Hello, David, good to see you again," I said, and David Morgenstern finally looked at me and turned red.

"You thieving bitch," he said, and Tolliver hit him.

SIXTEEN

The blow was not premeditated in any way. Tolliver simply drew back his arm and hit David Morgenstern in the stomach as hard as he could. As David collapsed to the carpet, choking and clutching his stomach, Tolliver closed the door so no one in the hall could observe the recovery of our guest. Barney looked scared, and Victor looked about a thousand different things — astonished, envious, and angry being the most identifiable.

Tolliver was rubbing his hand and half-smiling. He stepped away to show me he didn't intend to keep beating on David.

"Did you want something in particular, Mr. Morgenstern, or did you just come by to call me names?" I asked as Victor finally crouched by his uncle and tried to help David get up.

"I saw you talking to Victor at the house yesterday," David said, when he could speak. "And then, when Victor came up here . . ."

"You followed me?" Victor asked incredulously. "I don't fucking believe it, Uncle David."

"Language," wheezed the man who'd just called me a bitch.

"So, you decided I had a sexual interest in Victor?" I said, with what I thought was remarkable dignity.

"I just wanted to be sure he was okay," protested David. "Joel and Diane are so wrapped up in the situation about Tabitha, and Felicia went to work, and my parents are at home . . . my mother's having a bad day . . . so I thought someone should be watching out for what Victor was doing. He doesn't need to be around people like you."

"And you thought calling me names fell into the category of watching out for Victor?" Tolliver had come to stand beside me, and I felt like kissing the hand that had hit David.

"I thought," he began, and then he turned so red I thought his blood pressure had soared. He cleared his throat, leaned over so he could clutch the back of a chair for support, and began again. "I thought the boys had come up here for . . ."

I wasn't going to help him out. Tolliver

and I waited obviously and patiently for David to finish his sentence. Barney and Victor exchanged glances that fully expressed how lame this idea had been, and how stupid Uncle David had been to follow Victor. Grown-ups!

"I thought they were going to hang out with you two because they think you're cool," David said weakly, which was a big fat lie.

"We are," I said. "Aren't we, Tolliver?"

"Sure," he said. He patted my hand with his bruised one.

David finally recovered enough to move around the back of the chair and sit down, though we hadn't asked him.

"Maybe you could tell us why you thought you could call me names, and that would be okay?" I asked, my voice sweet and gentle.

"I am sorry," he said finally, just when my patience was running out. "Though I don't know why your brother had to hit me."

"He's not my brother, but he is my best friend," I said, to my own amazement. "And he doesn't like it when people call me names. Wouldn't you want to hit someone who called Diane a thieving bitch?"

"She got some phone calls after Tabitha vanished," David said unexpectedly. "People called her all kinds of things. Especially after the story got out about her quarrel with Tabitha that morning. People can be so ugly, you wouldn't believe."

"Actually, I think I would," I said.

It took David a minute to get that, but when he did, the red crept over his face and shoulders like a tide rolling in. "Okay, I'm feeling pretty bad now," he said. "I did a stupid thing. I can see Victor's okay, he's got his best bud with him, everything's cool. I know I acted like an idiot. Hey, Barney," David said, with a pretty pathetic attempt at regaining his superiority. "How are you, guy?"

Barney looked embarrassed. "Fine, Mr. Morgenstern," the boy said. "You?" Then he gasped and choked back a laugh at his automatic question.

"I've been better," David said, a bit more steadily. "Victor, why don't you and Barney run along? I've got to talk to Miss Connelly and Mr. Lang."

"Okay, Uncle David, if you're sure you're going to be okay," Victor said, with false solicitousness.

David gave him such a sharp look I thought Victor would probably end up paying for his moment of fun, but Victor maintained his serious look quite well.

"Come on Barney," he said. "The grown-ups want to talk." They put their letterman jackets back on and left the room, giving each other secret grins as soon as they were out of David's eyesight.

The door closed behind them with a thunk. We might as well leave it open, we were getting so much traffic.

Tolliver and I sat on the love seat and waited for David to flounder ahead.

"Diane says you're getting the reward for finding Tabitha's body," David said.

We waited.

"Why don't you say something?" he asked, his temper flaring up again. Just when you thought the fire had been stomped out, it popped up again.

"What's to say?" I said.

"You're taking money from my brother and his wife," David said. "Money they need."

"I need it too," I pointed out reasonably. "And I earned it. I'll bet not all the money came from Joel and Diane, either."

He was taken aback. "Well, there were donations," he said. "A lot from Fred, and a chunk from our parents, of course."

I couldn't have had a better lead-in if I'd ordered it. "Was your father especially close to Tabitha?"

"Yeah, he was," David said. His blue eyes were focused on another time, and he said, "My dad is a great guy. When he and Mom would go to Nashville to visit Diane and Joel, Dad would take Tabitha all the way out to the stables for her riding lessons. He went to her softball games."

"And your mother went along?"

"No. I'm sure you noticed yesterday that she was too sick to do that much. The Parkinson's is eating her up. Sometimes she'd ride over to Nashville, but she'd just stay at the house with Diane. She's nuts about Diane. Of course, she liked Whitney, too."

"And your dad has a Lexus like Joel's?"

"Why are you asking me all this?"

I couldn't believe he'd told me this much without asking why. Maybe David was lonely within his own family. As I looked at him, I wondered suddenly if David was the reason Felicia clung so closely to a family that had little connection to hers any more. My brother was looking at me strangely, with an expression I couldn't read.

"What do you do for a living, David?" Tolliver asked. You would never have thought that ten minutes before, he'd socked this guy in the stomach like he wanted his fist to come through the back.

"I work at the *Commercial Appeal*," David

said. "In the advertising department."

I didn't know exactly what such a job would consist of, but I was pretty sure David wouldn't make as much money as his brother, Joel. Joel was a CPA with a large firm, and he was obviously doing well at his job if his consumer goods were a reliable yardstick. And Joel had had not one wife, but two; both pretty, if the picture I'd seen the day before at the house hadn't been ridiculously touched up. Joel had a son and he'd had a daughter. I wondered what David had. A huge pile of envy? A case of jealousy?

"You drive your dad's car often, David?" I asked.

"The Buick? Why would I?" he asked.

"Wait, you said he had a Lexus."

"No I didn't. You asked me if he had a Lexus, and I asked you why you wanted to know."

Then I remembered Tolliver had said he'd been talking to Fred about his car. I'd misunderstood. And Victor had said his grandfather had a Lexus, but he hadn't specified which grandfather. I'd made a series of assumptions, and had gotten the usual result. Assumptions were dangerous things.

I'd been staring at David while I thought,

and he was getting antsy. "What's up with you?" he asked. "I made a mistake coming here, and I apologized. I'm leaving now."

"Were you really following Victor?"

"No one is watching out for him," David said. "I need to."

I noticed that was yet another response that didn't really answer the question: a David Morgenstern specialty, apparently. "It seems to me that *everyone* says they're watching out for Victor. Certainly Felicia is, and you are. Both of his grandfathers mentioned their concern about him."

"Oh, Felicia talks about Victor a lot," David said bitterly. "But if you ask me, she's using Victor as an excuse to keep hanging around Joel . . . and Diane." He tacked Diane's name on hastily, as if that would mask what he was implying.

That was an interesting thought, but I stuck to my course. "Is everyone so worried about Victor because there's reason to think he had something to do with what happened to his sister?" I had caught myself considering, as Victor sat across from me ostensibly spilling his innermost fears, that he could be performing the whole scene as a cover-up for his own guilt.

"We wondered . . . I talked to Joel about

this . . . Victor's so secretive. He vanishes and then he won't say where he's been . . . he hangs out with that kid Barney so much, and Barney's parents aren't . . . they're Christian, and they go to one of those churches where people wear Birkenstocks to the service. He locks his door a lot. We'd been wondering if Victor and the boy are into drugs, but his grades are good. He's on the wrestling team, and he's a strong boy, but we worry . . ."

"You sense there's something different and unknown about Victor," I said.

David nodded. "Do you know what it is?" he asked me baldly. "After all, for some reason he came to talk to you. If he didn't come to you for sex . . ."

"It's unthinkable he'd come to me for any other reason," I said gravely. "Is that it?"

David looked ashamed all over again.

"I don't have sex with teenagers," I said. "Not one of them, not two of them at once. I'm not interested in that."

Since I kept my voice cool and level, David didn't have any fuel to feed his anger, and he lapsed into his backup emotion, befuddled concern. "Then why was Victor here?"

"You'll have to ask Victor that," I said. Considering Victor had spent months thinking his father might have had something to do with Tabitha's disappearance, he was a model of mental health. He'd seemed so relieved to share the burden. He'd also seemed happy to tell someone about his sexual orientation. Victor needed a therapist. I couldn't believe he hadn't been visiting one. I said as much.

"Oh, he went for a while," David said, anxious to assure me that they'd done their best by the boy. "But Fred, he's an old-school kind of guy. He thought Victor should suck it up and get on with his life. I guess maybe he talked Joel and Diane around to his point of view, because when Victor moved here from Nashville, they never got him another therapist. Truth be told, Victor did seem a lot better once he was in Memphis."

"So Fred didn't want him talking to anyone," I said.

David looked surprised. "Not to a therapist. He's just an old fashioned man, the kind who thinks you need to keep your problems to yourself and let time heal you."

I was ready for David to be gone. In fact, I really didn't want to see any more of this extended family. In fact, I wished I'd never heard of Tabitha Morgenstern. I wished I'd never stood on the grave in the corner, but

I couldn't help having the idea that I'd been herded toward that grave, I'd been asked to Memphis to find the child, and I'd done exactly what somebody wanted me to. All along, I'd been manipulated.

"Goodbye, David," Tolliver said, and David actually looked a bit startled that we were ready for him to leave.

"Once again," he began as he stood up.

"I know. You're sorry," I said. I felt so tired I thought my flesh might fall off my bones. It wasn't bedtime yet, and I didn't think I'd eaten since a long-ago light breakfast.

Finally David was out the door, and Tolliver said, "We're getting food right now." He called room service and placed an order, and though we'd called at a strange time, our food arrived quickly.

As we ate silently, I thought. We have a lot of thinking time, since we're on the road so much. Somehow when we're in a town, when we're not moving, we do anything but think.

I went back over everything I knew.

Tabitha Morgenstern. Eleven. The much-loved child, as far as I could tell, of upper-class professional Jewish parents. Abducted in Nashville, to end up interred in an old Christian cemetery in Memphis. Neither of her parents, the papers had told me, had

321

ever been arrested for anything. Her older half brother, either. But that half brother thought he'd seen his father's car close to the house the day Tabitha had disappeared.

Tabitha had grandparents who lived in Memphis, but had visited in Nashville frequently. Her grandfather and grandmother Morgenstern seemed to adore her. In fact, Victor had told us her grandfather often took her places by himself. Did I have to suspect Ben Morgenstern of fooling with the child? I sighed. And Tabitha had a sort of step-grandfather, Fred Hart, who seemed to have remained close to his former son-in-law. Fred Hart, a Bingham alumnus, owned a pearl Lexus, like the one that Victor had seen in the neighborhood the morning of the abduction. Victor had assumed he was seeing his dad, because it would have been reasonable to see his dad in that location, but what if he'd seen his grandfather's Lexus instead?

Tabitha had a step-aunt, too, Felicia Hart, and an uncle, David Morgenstern. Both had gone to Bingham. David seemed to resent his brother's successes, though as far as I could tell he also seemed to have cared for his niece. The attractive Felicia seemed to have quite an appetite for the male gender. There was nothing wrong with that. She was also very protective of her nephew, and there was nothing wrong with that, either.

I rubbed my face with both hands. There had to be something I could glean from this information, something that would help me lay Tabitha to rest. Being shut up with Tolliver, now that I'd had so many thoughts I shouldn't have had, was becoming intolerable. I dropped my hands to the table and looked over at him. He happened to look up at that moment, and our eyes locked. He put down his fork.

"What are you thinking?" he asked. His voice was very serious. "Whatever it is, I think you'd better tell me."

"No," I said, equally seriously.

"Then what are you willing to talk about?"

"We have to find out who did this, and we have to leave this place," I said. Movement would bring relief, being on the road again. "Don't you think a random stranger is completely ruled out?"

"Yes, because of where the body was found," Tolliver said. "It's impossible that it was a random act."

"Do you think I was meant to find the body?"

"Yes, I think that was why you were called here."

"Then it has to follow that Clyde Nunley

was killed because he knew who'd suggested I be the next guest in the series."

"Maybe," Tolliver said slowly, "the key was finding of the priest's records."

I mulled that over.

"After all, it was the finding of the records that made St. Margaret's such a good subject for a reading. It was a controlled experiment."

"Sure. Dr. Nunley had to know if I was getting it right or not, and there was a way to prove that. There usually isn't."

"So she was put there for me to find. Maybe months ago, when the records were discovered." I groped my way through the thought. "Someone wanted her to be found."

"And that someone had to be the killer."

I combed over that one, too.

"No," I said at last. "Why would that have to follow?"

Tolliver was taken aback. "Who would know and do nothing?"

"Someone you loved. You might not do anything, if the killer was someone you loved."

"Not just someone you loved. A member of your family." Tolliver's face was very grim. "Your mom or dad or wife or husband or sister or brother . . . that's the only way you'd hide it."

"So we have a couple of ways to go," I said. "We can sit here and wait for the police to work their way around to the solution. They'll probably get it, sooner or later. Or we can skip out on this."

"Let's try to find out who could have put your name in Clyde Nunley's ear," Tolliver said.

SEVENTEEN

Mrs. Clyde Nunley was certainly not Jewish. She was aggressively Christian. There were crosses and crucifixes in every room in the Nunley home, and a painting of a saint on every other wall. Anne Nunley was thin and dry and hollow, and she had few friends. She was even glad to see us.

We thought the professor's widow might not be willing to talk, especially after we saw all the crosses. Anne might not have wanted to talk to another faculty wife, or a neighbor, but she sure wanted to talk to us. Anne was a True Believer in spiritualism.

I've met all kinds of true believers: Christian, Jewish, Wiccan, atheist. I don't think I've ever met an Islamic true believer, because I don't think I've ever met a follower of Islam. What I'm trying to say is, your basic religion doesn't seem to make much of a difference to your belief (or lack of it) in the things that are more in my bailiwick, which is any kind of contact with the dead. You wouldn't think atheists would believe in the spirit surviving death, but some of them do. It's like people just can't help believing in something.

Anne Nunley, it appeared, was an aggressive Christian mystic.

After she'd appeared at the door to greet us, and invited us in, Anne had begged us to be seated. Without asking us, she'd brought in a tray of coffee and cookies. It was about ten in the morning by then, and the day was much brighter than the preceding days had been. It was warmer, too, in the upper fifties. Sunshine poured through the old house's eastern-facing windows. I almost felt I could find a rock and bask like a lizard.

Tolliver and I eyed the laden tray Anne set on the coffee table before us, and I recognized this as sheer overachievement. Anne Nunley was determined to be the best widow in the world. And I also thought Anne Nunley was running on empty. Her husband's sudden and unexpected death had sparked a little explosion in her brain.

"Tell me, do you think Clyde's spirit is at the cemetery still?" she asked in a chatty way. "I wanted him to be buried on campus; I think it's fitting. I've called the campus board that has St. Margaret's under its wing. I don't think I'm asking much, do you? He worked at Bingham for ten years, he died there, and he was practically almost buried there anyway!"

I blinked. "His spirit is not at the cemetery," I said, answering her original question. My simple statement was the springboard for a five-minute ramble on Anne's beliefs about life after death, the prevalence of ghosts in Irish folklore (no, I don't remember how that came into the conversation), and the absolute reality of a spirit world. I certainly wasn't going to argue the other way on that one.

Tolliver just sat and listened. Anne wasn't interested in him at all; she saw him as a shadow at my elbow.

"Clyde wasn't faithful to me at all," Anne said, "and I had a hard time dealing with that."

Total disclosure seemed to be the order of the day. "I'm sorry you had to endure that," I said carefully.

"You know, men are just pigs," she said. "When I married him, I was sure everything would happen the way it was supposed to. We wouldn't have much money, because after all, being a college professor is not the most remunerative of occupations, but we would have lots of respect, because you have to be smart to be a college professor, right? And he had his doctorate. I thought I would have children, and they would get to go to Bingham free, and they would grow up and bring their children home; this house is so big."

It was a big house, and decorated in just-turned-antique furniture I suspected had come from Anne Nunley's parents, or perhaps Clyde's. Everything was polished and neat, but not fanatically so. Everything was comfortable, and nothing was expensive. It was a good house in an old neighborhood with big trees that had lifted the sidewalks. The big hallway that we'd entered had two large open archways on either side; we'd gone right, into the living room. The other archway revealed another good-size room that appeared to be Clyde's home office.

"But the children didn't come, and Clyde didn't want to be tested, and there was nothing wrong with me. But he was seeing other women. Not students, you know, at least not while they were taking his classes. After they graduated, you know, he might see them."

She explained this very carefully, as if the exact details were important to me.

"I understand," I said. And I'd thought we would have trouble getting her to talk to us. The problem was going to be getting her to shut up.

"But of course, he never knew the little girl," she said. "His being in her grave is just a terrible . . . invasion. Is she still there?"

The sudden question took me by surprise. "No," I said. "But the man in the grave, the original burial, is still there."

"Oh, then our Lord wants you to lay him to rest," she said.

"I believe that's true."

"Why have you come to see me? Do you need me to be there when you do it?"

Since I had no idea what I could do about Josiah Poundstone's ghost, or essence, or whatever you want to call it, I shook my head. "No, but I did want to ask you about a few other things."

She fixed her mad eyes on me. "All right."

I felt I was taking advantage of a woman who was not in her right mind. But here I was, and she was eager to talk.

"Did your husband see Felicia Hart or David Morgenstern, socially?"

"Yes, from time to time," she said, in a surprisingly matter-of-fact way. "And Clyde and Fred were on a committee together. Fred is active in alumni affairs, you know.

His wife was, too, before she died."

"She died of what?" The women in this family seemed to have extraordinarily bad luck. Joel's first wife had had cancer, his mother had Parkinson's, Tabitha had been abducted . . . it made you wonder about Felicia's and Diane's futures.

"She had a heart attack," Anne said.

"That's awful," I said. I really couldn't think of anything else to say.

"Yes," she agreed. "Poor woman. It happened when no one was home, about the time Tabitha was taken. She was gone when he found her. What a sad family."

"Yes, it is." Though this family seemed to have a lot of tragedy, in Mrs. Hart's case, maybe a heart attack was exactly what it had been, and nothing more sinister.

"Do you think Felicia was seeing your husband as a girlfriend?" Tolliver asked. He tried to keep his voice smooth and unobtrusive so he wouldn't stop the flow, but Anne gave him a sharp glance.

"He may have been," she said, and now her voice was cold and hostile. "But then again, he may not have been. He didn't tell me names, and I didn't want to know. Felicia was here a time or two for one of our parties. We used to give parties."

That was too hard for me to imagine,

Anne getting the house ready for a party, maybe wondering which of her husband's "girlfriends" he would invite into their home. Clyde, I knew instinctively, would have been embarrassed by his wife's Christian religious paraphernalia, while Anne would never have considered taking it down for a party. I hoped for her sake that he had simply let it go without comment, but my slight knowledge of Clyde Nunley convinced me he would have made secret sneering comments to his guests.

"Would Clyde have done something for Felicia if she'd asked him?"

"Yes," Anne said, pouring some more coffee in my cup. Tolliver had quietly been eating the cookies, Keebler's Fudge Stripes, which he loved. "Clyde liked doing favors for people, if it would give him traction with them. Felicia is pretty and she has a high-profile job, and she's active in the alumni club, so he would have done what she asked. He's been sorry David Morgenstern doesn't seem to be his friend, anymore, too."

She was slipping into the present tense, I noticed.

"Do you know why they weren't friends anymore?"

"Clyde made some comment about David's nephew not being Bingham material,"

Anne said promptly. Maybe there was Sodium Pentothal in the coffee?

"Would you know why he said that? Why he thought Victor wasn't appropriate for Bingham?"

"He'd seen the boy with another young man at a cinema," Anne explained. "He was sure they were, you know, in a relationship. Gay," she elaborated. "Though of course, they're not. Gay. They're sad, is what they are."

If Victor was sad, I didn't think his gayness had much to do with it.

"Of course, that made David angry, and he told Clyde if he ever heard Clyde say anything else about Victor, he'd make sure Clyde never opened his mouth again. Clyde was mad about it, but sorry, too. David had been a friend of his, way back. So, he would have done a favor for David, too, to get him back as a friend."

Had this woman had any illusions about her husband? Surely you needed some?

Anne had found her way back to the original topic like a homing pigeon, when I'd quite lost track of it. "So," she said, "If you're asking me if I'm sure about Felicia, no, I'm not, and I don't want to be judgmental."

I bit my lip, and Tolliver looked off in

another direction entirely. I didn't know if Anne was being one of the most judgmental people I'd ever met, or simply realistic, but I had a terrible impulse to laugh.

"Have you completed the funeral arrangements?" Tolliver asked.

"Oh, yes, part of Clyde's belief system was preparation for your funerary rites," she said. "He's got it all written down somewhere. I just have to find the file." She pointed to a file cabinet across the hall in Clyde's home office. "It's in there somewhere. Since he was an anthropology professor, he was really into death rituals, and he put a lot of thought into writing down what he wanted. Most funerals involve a church. And a minister of some kind. At one time, Clyde wanted a gathering of the clan elders with a feast and distribution of his goods."

"The clan elders being?"

"Professors senior to him in the anthropology and sociology departments," Anne said, as if it were quite evident.

"You would have to provide the feast, I take it?"

"Yes, dammit. Excuse me for swearing. And then all his office stuff to give out! As if anyone wanted his old pencils! But that's what he wanted, the last time I heard. Maybe he changed his mind after that. He liked to play around with ideas."

I looked across the hall. The file cabinet and desk sat in disarray with all the drawers pulled open, and files were scattered here and there on the floor. For a crazy moment, I wondered if I should offer to help search for the documents containing Clyde's last funerary wishes, but I decided that was too much. I didn't want to know what Clyde's instructions had been about the final disposition of his body and possessions.

I couldn't think of anything else to ask Anne. I glanced at Tolliver and gave a tiny shrug, to show I was finished. Tolliver thanked her for the cookies and the coffee, and then he said, "Do you know who told your husband that my sister would be a good person to invite for his course?"

"Oh, yes," she said. "I know that."

"Who was it?" I asked, thinking that at least we were getting somewhere.

"Why, it was me," she said simply. "After Felicia met you in Nashville, she talked about you at a party, and I was so interested. She really believed in your powers. So I read about you on-line, and I thought that finally someone would be able to give Clyde some of his own back. He's been teaching that course for two years now, and he just loved exposing all those people as frauds, or at least as less than reliable. It wasn't that Clyde disagreed with their beliefs, either; he just didn't want anyone to be able to do anything different. But you, I knew you were real. I read the articles and I saw some pictures. That day you found the child's body, he was just furious at you. The night he died, he went out once, and then he came back even angrier, and I gathered he'd seen you at your hotel?"

I nodded.

"So then he made a phone call or two on his cell phone, and off he went again," she said drearily. "I went to sleep in my room. And that time, he never came home."

"I'm sorry for your loss," I said after a moment, when I saw she'd said all she wanted to say. But I wasn't sure she wasn't better off without Clyde Nunley.

Anne remained seated while we showed ourselves out. She was looking down at her hands, and all her manic energy seemed to have faded away, leaving her melancholy. She shook her head when I offered to call a neighbor or friend for her. "I need to keep looking through Clyde's papers," she said. "And that Seth Koenig said he was coming over later. The federal agent."

We were both quiet for a few minutes after we got in our car.

"He was mean to her," Tolliver said. "Surely she'll be better off."

"Oh, yeah, Clyde was rat poop," I said. "But she's going to miss him, anyway."

I couldn't see any wonderful future for Anne Nunley, but I would have to put that in the file of issues I couldn't do anything about. As we drove, I mentally constructed a future for the widow in which, at Clyde's funeral, she met a wonderful and kind doctor who had a great weakness for thin, needy women who lived in big comfortable houses. He would help her struggle back to emotional health. They would never have parties.

I felt much better after that.

EIGHTEEN

We'd learned a lot more about the professor during our strange talk with his widow, but I wasn't sure that what we'd learned would be of much help in narrowing the search for his murderer. Not that I cared a whole lot about who'd killed Nunley — but I did care who'd killed Tabitha.

There was a basketball game I wanted to watch in Texas. I wanted to be free to go to it. I wanted to look for a house in Texas, a house that wasn't too far from where my sisters lived. So I wanted to be free of this situation, both for the sake of the Morgensterns and for my own reasons.

Tolliver was outside tipping the valet as I walked through the Cleveland lobby. I was so lost in thought that I didn't even notice Fred Hart until he called my name.

"Miss Connelly! Miss Connelly!" His heavily southern voice pulled me back into the here and now, though I wasn't happy about it. Maybe the look I gave him wasn't very friendly, because he stopped in his tracks.

"Did you need to see me?" I asked, which was a stupid question, but I had to say something.

"Yes, I'm sorry to disturb you," he said. "Joel and Diane asked me to deliver something to you on behalf of the Find Tabitha Fund."

It took me a few seconds to understand what he was saying, and by that time Tolliver had caught up me and shaken Mr. Hart's hand. Standing in the middle of the lobby didn't seem to be a good place for such a conversation. I suggested Mr. Hart some up to our room with us. He wasn't very enthusiastic about accepting, but he trailed along after us into the elevator.

The close quarters made me aware that Mr. Hart had been lubricating himself with bourbon. I tried not to make a face as the all-too-familiar smell caught at my throat, and I saw Tolliver's face tighten. Tolliver's father had been very fond of bourbon. We both had a great distaste for bourbon.

"I understand that you two met my daughter before," Mr. Hart said. In the mirrored surface of the elevator wall, I stared at a man who seemed to be aging by the minute.

Fred Hart was grim and gray.

"Yes," I said. "Tolliver dated her for a while."

I don't know what demon prompted me to add that, but I think I was feeling needled by Fred Hart, by his reluctance to come to our room. I decided that was because he thought there was something distasteful and shoddy about us, and I wanted to get back at him. That was a stupid thing to do.

"Did he now? Felicia is so focused on work . . ." his voice trailed off. He should have finished the sentence by saying "that I'm glad she found time to go out," or "that she seldom seems to date." Those were the words that would have made sense of the thought. But it was like his heart gave out before he could complete the idea. We both tried hard not to look too startled.

When we finally got into the room, I, for one, was thinking we should maybe call the older man a cab, not let him drive home. I was really concerned. He'd seemed such a nice guy at the Morgensterns' awful luncheon; very serious and sad, true, but also caring and thoughtful. What had happened to Fred Hart?

"Mr. Lang, Miss Connelly," he said ceremoniously, standing in the middle of our little temporary living room, "Joel asked me to give you this." He took an envelope out of his inner jacket pocket and handed it over to me.

I stared at the white envelope for a moment before I opened it. There was no way to do this that wasn't awkward. The envelope contained a check for forty thousand dollars. It was the reward money for finding Tabitha's body. With this money added to what we had in savings, we'd be able to buy a house. My eyes filled with tears. I hadn't wanted to earn it this particular way, but I was glad to have it.

"You're shaken, I can see," Mr. Hart said, sounding pretty shaken himself. "You may not want to accept this, Miss Connelly, but you did the work and you deserve it."

I did want to accept it, and I had every intention of accepting it. I did deserve it. But somehow his words shamed me, and I felt abruptly sick.

To my horror, I saw a tear trail down Fred Hart's cheek.

"Mr. Hart?" I said, in a very small voice. I was not qualified to deal with a weeping man, especially since I didn't know the trigger for his tears.

He sat down heavily in the closest chair, which happened to be one of the wing chairs. Tolliver settled in the other, his face unreadable, and I perched on the edge of the love seat across from them. We had just had a very strange talk with Anne Nunley; now it looked as though we were going to have one with Fred Hart.

Of course, alcohol was playing a major role in opening Fred Hart's emotional conduits.

"How are Joel and Diane?" I asked, another stupid thing to say. I was trying to divert him, since I had no idea what to do.

"Bless them, they're fine," he said. "Diane is such a good girl. It was hard to see him marry again, see someone take Whitney's place. Diane should never have married him. I never should have let Whitney marry him. Out of her league, and I knew it."

"What do you mean? Was he mean to Whitney?"

"Oh, no, he loved her! He was good to her, and he adores Victor, though he doesn't understand him at all. That happens a lot with fathers and sons, though . . . and fathers and daughters, too."

"You mean Joel didn't understand Tabitha?"

He looked at me with a face that was still wet, but now impatient, too. "No, of course not. No one 'understands' a girl that age, especially the girl herself. No, what I mean is . . . it doesn't make any difference what I mean."

My heart was pounding fast with anxiety. I felt we were close, so close, to understanding what had happened at the Morgenstern house that spring morning.

"Are you saying Joel molested Tabitha?"

I knew I'd made a terrible mistake the minute his face shut down.

"What a dreadful suggestion. Abominable. I'm sure you see a lot of that kind of thing in your work, but it's not something that's happened in our family, young lady."

I'm not sure what he was referring to when he said "my work," and I'm not sure Fred did, either, but the point was, he now felt entitled to be angry with me, and he was taking full license.

"Something awful did happen in your family, though," I said, as quietly and gently as a snowflake falling.

His face crumpled for a minute, like tissue paper. "Yes," he agreed. "Yes, it did." He heaved himself to his feet. "I have to go."

"You sure you're okay to drive?" Tolliver asked, in the most neutral voice possible.

"Actually, I don't believe I am," Fred admitted, much to my surprise. I don't think I'd ever heard a man admit he was incapable of driving, and I have watched scores of men in many states of being high. They all thought they could manage a car, or a truck, or a boat.

"I'll get him home in his car, you follow us," Tolliver said.

I nodded. I wasn't especially pleased at the prospect of getting the car back out of the hotel garage, but I didn't see anything else we could do.

I stored the check in Tolliver's laptop case for safekeeping while Tolliver called downstairs about the cars. We got Mr. Hart up between us, and we went to the elevator. He kept telling us over and over how much he appreciated our help, and how sorry he was he'd spoken to me in an angry way.

I couldn't figure out Victor's grandfather. Finally I stopped trying. It was obvious to me that this man was under a nearly unbearable strain, and the weight of it was crushing him. But why Fred Hart? If our distraught caller had been Joel, I could have understood it better. After all, it was his daughter who was dead, it was his family who was under suspicion, it was his wife who was about to give birth under extremely unhappy circumstances.

With some difficulty, and a little help from the bellboy, we got the older man into the passenger's seat of his car. He was driving his Lexus hybrid, the one like his son-in-law's, and even under the circumstances I could read Tolliver's flush of pleasure at getting to drive the car. I was smiling to myself as I slid into our car, which was very humble in comparison.

Fred had given Tolliver directions, though he was speaking less and less and seemed ready to go to sleep. I followed Tolliver east, again, this time past the Bingham College area to Germantown. We turned so many times I was worried about Tolliver and me escaping from the suburb after we'd deposited Fred at his home.

When Tolliver pulled into a driveway that led into a large corner lot, I was trying not to be stunned by the obvious richness of the area. Fred Hart's place had been new maybe twenty-five years ago. The whole neighborhood appeared to date from the same era; the homes looked fairly modern in style, but the trees showed a good growth and all the landscaping seemed well-established.

What astonished me so was that all these houses had taken steroids. Not one of them would have less than four bedrooms, and that would only be the beginning of it. I imagined each one of them cost a million, probably way more; this was not the kind of place I planned to look at when Tolliver and I began house hunting. I pulled into the multi-car garage, which could hold two more cars besides the Lexus and ours. Besides being big enough to hold four third-world families, the garage had a large closet at the far right side that must act as a toolshed. And there wasn't a single oil stain.

I jumped out to help Tolliver, who was having trouble getting Fred out of the car.

"He pretty much passed out during the drive," Tolliver explained. "At least he'd already given me directions. I hope the house key works. If we're at the wrong house, we're screwed." We both laughed, but not too merrily. I sure didn't want to have to talk to the police again, for any reason.

Tolliver handed me a key ring he'd extracted from Fred's pocket, and while he resumed pulling Fred out of the car I hurried over to the door. The second key I tried turned in the lock, and his security system, if he had one, wasn't on, because nothing began to tweet or blare when Tolliver got the stumbling man into the house. I moved ahead to find the best place to stow him. I had to stop and gape. I'd thought the Morgenstern house was so pretty and big, but this house was overwhelming. The kitchen we'd entered was huge, just huge. I passed from there into the family room, or den, or living room. I didn't know what to call it. It had exposed beams in the cathedral ceiling, an enormous fireplace, and conversation groupings.

"If I had been brought up here, I would believe I could have anything I wanted," I said, stunned.

"Where do we go?" Tolliver asked impatiently, not in the mood to listen to sociological reflections. I made my feet move. The master bedroom, I discovered, was downstairs, which was a great relief. Together, Tolliver and I got Fred onto the (of course) king-size bed, got his coat and shoes off, and covered him with a soft afghan that had been thrown artfully over the back of a huge leather chair . . . in front of the master bedroom's very own fireplace and conversational grouping. I didn't know who was supposed to have conversations here, since Fred appeared to live by himself. I predicted I'd find a walk-in closet and a bath with a sunken tub somewhere very close. I opened the closet door, and then the bathroom door. Yep. All that and more.

"Watch out!" a voice called from the bed, and I swung around, startled.

Fred Hart had roused himself to give Tolliver a big caution. He'd grabbed Tolliver's arm while Tolliver was trying to arrange him comfortably.

"You have to watch out. I'll tell you the truth. You just don't know what happened . . ." the older man said, and then he conked out again.

"I know you drank too much," I muttered.

Tolliver hung up Fred's coat and looked around for any other little thing we should do. "That's it," he said. "Let's go. I feel like I broke in, this is so much not our kind of place."

I laughed. We left the bedroom, and the sleeping man, and began making our way back to the kitchen. I just had to stop while we were going through the family room. It was so pretty, all dark browns and coppery colors with bright blue touches here and there. I sighed, and turned to look out the huge window into the back yard. I was a bit surprised there wasn't a pool. I decided the lack was due to Fred's gardening habit.

When Ben Morgenstern had told me Fred liked to garden, I had not imagined anything like this. The high red brick wall that enclosed the back yard was covered with vines, carefully pruned and directed. Running all around this wall was a flower bed full with bushes and probably with bulbs that would bloom in the spring and summer. Aside from this, there were groupings of bushes and flowers, much like the groupings of tables and chairs inside the family room. In the more established beds, the bushes were high and thick. There were a couple of beds that looked newer, because the brick edging looked brighter and the plants smaller. I was seeing this garden in November, when it was not flourishing, but I was deeply impressed. Maybe this was why Fred had held on to such a house after the deaths of his wife and daughter.

On a wrought iron table on the flagged patio right outside the windows, I saw gardening gloves, some kind of spray device, and a gardening hat. These things were laid out with precision, and a folded newspaper by them with today's date indicated Fred had been working in his garden this very morning.

Leaning against the table was a spade, covered in dirt. Digging a new flower bed in November? He was enthusiastic. I wondered why he'd left the spade dirty, when everything else was so clean. Maybe he'd intended to finish some job when he'd put it down.

I didn't know much more about gardening than I did about astrophysics. I shrugged. Maybe November was a good time to turn the dirt over so it breathed all winter, or something esoteric like that. To my right, just where the brick wall ran up to the wall of the garage, was a wooden gate. It was placed there so Fred could wheel his gardening stuff back to its place in the tool closet in the carport, I figured.

Tolliver was using our cell phone. "Hey, Felicia," he said. "This is Tolliver. I don't like to leave this as a message on your machine, but I guess I better tell you that your dad is at home, and he could probably use some company. He was feeling kind of sick when he came to see us at the Cleveland, so we brought him home. He seemed pretty upset about something. He's asleep right now." And with a snap of the phone, Tolliver ended his message without a good-bye.

"Good idea," I said. "She should come by and check on him. I wonder if they see each other very much, in the normal course of things. It's quite a drive out here from midtown, and apparently she has a really high-pressure job." My voice trailed off. I should shut up.

Tolliver looked at me without expression.

350

He didn't want to talk about Felicia. Okay. I got that.

A final glance around left me feeling more than ever like a ragged orphan in a Dickens novel. We left through the kitchen, locking the back door behind us. Considering the cold weather, it wasn't too surprising that we didn't see a soul as we backed out of the garage and drove to the end of the street to turn right, to get back to more familiar territory.

We had to stop at a Walgreen's to buy a few things, and we filled the car's tank with gas while we were taking care of odds and ends. We'd gotten tired of room service, not only the menu but also the expense, so we had a leisurely meal at a chain restaurant. It was a simple pleasure, doing something so regular and normal. The cell phone didn't ring and there were no messages for us at the front desk or on our voice mail when we finally went back to the Cleveland. The day had sped by.

"You know, now that we've gotten the check, would the police really need us any more?" I asked. "I don't think so. I know we don't have anything on the schedule until next week, but we could leave Memphis. Stay somewhere cheaper. Maybe get to Texas to see Mariella's basketball game."

"We should stay here a day or two longer," Tolliver said. "Just to see."

I bit my lip. I'd like to take a big bite out of Felicia Hart, whom I blamed for Tolliver's preference. The bitch was stringing Tolliver along, I just knew it. Now that I'd seen the house she'd grown up in, I was sure. Women like that don't bond with guys like him, not in real life. He'd denied any real attachment to her, but here we were.

Then the cell phone rang.

Tolliver made a big deal out of answering it casually, but I could see that he was tense.

"Hey," he said. "Felicia . . . oh, how's he doing? He what? Okay, I'll come."

He listened for a few seconds. He looked unhappy, puzzled.

I could kill her.

"But she . . ." Tolliver covered the receiver. He looked at me, his face dark and troubled. "She wants us to come back out to Fred's house," he said. "She says she has some questions she wants to ask us about his condition and what happened today."

"He got here drunk and we took him home," I said. "What more is there to say? You can tell her that over the phone. You *are* telling her that over the phone."

"She seems pretty insistent," he said.

"I don't want to go. If you have to talk to

her, you go."

"Harper isn't here," he told the telephone. "No. She's out on a date. What difference does it make, with who? All right. I'll be there in a little while." He ended the call, and went to his room to get his coat without a word to me.

I made a face at the mirror by the door.

"Here, keep the cell." He tossed it onto the table. "I'll call you from the house if I need to tell you anything. I'll be back before long," Tolliver said briefly, and he left.

The room felt very empty when the door closed behind him.

I don't often do this, but I cried for a few minutes. Then I washed my face, blew my nose, and slumped on the love seat, my head empty and my heart sore.

Too much had happened to us in the past few days.

I remembered when I'd first searched for Tabitha Morgenstern. I remembered the stale feeling of the Morgenstern family, the feeling that they could feel nothing new, nothing vital.

They'd recovered, to an amazing extent. They'd started a new life. They'd moved to a new location, reestablished ties with Joel's family that had never been weak, since Nashville and Memphis aren't far from each other. Victor had started at a new school and found a new friend, Joel had worked at a new job, Diane had created a lovely home.

Now, what would happen? Of course, Diane would give birth, and maybe this baby would help them to heal. Maybe knowing what had happened to Tabitha would, too. In time, maybe Victor would be able to share his big secret with his parents, and possibly they'd understand.

It must be hard to have a dad like Joel, after all. He was just . . . outstanding. Even if he left me unmoved, I could see that he was handsome, I could see that he was bright, I could see that women adored him. I also saw that he loved one woman in particular, loved her devotedly, but if I hadn't somehow acquired immunity to the Joel mojo, I might not be able to comprehend that. I wondered how often he'd had to fend off serious passes from other women, how many burning glances he'd deflected simply because he seemed ignorant of his attraction.

I tried to remember what Fred, Joel's first father-in-law, had said about Joel that morning. Something about the marriage of Whitney and Joel? He'd said something like, "I never should have let Whitney marry him. He's out of her league." He'd also said Diane shouldn't have married Joel. Why would Fred think that? Joel so obviously adored Diane.

I got down on the floor to do some leg lifts, thinking all the while. What was so wrong with Joel, that Fred shouldn't have approved his marriage to Whitney Hart? Did Fred know something bad about Joel, or had it been a bad marriage? But every comment I'd heard and read about Joel's first marriage had emphasized how close the couple had been, how heartbroken he'd been when Whitney died. And then, in less than two years, he'd married Diane. That seemed like a good marriage, too, at least as far as I was any judge. The abduction of Tabitha would have broken up a weak marriage, right? I'd read in several places that the death of a child often caused couples to separate, for a multitude of reasons.

Given the argument Diane had had with her daughter before Tabitha vanished, many husbands in Joel's place would have found reason to blame Diane, to assume the argument had everything to do with Tabitha's disappearance. But Joel was a faithful guy; probably Diane had never thought of leaving Joel. Because women loved Joel.

Women loved Joel. Fred Hart had a Lexus, just like Joel's.

I sat up. I stared at nothing, thinking furiously.

NINETEEN

It was lucky I remembered the route to Fred Hart's house, because the cab driver didn't know Germantown from shinola. He dropped me off a block away, and I paid him the equivalent of a small fortune. He sped off, probably anxious to get back to the world as he knew it. I was wearing dark clothes and I was using the hood on my jacket, a very reasonable thing to do in the cold weather. I had pulled on my gloves, too.

Away from the main arteries, the night was still and silent. We were way into the burbs, and every soul was shut inside on this freezing night. The huge fireplaces were fired up, the ovens were cooking good meals, hot water was heating the thousands of showers and tubs. Nothing was lacking, inside, to perfect the comfort of the people who inhabited these homes.

And yet, Fred had lost his wife and one

daughter, and a step-granddaughter. Nothing could stop tragedy from visiting your home. The angel of death would not pass over, leaving you unscathed, no matter how large your house was.

I crept up to the garage on the side of the house. Our car was there; Fred's car; and another car that must belong to Felicia. I ran silently across the white concrete to the wooden gate in the brick wall. I turned the knob very carefully. It was locked. Sonofabitch.

I looked at the brick wall. It had an occasional gap, part of an openwork design in the bricks. I took a deep breath. I fixed the toe of my right sneaker into the little gap, and I threw myself upward. It didn't work the first time. The weak right leg didn't hold. So I put the left foot in, and with my mouth clenched in determination, I heaved again. This time I clutched the top of the wall with both hands. I pulled myself up while I swung my right leg, and by some miracle I got myself on top of the wall. I was very close to the gate, which was at the angle formed by the house and the wall, and I would only be visible from the family room if someone was standing right up against the window looking outside. It was dark, and this part of the wall did not catch the spill of light from inside. I stayed very still, trying to calm the hammering of my heart. I drew a deep breath. Then another.

I risked moving enough to peer down below me as I lay full-length on the narrow wall. It was hard to make out exactly what was directly underneath, other than that it was vegetation. I figured I was going to have to drop into some rose bushes, but that was just going to have to be their fate.

As it turned out, my landing hurt me more than it did the roses. A thick central stalk jabbed me savagely in the thigh, and I was sure that it had torn my pants and the skin underneath. And I couldn't make a sound. I bit my lip as I extricated myself from the bushes. After a second to collect myself and to let my thigh stop throbbing, I stepped out of the soft earth of the bed, across the neat brick border, and onto the grass. The ground was damp from the previous days' rain, and I knew I was smeared with mud. I crouched and duckwalked over to the huge picture window. The lights were on inside.

Felicia had her back to me, thank God. She was facing Tolliver, who had his hands up.

That wasn't good.

That meant Felicia had a gun in her hand. It was also bad that Felicia had blood all over her. She was wearing off-white pants and a dark green sweater, and the pants were smeared with dark stains — it was harder to tell what shape the sweater was in.

There was a sliding door in the expanse of glass, but I didn't know if it was unlocked or not. If Fred had gardened that morning, he might have left it open. Or he might have automatically locked it before he started off for our hotel to give us the reward money. I hadn't thought of checking, earlier.

It was locked. Of course, it was locked.

"Why doesn't he love me?" she screamed, her voice so loud I could hear her clearly through the glass. "Why the hell doesn't he love me?"

She wasn't talking about her father. She meant Joel, of course. This was all about Joel.

"They'll blame you," she said. "They'll blame you for this, and I'll have another chance." And she raised the gun in her hand.

Even if I'd been able to get into the room, there would have been a chair and a table between me and her. There was nothing between Felicia and Tolliver. I saw what I had to do. I pulled one of the bricks out of the border. I tucked it under my arm while I punched in 911. When a voice answered, I said, "I'm Harper Connelly, and I'm at Fred Hart's house at 2022 Springsong Valley. Felicia Hart is about to shoot me." Then I put the phone down on the ground, very gently, and I braced myself. I stood up straight and looked Tolliver in the eyes. He stared over Felicia's shoulder at me, his face full of horror. He shook his head, a tiny shake meant to warn me off.

"Felicia!" I screamed, and I slammed the brick into the glass as hard as I could. A web of cracks began running out from the impact point.

The big noise startled her, and she wheeled around and fired without hesitation.

I saw Tolliver begin to launch himself at her back as the glass shattered in front of my face. I felt the bullet go by my ear. I heard it.

I saw the glass shiver, and I thought it would all rain out on me and I would be sliced open.

Fragments of glass struck me in the cheek, and I felt blood begin to trickle down onto my neck as I leaped backward on the flagstone patio. Before I covered my eyes, I saw Tolliver wrench the gun from Felicia's outstretched hand and bring the butt of it down on her head.

Only once.

Then I was under the patio table, and there were pieces of glass around me and covering the top of the table, and I was shaking all over.

Tolliver unlocked the door from the inside and then he was asking me if I was all right. He was pulling me into the house to drag me into the kitchen where he grabbed up a washcloth and began to dab at my face. There were bits of glass in the cuts on my face, and that hurt quite a bit, as I tried to make clear to him. Then we heard the police sirens, and then he was holding me. And it was all over.

The EMT was doing painful things to my cheek. She was getting the slivers of glass out, and it was hurting, but not as much as getting shot would have hurt. She had pointed that out several times, and I had agreed each time, though with less enthusiasm on every repetition.

The Germantown police had kindly let Detectives Lacey and Young come to the scene of the crime, and they were all listening to Tolliver's story. He'd covered the part about Fred Hart visiting us that morning, and Fred's inebriation.

Then he talked about Felicia's phone call.

"She said she wanted to talk to me here, that she wanted to know all the details about her dad's visit, and so on. I thought she wanted to see me again, because we'd had a . . . we'd hooked up a couple of times. She'd been calling me pretty steadily since. I think she was trying to keep tabs on Harper and me, to know where we were in case she needed us again. Which she did."

"What did she need you for?" Brittany Young asked. She'd been pulled away from some home activity. Her hair needed a brushing, and she was wearing a sweatsuit and Reeboks.

"She needed us to find Tabitha." Tolliver took my hand, and I tried to smile.

"You're saying she confessed to taking her," Detective Lacey said.

"Yes, she did. She knew Tabitha would get in the car with her. She borrowed her father's Lexus, so no one would see her own car. She thought that someone might see the Lexus and report it, and that Joel might be suspected; but she knew he would have an airtight alibi because she called him at work that morning and made sure he was staying put. She thought if Diane suspected Joel, she'd divorce him; or maybe Joel would suspect Diane, and he would divorce her. Felicia thought maybe the stress of the whole thing would rip the marriage apart, even if mutual suspicion didn't. Plus, she didn't like Tabitha. She thought the girl was getting preferential treatment over her own nephew, Victor. And she couldn't just kill Diane, to make way for herself. That hadn't worked when her own sister died."

"You're saying she had something to do with Whitney's death?"

"I don't see how she could have caused Whitney's cancer. But that kind of opened the door for her, she thought. She made her best play for Joel after her sister died. She came over from Memphis to Nashville a lot, she was as good to Victor as a mother could be, she offered to move in for a while to help Joel out."

"And he wouldn't bite," Young said.

"He wouldn't bite," my brother agreed. "So Felicia worked on this plan, worked on it for a long time. She took Tabitha back to this house, smothered her there on the couch."

And then I recognized the cushions. The blue cushions. No wonder they had struck me so much when I'd seen them that afternoon. I hadn't been listening to my inner chimes, and they'd been ringing away.

"And then Felicia buried Tabitha in this garden, wrapped in a black plastic bag. Her dad was putting in a new flower bed, and Felicia put the body in there, deep."

"Why'd she decide to bring her up?"

"One strategy hadn't worked. And Diane got pregnant, which was a stake in Felicia's heart. It was time to shake things up again. She had her ace in the hole; my sister. Probably, what sparked the whole plan was the discovery of the death records the parish priest had left. She knew Clyde Nunley, and knew he'd do almost anything for her if she worked him right. So she got him to invite Harper to the college, and she waited till her dad was out of town, and she dug up her niece. This was maybe three months ago, she wasn't clear on that.

"And her father caught her in the middle of it. He didn't know what to do. This was his only remaining daughter. So he did what she asked. He helped her take the plastic bag to St. Margaret's. They reburied Tabitha."

I shuddered, and Tolliver's hand tightened on mine. The EMT finished working on my face and put a butterfly bandage on the worst cut. The rest, she dabbed with antiseptic. She wrote down a few instructions and shook her head. "You're lucky," she said for maybe the twelfth time, and I nodded. "You're gonna come out of this much bet-

365

ter than the woman who shot at you."

Felicia was in the emergency room getting her head checked.

Her father was on his way to the morgue. Felicia had killed him every way a daughter could kill her father. All these months, he'd known what his daughter had done. I was surprised he'd lasted this long. Three months' worth of days in this big house, thinking about what Felicia was capable of. It made me shiver just to imagine it.

"So what else did she tell you?" Lacey asked. He was wearing jeans and a cowboy shirt, oddly enough, one with pearl snaps instead of buttons. He had on cowboy boots, too, though I didn't know how he'd seen over his belly to put them on.

"She said that she planned on blaming her father's death on me. She'd kept hold of the shovel they'd used to dig the grave in the St. Margaret's cemetery. Today she planted it in the back yard to be found, because it still had dirt on it from the cemetery. When we told her that her dad was here and passed out, she hared out here and hit him in the head with that shovel. She figured he was about to break and give her up. After he was dead, she planned to blame his murder on me, and Tabitha's on him."

"Why would you kill Fred Hart?"

"I'm sure she would have thought of something," Tolliver said wearily. "After all, if a man like me kills a man like Fred Hart, I don't think there'd be too many questions. She would have thrown away her bloody clothes. Maybe if she couldn't figure out how to get blood on me that looked natural, she would have shot me, said she'd caught me in the house after I'd killed him. Who would you have believed?"

The police didn't like that. But I thought my brother was telling the truth.

"What Felicia didn't count on was Harper," Tolliver said, kissing me on the cheek. "I was never happier in my life to see anyone, as I was to see you when you popped up by that window."

"You came out here without a gun or nothing?" asked one of the cops.

"I don't like them," I said. "We've never had a gun."

He shrugged, like I was pretty stupid, and maybe I was.

But if I'd had a gun, I would have shot Felicia until I didn't have any bullets left. As it was, she was alive to stand trial for all the things she'd done.

I got a lot of satisfaction out of that.

TWENTY

"You look like a cat attacked you," Victor said.

I just stared at him.

"Okay, not funny," he said. "I'm just really nervous."

I started to tell him we were, too, but I decided that wouldn't be a calming statement. And Victor really needed to calm down.

I'd figured it might help Victor take his mind off his family situation and at the same time broaden his horizons a bit, so I'd asked him if he wanted to come to the cemetery to help lay Josiah Poundstone's ghost. I was regretting that idea, at the moment. Victor was a little too excited, though he seemed thrilled that I'd asked him. He'd given me a big hug, which surprised the hell out of me and caused Manfred to raise his eyebrows.

I didn't know anything about the business

of laying a ghost. So I'd called Xylda Bernardo, and Manfred had brought her. Manfred, resplendent in black leather and silver, had greeted me with a kiss. He'd shaken Victor's hand a little too long. I thought he was trying to get a reading; he wasn't making a pass. Manfred wasn't that diverse. At least, I thought so.

Xylda gazed around the cemetery. "Tell me about it," she said.

I explained what I'd seen and felt that night to Xylda, who seemed alert and attentive.

"So, his body is here, and so is his soul. He died of blood poisoning, you think? From a knife cut, given him in a fight."

"Yes. Really, he was murdered. I don't know who stabbed him, but I suspect it was his Beloved Brother," I said, because that was something I knew about. "I think the headstone might indicate guilt. Of course, it could just mean his brother loved him a lot. But I guess that doesn't matter. What really matters is Josiah's ghost being restless, because he wonders why he had to die, and then why his grave was disturbed so often."

"So, you want his spirit to pass on?"

I didn't even want to consider what other options Xylda could offer me. "Yes, that's what we want."

"Good," Xylda said enigmatically. "Do you sense him here now?"

It was another cold night, but at least it was clear and not raining. The old cemetery felt just as scary as it had the other time we'd come in the dark. The muted sounds of the city, the uneven ground — but at least the open grave had been filled in. We'd checked that out in the good old daytime, with the sun shining.

I stood once again on this much-used grave and felt downward. I felt Josiah Poundstone's presence not only below me, but around me. "Yes," I said. "He's here." Victor shivered and looked around as though he expected a murky white figure to approach the grave.

I glanced at my watch. We needed to get a move on. We weren't exactly supposed to be here.

I'd thought about calling the college for permission, but I'd figured it was something they'd never give us. I wanted to get this over with and get off Bingham property before the security guards came by.

Following Xylda's directions, we circled the grave that had held Tabitha's body. We formed a narrow circle around it, and we joined our hands. Manfred's small hand had a strong grip, and his many silver rings pressed into my flesh. Victor had a much lighter grasp on my right hand.

Xylda began saying something in a language I didn't understand. I don't even know if Xylda understood it. But it was effective, whatever it was, because there was a mist forming in front of me, between me and Xylda, and in the mist I could see a face. It was a face I had never seen mobile, animated.

"Jesus," whispered Manfred, and "Name of God," said Victor.

I was not frightened.

"Thank you," I said. "Thanks, Josiah." He'd saved me from falling into the grave, after all. "No one's going to bother you again. Everyone you knew here has passed on ahead of you. You need to go, too."

I thought he smiled.

"Don't seek justice, seek peace," Xylda said, and the face wavered. The eyes turned to Xylda in confusion. And then I saw the lids fall and remain closed. Victor made a gasping sound, and I knew he was weeping as Josiah made his final departure. The face lost its clarity, became less defined, and then the shape of it gradually dispersed. In five minutes, there was no more mist. And the air was clear.

And the cemetery felt empty of anything but us.

I couldn't explain this to anyone, ever.

I'd never believed in anything like this. Souls, I knew; I'd seen them and felt them. But I'd never known one that had lingered for over a hundred years, one that had been strong enough to manifest itself physically. Josiah Poundstone must have been a remarkably vital man, maybe one of the men who charmed everyone, like Joel Morgenstern. Seeing the ghost changed me. Maybe it changed everyone there that night.

I wondered what Fred Hart would have told me if I'd asked him, "What do you see in your garden at night?"

Detective Lacey told me something interesting. Clyde Nunley's will really had requested a burial at St. Margaret's, saying he had loved the college so much he wanted to be on its grounds forever. I thought this was amazing, and I thought Bingham's agreement to this was even more amazing. Detective Lacey didn't have any information on the kind of graveside service Clyde had settled on, and I really didn't want to ask.

Felicia thought so little of Clyde Nunley that his death seemed only incidental to her.

Detective Lacey, who had actually developed some respect for me, told me Felicia confessed to killing Clyde almost casually. He was very much an afterthought, a footnote in her grand plan. "He started acting like he had a claim on me," she'd said. I suspect he tried to blackmail her; the social-climbing Nunley may have thought of divorcing Anne and marrying Felicia. Perhaps he told her he might tell the police exactly who had suggested that he call me to "read" the cemetery. If he'd had a true understanding of her character, he would have known he was signing his death warrant.

Felicia had slept with other men only as part of her grand design. Tolliver she'd seduced so she could have a good reason to keep tabs on our whereabouts when she needed to have Clyde call me. It was only a bonus for her when Anne Nunley turned out to be interested in the accounts of me she'd heard, and Anne had also suggested my presence to Clyde when he was discussing the priest's graveyard material he'd found in the archives of the college. Felicia had hooked up with Clyde to have a conduit into the course study, so she could be sure we were brought there. She didn't consider having sex with either Clyde or Tolliver to

373

have any bearing on her love for Joel, which was so much purer, so much finer.

The media feeding frenzy could hardly get enough of the story, right up until the time Diane delivered her son. Joel called us to tell us, and we sent a little gift, though we weren't sure Diane would be glad to get it. We felt obliged. Somehow, their marriage held, even though Diane had to find out that it was for love of Joel that her daughter had died. Diane was evidently a big-hearted woman who could see that none of this was Joel's fault.

At the trial, Joel steadfastly denied giving Felicia any encouragement at all, despite all her attorney's badgering. We had to be there for part of it, and it was as unpleasant as you can imagine. Of course, the women on the jury loved Joel, and I was pretty sure Felicia would be convicted on all counts. The police had come up with some forensic evidence that confirmed some points in the story Felicia had told Tolliver.

Rick Goldman got a ton of business as a result of his small part in the whole thing. Goldman had a way of making a mountain out of a molehill, and his reputation as a private eye soared. He sent us a letter enclosing a brochure and business card with his website address included.

Agent Seth Koenig resigned from the FBI that year and went into private practice. He specializes in tracking down missing children. He sent us a brochure with a business card attached. He doesn't have a website, yet.

So far, Tolliver hasn't talked about Felicia. I hope he didn't love her; I don't think he did. If there's something that needs saying, some day he'll say it.

We made it to Mariella's basketball game, and her team won. She scored twice, and she was elevated to unbelievable heights by this triumph. She was even happy to be in our company for one whole evening. Gracie sang for us, and we managed not to wince. Iona and Hank were half-way civil, which was the best we'd ever gotten.

Sometimes, Manfred calls me. He always keeps the conversation short and teasing. He tells me about his grandmother's doings, and he tells me about any tattoos and piercings he adds to his collection.

"I think he's making those up just to have a reason to talk to you," Tolliver said one evening in Tucson.

"He's a boy who's got a crush," I said.

"You know better. He's a guy, and he cares about you. Maybe on a superficial level. But he admires you."

"I know," I said with contrition. "Manfred's not high on my dance card, though."

"Someday," Tolliver said, and paused. A knot formed in my belly. "Someday you're going to meet someone, and you won't want to be on the road with me any more."

"Then you'll find someone, too," I said. "Anyone would be lucky to have you."

He laughed.

After that, we rode a good ways in silence.

ABOUT THE AUTHOR

Charlaine Harris is the author of the Sookie Stackhouse books and several other mystery series. She lives in southern Arkansas with her husband, her three children, three dogs, and a duck. She is an avid reader, mild cinemaphile, and occasional weightlifter. Her favorite pastime is cheering on her children in various activities.

We hope you have enjoyed this Large Print book. Other Thorndike, Wheeler, and Chivers Press Large Print books are available at your library or directly from the publishers.

For information about current and upcoming titles, please call or write, without obligation, to:

Publisher
Thorndike Press
295 Kennedy Memorial Drive
Waterville, ME 04901
Tel. (800) 223-1244

or visit our Web site at:

www.gale.com/thorndike
www.gale.com/wheeler

OR

Chivers Large Print
published by BBC Audiobooks Ltd
St James House, The Square
Lower Bristol Road
Bath BA2 3SB
England
Tel. +44(0) 800 136919
email: bbcaudiobooks@bbc.co.uk
www.bbcaudiobooks.co.uk

All our Large Print titles are designed for easy reading, and all our books are made to last.